My Name is
Eva

SUZANNE GOLDRING

My Name is Eva

bookouture

Published by Bookouture in 2019

An imprint of StoryFire Ltd.

Carmelite House
50 Victoria Embankment
London EC4Y 0DZ

www.bookouture.com

ISBN: 978-1-78681-969-7
eBook ISBN: 978-1-78681-968-0

There was things which he stretched, but mainly he told the truth.
The Adventures of Huckleberry Finn – Mark Twain

Sweet is revenge – especially to women.
Don Juan – Byron

In memory of Nora and Tiny Wall,
whose tender letters survived
and
with thanks to Lyndsay Sellars and
Betty Talbot, who gave me tantalising
snippets about their wartime exploits.

Part One

Quiet! Tall gin mixer required for full menu (3,6)

Chapter 1

Mrs T-C, 6 October 2016

We Never Have Fish

Mrs Evelyn Taylor-Clarke, Evie to loved ones long gone, Eva for a brief but special time and Hilda, during her temporary stay in the nursing home (where staff always used the first Christian name recorded on patient notes), is thinking. Danielle, catering manager at the Forest Lawns Care Home, will be back again soon with her clipboard of menus, asking her to decide what she would like for lunch.

'What will you have today, Mrs T-C?' she'll say, tapping her board with her ready pen, impatient for a decision.

The care home caters very well for its residents, with three options of main course every day for lunch and two choices at teatime, which Evelyn still prefers to call supper.

Should she choose the chicken or the fish today? Fish or chicken? What should it be? Evelyn knows she had fish yesterday, cod mornay it was, with a lovely cheese sauce and mashed potatoes. The day before she chose smoked haddock with a soft-poached egg and spinach. Today, there is a choice of fish pie, vegetarian lasagne or roast chicken, but it might be helpful if she tells Danielle she wants fish again and complains that she hasn't had any for a very long time.

Pat is coming again this afternoon and there might be more questions. She has been turning up with questions ever since she began preparing to put the estate on the market. She never had any questions while Evelyn still lived at Kingsley Manor – in fact, she hardly ever visited – but that was before she had power of attorney and thought she knew what was best.

The drawing room is quiet this morning; only a couple of other residents have settled themselves in the high-seated, winged arm-chairs after breakfast. Evelyn shakes her *Daily Telegraph* to straighten the pages and turns to the back. She always reads the obituaries first, although most of her acquaintances are long gone – she has outlived so many. Then she turns to the weather forecast and the crossword. She studies the clues, both those across and those down, turning the newly sharpened pencil in her fingers. She likes to keep her pencils dagger-sharp. Yesterday, she asked Sarah, the Forest Lawns activities organiser, for a supply of pencils with rubbers. That's what she needs, sharp pencils with erasers attached to the end, just like they all had when she was training in the war. Doesn't anyone use them any more? So much better when you want to correct a mistake. But it wasn't a mistake, was it? Very little in Evelyn's life has been a mistake, apart from the one she can never forget.

With a quick light hand, despite her arthritis, Evelyn fills in the clues with pencil. Really, Mr Thursday is hardly challenging; even the anagrams are easily solved. She will have to pretend again, so once she has completed the puzzle, she finds a pen in her patent leather handbag and then scribbles over the pencilled words in each white square of the grid with black ink, changing the letters so they no longer link up in a tidy and comprehensible pattern; they are no longer words, just nonsense.

On Monday, she noticed Fay, one of the regular nurses, glancing at the paper after she had finished rewriting the words in the puzzle. She looked at the crossword, frowned, then gave Evelyn a pitying smile and said, 'Well done, Mrs T-C. You're still keeping your hand in, I see.' And Evelyn smiled back, but her smile was for herself, for her own amusement, at the thought that Fay would never realise she had sprinkled the squares with the odd letter from the Cyrillic alphabet, and nor did she notice when Evelyn occasionally popped in a word or two of German.

Last week, waking from a nap in the lounge, Evelyn had decided to have fun when Mary brought her a cup of afternoon tea. 'Danke, liebling,' she said. 'Du bist sehr gut für mich.' And she had enjoyed seeing the woman's look of confusion and relished hearing the words she spoke to her colleague standing by the tea trolley, pouring more cups for other residents slumped in their armchairs. 'Bless her,' Mary had said. 'She must be dreaming she's back in the Old Country.' And the two women cast fond looks at her as they poured and stirred the tea and placed mugs in the shaking hands of those who were unsteady with cups and saucers.

And now Evelyn hears the rattle of the morning trolley, bearing coffee, biscuits and the post. The Forest Lawns Care Home is very predictable and every hour of the day has a function. Wednesday morning it was chapel and every Thursday afternoon a young physiotherapist in Lycra leggings appears in the drawing room and encourages everyone to try some simple armchair exercises. 'Stretch out, stretch up and flex those toes,' she repeats, as they follow her instructions with trembling limbs. For those residents whose memories are unreliable, routine is comforting, reassuring. It helps them to feel safe in an increasingly uncertain world, which shrinks day by day until only the familiar surrounds them.

Evelyn's neighbour, Phyllis, is awake in her armchair and is turning the pages of *Good Housekeeping*, the October edition, full of recipes for puddings and preserves made with autumn fruits. Phyllis is humming 'We'll Meet Again' as she flicks over the pages with a dampened forefinger. She is quite happy, although Evelyn is tiring of that much-repeated tune and wishes she would hum something else or stop humming altogether. It might stop if she snatched the magazine away. Phyllis has been pawing that issue for two weeks now and can't possibly remember reading any of the articles. As she says herself, quite cheerfully, 'I can start reading it and forget what it's all about by the time I get to the bottom of the page.'

But Evelyn doesn't take the magazine away, much as she would like to. Instead, she observes Phyllis, just as she observes other residents whose minds are not as sharp as they once were. They come and go, these neighbours; some disappear in the night when an ambulance calls, never to return. But however short their period of residence at the home, she can remember all their names, though she doubts any of them could recall hers. Over there, across the room is Maureen Philips, a round rosy apple of a woman, who has an appetite for sweet things. She will immediately eat any treats brought by visitors, complaining that she hasn't had anything to eat at all that day, and is always determined to win the chocolate bar prize in musical bingo. Near the fireplace sits Horace Wilson, in his dark blue blazer and flannels, telling anyone who will listen that he is going home in the morning; and Wilf Stevens dozes, then often looks up from his knees and asks if anyone has taken Molly out for her morning walk yet.

Evelyn watches them all, storing the signs of vagueness, their slack confusion, for future use. Take note, Evelyn, take note, she tells herself. See how Maureen pauses before she answers questions, look how Wilf is proudly showing his pocket watch to the nurse again, telling her it was awarded to him for a lifetime of service. Horace can't choose what he will have for lunch and asks again and again if he had breakfast today. Repetition and indecision are your defence, Evelyn. But she thinks she won't let herself decline completely. She will still have her hair set when the hairdresser calls round once a week, she will dress with care, as far as she is able, but maybe she will let a button or two miss their buttonholes, sometimes wear odd shoes or even misapply her lipstick. No, that would be going too far – as long as she is able, she will colour her lips and her Cupid's bow, less defined than it once was when it was described as the 'kiss of an angel'. No, lipstick will be the last thing to go.

Chapter 2

14 October 1939

My dearest darling Hugh,

Mama has written to me again, asking me to give up my job here and go home. She is worried about the raids, I know, but I worry I will die of boredom while you are away being heroic if I have to abandon my at least gossip-filled office life and my evenings with the girls for the tediously safe hills of Surrey. I adore being back at Kingsley, you know I do, but I don't know how Mama thinks I would fill my days when she and Mrs Glazier are totally in charge of providing for the household and probably the entire village too, knowing them.

I've said it before and I'll say it again, I am not going to be one to sit around knitting socks (though I'd knit pair after pair of dreary khaki socks for you, my darling, if I thought it would help) but I do so want to 'do my bit'. I wish you would change your mind and agree that I should join the Wrens or something. I don't see how that could be an unsuitable occupation for your wife, and it certainly couldn't be any more dangerous than staying here in London in the flat. I must say, I really rather like the Wrens uniform – well, their darling little hats, at least.

If things in London get much worse I may make the effort to spend more nights at Kingsley (though if I do,

Mama will never leave off asking me to stay), but don't ask me to abandon my London life completely, as it helps me to feel more like a proper grown-up married woman while you are away in France.

In your last letter you asked me to look after McNeil when he arrives in London, so I have alerted Grace and Audrey as they are not sweethearts with any fellows as yet and will be eager to take him under their 'wings' as it were. I hope he will be man enough to withstand their enthusiastic attentions!

Well, darling, I must sign off now as Miss Harper has been giving me stern looks for at least five minutes. She clearly thinks I should have finished my lunch break and returned to my work. What she would think if she realised I was using company paper as well, I dread to think.

Your ever-loving wife,
    Evie xxxxxxx
    Ps I love you

Chapter 3

Mrs T-C, 6 October 2016

Everything In Its Place

Evelyn's room at Forest Lawns has a view of the garden. She was determined that if she had to live in a care home then she would not be completely separated from her lifelong love of gardening. She might no longer be able to kneel to weed herbaceous borders, hack at overgrown honeysuckle or double-dig a vegetable plot, but she can still offer advice on the pruning code for different varieties of clematis, suggest the removal of old hellebore leaves to reveal the budding flowers or recommend a supplement to improve a sickly yellow camellia. But now she wonders, should this knowledge also still be within her grasp?

She stands by the window gazing at the small improvements, which have been made at her suggestion since her arrival early in the year, after that final critical fall. The hot late-summer border filled with blood-red crocosmia, orange heleniums and burgundy sunflowers was a great success after just one season. Under the oldest oak tree a newly planted carpet of pale narcissi will emerge in spring, but for now a sprinkling of deep-pink miniature cyclamen brings a shot of colour to that corner of the garden.

But do I really have to pretend I can't remember the Latin name for wormwood or the right time to plant tulip bulbs? And am I going to have to act as if all that preciously grown knowledge is now lost to me?

A gardener is blowing the fallen leaves into heaps, then scooping them up with two boards between his hands into a barrow. She can see a thin stream of smoke spiralling from the farthest corner of the grounds. *He should be composting those leaves*, she thinks. *Leaf mould is so good for the garden. Helped me establish lily-of-the-valley in several awkward spots.*

But Pat is coming soon for her afternoon visit and Evelyn must be ready. She tidies a hair that has strayed from her weekly shampoo and set, looking at her reflection in the mirror of the dressing table that stood in her mother's bedroom for as long as she can remember, oh, ninety years probably. It must be well over a hundred and fifty years old. The mirror is framed in a mahogany stand, and has three sections, with a little drawer in the middle for Evelyn's hairpins and odd buttons. She opens it every day, after the cleaner has whisked around the room with her duster, to check that a particularly special button is still there, untouched in its little box.

On either side, on the polished surface, on linen mats embroidered by a long-dead relative, are silver brushes and a sturdy hatpin, which Evelyn tells everyone is an old letter opener. They'd never guess why it was issued to her and she laughs inside at comments about such an indelicate hatpin. On the middle mat lies a silver-backed mirror, engraved with the initials M.M.H., matching those on the brushes. 'Mama's initials,' Evelyn murmurs, 'Marjanna Maria Hutchinson,' tracing the curling letters with the tip of her finger. She holds the hairbrush to her nose, and it seems to her that deep within the bristles there is still the faint scent of lavender water.

She thinks of Mama often when she sits here to brush her hair, powder her nose, apply some cold cream. 'A lady always has a fresh handkerchief,' her elegant mother would say, admonishing the child before her, with grass seed in her hair and grazed knees, as she brought a clean square of lace-edged linen from her pocket to wipe her daughter's smeared and grimy face.

Evelyn still has some delicate hankies, but they are more for show than practical use; a wisp to tuck into a cuff, a message to drop into a handbag. Everyone uses tissues now. Much more practical, but so much less significant, Evelyn thinks. No one's going to convey anything other than germs with a dropped tissue; people will shy away from it or throw it in the bin.

A last check reassures her that she is presentable. Her hair is tidy, her lipstick is red and she blots it to avoid smudging. So common leaving marks on cups. But she lets her collar crumple and slip inside her cardigan, so Pat can fuss and straighten it for herself.

Evelyn steadies herself with her walking frame as she rises from the dressing table stool, then checks that all the drawers in her room are closed. Such a blessing that she was able to bring her own furniture here and didn't have to accept the light oak and beech furnishings used in most of the home's other rooms. Not the bed, of course; they like residents to have beds that can be adjusted when there are problems and Evelyn now has a rippling wobbling water mattress to soothe her aches and pains. Sometimes she tells herself it is talking to her as she turns in the night and it automatically bubbles and readjusts to her position. But the other furniture, the dark mahogany that gleams and tells her if any hands other than hers have pried, that bears traces of white talcum powder (so much more convenient than a slip of paper), the chest of drawers, bedside cupboard, dressing table and mirror, are all old friends from home and glow with remembered firelight.

A final look reassures Evelyn that all will be the same when she returns. She bids goodbye to the silver-framed photograph of the handsome man on her bedside table and checks that the photo she always keeps hidden is safely stowed in the drawer beneath, then she shuffles into the corridor with her walking frame to meet her niece.

Chapter 4

16 December 1939

My darling,

Thank you so, so much for the gift of the L'Opera perfume and for the beautiful little manicure set. How you are able to find such treasures at the present time, when you and all the boys are so short of essential clothing, I cannot imagine. All the girls here are madly knitting and I have sworn to join their ranks although I fear their efforts will far outstrip mine. But I cannot bear to think of my darling husband down to his last pair of decent socks and facing the prospect of being barefoot by Christmas. And if, as you say, the Company cobbler is now out of leather, you may be truly barefoot, all of you, before very long.

Now I don't want to bore you with my own petty grievances when yours are so much greater than mine (I had my shoes mended and bought new stockings), but I have to say I am terribly fed up with this job and keep wishing I was doing something more worthwhile. You know how tired I am of office life and would like a change if I can, despite your objections.

I have been thinking I would like to join the A.T.S (they are paying £2 a week, 1/6 food allowance daily & all uniform & board provided) or the Women's Land Army (you've always said you think I look attractive in jodhpurs) or the River Ambulance or something. So I have decided

I will go up on Monday & have a look around. The British School of Motoring are offering special courses at reduced fees for women who will do National Service & the Motor Transport Training Corp said when I enquired that they would place me (where secretarial knowledge was useful) if I could get a driving licence, as they won't take my word for it that I can already drive. They don't seem to think that pootling around the estate counts if one is driving important officers around. But wouldn't it be nice if I could get one of those secretary-cum-chauffeuse jobs to a sweet little general or something? Can't you just see me in a smart uniform, cap at a jaunty angle and all, saluting as I drive past?

Darling, I suppose it is hard for you to understand why I feel I must 'do my bit', but it's like this. Right now, there are opportunities for doing something different, which will never come again. At least I sincerely trust they won't, but the fact remains that the opportunities are here now. I know you want me to stay where I am safe, waiting for your return, but this war is not like the last one. Women aren't just sitting at home knitting, or dashing out with white feathers, they are making a real contribution, I know they are. And it feels as if times are changing for us and I want to be a part of that.

I promise I will let you know how I get on and won't let them send me anywhere hazardous where I might risk not seeing my darling husband when he is finally home on leave and we can spend some precious hours dreaming of having our very own home in the country one day.

Much love, my darling one, with umpteen kisses,
    Yours, Evie xxxxx
    Ps I love you xxxxxxx

Chapter 5

Mrs T-C, 6 October 2016

Keys and Puddings

'You've got your collar all skew-whiff again,' Pat complains, slipping her hands either side of her aunt's neck, then turning the collar up and then down again, smoothing the material and pursing her lips. 'Didn't you look in the mirror before you left your room?'

''Course I did,' Evelyn says, looking at her niece in her old checked golfing trousers covered in dog hair. 'Don't make such a fuss, dear. There's plenty here worse off than me.' She nods towards her fellow residents on the far side of the drawing room, asleep in their armchairs.

'Oh, don't I just know it! I saw quite a commotion as I was arriving this afternoon. I was standing outside waiting for someone to let me in and there was an old gentleman bashing away at the buttons on the keypad by the door, trying to get out. He was shouting and hollering something about being expected at home for lunch and how he was going to be late. Then one of the staff came along and persuaded him to go back to his room.'

Evelyn sniffs. 'It's lucky he didn't get out then. They'd be in almighty trouble if someone actually escaped.'

'They certainly would be. It's their responsibility. I expect they have to change the security codes all the time, just to be on the safe side.'

Evelyn doesn't correct Pat and tell her she knows the numbers are never changed. One, two, three, four. That's been the entry code for months, ever since she first arrived at the Forest Lawns

Care Home. It shows such a lack of imagination. If she were in charge, she would choose something with a bit of history: 1066, the Battle of Hastings, perhaps, or maybe the Great Fire of London, 1666. That would make it so much more interesting as well as being memorable.

She knows the code is unchanged, because she's watched the staff tapping at the buttons often enough. If she sees anyone using the keypad as she shuffles through the entrance hall (taking her exercise, she calls it), she deliberately slows down so she can check the code is still the same. She doesn't like to think that she might not be able to leave when she needs to.

But she can guess why the numbers never change. It's because the staff think the residents wouldn't remember the code, even if they were told, so what is the point? Otherwise they'd have to keep reminding each other of the new number and passing it on to approved visitors and volunteers, who are allowed to come and go freely. Too much trouble for them.

Evelyn knows the code, though, but keeps that knowledge to herself. She can't let Pat suspect or she might wonder how well she remembers other details, so she just says, 'Probably dear, probably,' and waits for what might come next.

'So, have you thought any more about what we were discussing the other day?' Pat leans forward with an encouraging smile. 'You know, about the keys?'

Evelyn knows perfectly well what Pat means, but can't let her think that, so she tries to look mystified before she answers. 'Keys… what keys are you talking about?'

The smile disappears and Pat frowns. 'Honestly, it's so hard trying to get anywhere with you. I asked you on Tuesday if you ever remembered having any keys to that lovely bird's-eye maple breakfront bookcase. A couple of the drawers are locked and I really don't want to force them open. It's such an important and valuable piece of furniture.'

'It was Mama's,' Evelyn murmurs. 'She kept her letters there. And her diaries. Have you read them?'

'How can I, if I can't open the drawers?'

Evelyn's reply is deliberately slow in coming. 'I don't think there's anything else in there.'

'You said that last time. But how can you be sure? You can't remember what you had for lunch half the time. Anyway, you said you'd think about where the keys might be.'

'Did I?' Evelyn looks away towards the view of the gardens through the drawing room windows. Smoke is still drifting behind the trees. Anything could be burning there. A bonfire is a very good way of gradually disposing of papers that might prove inconvenient – and other evidence.

'So, did you think about it? Where the keys might be?'

Evelyn is quiet for a moment, as if she is thinking hard, then says, 'What about the kitchen drawer? Did you look there? We always threw all sorts of bits and pieces in the kitchen dresser drawer. It was full of junk. They might have slipped down the back.'

'Of course I tried that drawer, then I tried every other darned drawer in the kitchen, the cellar, the workshop, the whole damn house. Honestly, Aunt Evelyn, the place is a total mess. Please remind me not to leave such a horrendous muddle to my kids when I go.'

'Then maybe the children would like to have a look around with you, to help you. It would be like a big treasure hunt for them. We always enjoyed a treasure hunt when I was a girl. I remember once, Great-Uncle Will—'

'Oh, Aunt, really! They're not kids any more, they're fully grown adults with important jobs and responsibilities. They can't take time off work to come and rummage through all your old rubbish. For goodness' sake, some days I'm sorely tempted to call in house clearance and have done with it. If it wasn't for the valuables and the family trust, I'd have happily done that straight away.'

Evelyn can see it won't help matters to let Pat get even more annoyed, so after a few seconds of silence she says, 'Chicken. I had chicken for lunch today.'

That almost makes Pat smile. 'Good for you. I'm glad you're eating well here. You certainly look as if you're enjoying your food.'

'I've always had a good appetite. Mama always said so. And Mrs Glazier said I had the best appetite of all of us, when we were very young.'

'Mrs Glazier? She was your mother's cook or housekeeper, wasn't she?' Pat knows that Evelyn can easily be persuaded to talk about the past.

'Cook mainly, we had Violet to help clean. Mama always said staff were hard to get and keep, but Mrs Glazier was there for years. I loved her steak and kidney pudding and she made delicious apple dumplings. We always had them with custard. Have you ever had an apple dumpling, Pat? Such a treat, I tell you.'

'No, I haven't ever had one. And I doubt I ever will now. I don't think anyone makes that kind of pudding nowadays. It's all ready-made cheesecakes or packet crumble mix, if anything. Most people don't have any kind of pudding these days and I certainly don't need to start eating them.' She pats her well-padded waist.

'Oh, we always had a pudding when I was a girl. It wasn't considered a proper lunch or dinner if there wasn't a pudding, you know.' Evelyn pauses, dreaming of puddings past but not forgotten, then says, 'Have you ever had a Sussex pond pudding, dear? It has a lovely lemon sauce.'

'No, Aunt.' Pat sighs. 'I haven't had one of those either and I'm really not likely to.'

'I could ask the cooks here to make one for us, as a treat one day. You'd like that, wouldn't you? They're always happy to cater for special requests.'

'No, no, I haven't come here to talk about puddings! I need to talk to you about the house and the trust.'

Evelyn knows this, but stares at Pat, then strokes her niece's hands, as if she means to comfort her. 'I know, dear. I know and you've been very helpful. But I'm not able to get out very much now, you see. I'm sure you'll make the right decision.'

Pat sighs again, straightens her back and says, 'Yes, well, I have to, seeing as I have that responsibility.' She bites her lip for a moment, then says, 'I don't want to cause the family any embarrassment. I'm trying to handle everything carefully. It wasn't so difficult deciding how to deal with the land and the outbuildings, but the house is a different matter entirely. There's so much personal stuff stored there, I feel I've got to check through all of it. And some of it – well, some of it I'm just not sure about. That's why I've been worrying about the keys.'

She stands up, then bends to kiss her aunt goodbye. 'Oh well, if I have to force the locks, I'll just have to. Shame though, as that bookcase is worth a fair bit.'

As she turns to go, Danielle appears in her chef's whites, her clipboard of menus under her arm. She smiles at Pat, who says, 'I hear the food has been very good again today, but don't let her twist your arm into making one of her stodgy old-fashioned puddings.'

Danielle smiles again and says, 'Mrs T-C has a very good appetite for her age. And she certainly likes her fish. She had fish again today.'

Pat's smile fades as she stares first at Danielle and then at Evelyn, then she says, 'But you just told me you had chicken for lunch.'

'No, I didn't,' says Evelyn. 'I had fish. I expect you weren't listening to me. You never listen to me.'

Chapter 6

My dearest darling,

Forgive me if I sound just the teeniest bit cross with you, but it is so very hard to stay cheerful when I haven't the faintest idea where you are and what you are doing. I really do try not to, but I sometimes begin to imagine the most awfully gruesome scenarios and lie awake half the night, thinking I shall never see you again. I know I must try to be positive, and I do, darling, really I do, and of course I just want this wretched war to be over and for you to return to me in one piece.

I think what has rattled me all the more are the things you told me when we had those two blissful days of leave in Ilfracombe last month. Don't worry, I'm not going to spell it out in this letter, otherwise the censor will come down hard on you and will score through your letters with even more black pencil than before, but you know you did say how you and some of the other chaps are extremely concerned that a 'certain person' is gambling with all your lives. He believes 'the end justifies the means' you said, but I simply can't agree. If that means you are being put at risk unnecessarily (and yes, I do realise that war is a risky business and there will be losses) then I shall never think well of 'he who cannot be named'. How could I, darling, when my precious husband's life is in his hands? I just hope you can all talk some sense into him for all our sakes. I know you can't tell me exactly what you are up to, but my guess is that you and the other chaps are performing some of the riskiest, most highly secret operations in this war.

Oh dear, this is all a bit miserable, isn't it? I promise I shan't whinge any more, darling. I just want you to know I think of you all the time and long to have you back safely. You have to come through this so we can look forward to all the marvellous plans we have made for our life together, you with your horses and me with my own garden, plus one or two little helpmates of our own in due course. So please take care, my darling, and come home to me safely.

Your dearest wife, Evie
    Ps I love you xxxx

Chapter 7

Mrs T-C, 20 October 2016

Who Can Tell?

She's at it again. Rosemary Jenkins, over there in the corner. She's chatting away to a visitor, probably one of the support group workers who come in to help with the musical afternoons. And she's telling her what she did when she was young during the war. Evelyn can't quite catch everything that's being said, but she can certainly pick up the gist of it.

'You never!' the visitor gasps.

'I know. I was never meant to tell anyone,' Rosemary says. 'None of us were. All of us had to sign the Official Secrets Act. We thought we'd be court-martialled or even shot if we didn't keep quiet.' She giggles. 'But I don't suppose I'll get into trouble now, at my age. My memory isn't what it was, so I really can't remember who I've told and what I've told them.' They both laugh at this admission.

'So, where did you work again?'

'MI5 to begin with, in London. They recruited me first and then later on, I joined MI6.'

'Ooh, how exciting! And what did you do?'

Rosemary shakes her head. 'Nothing very important. I'm not sure I was much use. We did a lot of filing mostly.'

'Oh, come on. There must have been more to it than that.'

Rosemary leans forward, her voice dropping a little. 'Well, I was on lookout during the war. You see, there were a lot of strange people in London at that time.' She gives a nod to emphasise these final words and her attentive visitor has a greedy smile, eager for more thrilling revelations. 'And with my connections, I was invited to all the embassy parties. I was quite the social butterfly.'

Evelyn hears it all quite clearly. Stupid woman. She shouldn't be saying anything at all. Evelyn will never tell. It just wasn't the done thing. Once you had promised to keep it secret, that meant, to her, secret for ever. Along with all the other secrets. Perhaps she should pass behind Rosemary's armchair and lean across to whisper in her ear. The words 'Treachery Act' should produce an interesting response.

Another shriek of laughter disturbs Evelyn's concentration on her crossword. It's not at all difficult, but she does have to keep her mind on it when she is lightly sketching in the letters, which she will transform with ink in her final version. Today's puzzle contains more anagrams than similes and she does rather like anagrams; all that shuffling and rearranging reminds her of coding, which was great fun, if a touch headache-making at times when there was such pressure to produce an answer urgently.

And now the music is about to start. Evelyn would really prefer to sit quietly in her own room or one of the other comfortable reception rooms provided by the home, but it is useful to be seen as part of the group, all trying to remember the words to popular tunes. Last month, there was a pianist who was probably more used to playing in a working men's club as he cheerfully pounded the keys and sang 'Roll Out the Barrel'. Today, a man has come in to play his ukulele for everyone. Really, as if George Formby was all everyone ever listened to during the war.

Evelyn is rather more fond of classical music, especially the lovely lunchtime concerts at St John's Smith Square, when she was still able to travel into town on her own. And she had continued attending those concerts even after everything that happened. It was nice to make a day of it. An hour or so of shopping in Peter Jones in the morning perhaps, for a remnant to make new cushion covers, or picking out coloured wools for Pat for her intricate needlepoint. Mid-morning, a nice coffee in their smart café. That and a Danish pastry usually kept her going without lunch.

She sighs; it is rather tiresome not being a free agent any more, relying on the care home's staff. However kind and helpful they all are, it just isn't the same as being able to drive to the station after the early morning commuters and the school runs have finished and take the train into London for a matinee or a quick peek at one's favourites in the galleries. If the weather was fine, after the lunchtime concert she would often stroll along Millbank to the Tate. She particularly liked the Turners and never tired of gazing at *Rain, Steam and Speed*. Such an atmospheric painting.

And in early summer, there was the Chelsea Flower Show, not when all the public thronged the place, of course, but when it was a members-only day. Hellebores and snowdrops were her favourites; the heralds of spring. But not with Pat. She had taken her once years ago and she was convinced Pat had grown bored only halfway through looking at the show gardens. Maybe that was because Evelyn loved to make notes of the planting schemes and jot down the names of new varieties. Pat was only interested in dog-proof gardens and golf greens. No, it was so much more enjoyable when she went alone and could focus on the beauty of the plants and the skill of the garden designers and specialist nurseries. Evelyn feels a lot of her life has been less complicated when she's accomplished tasks alone.

And now the music is starting and a song sheet in large print is thrust into Evelyn's lap. 'When I'm Cleaning Windows' is engraved on her memory and she knows the lyrics to that and other popular songs off by heart, but she has to be seen to mumble and peer at the printed words as if she is struggling. Her wavering voice joins the other croaking, trembling chords, faint above the rhythm of the music and the pseudo-Lancastrian accent being used by the musician, but grows stronger with the famous chorus.

'Shall I help you, Mrs T-C?' asks a kind voice at her side and a hand extends to help her hold the song sheet, then places Evelyn's crossword on the coffee table and picks up her pencil. Evelyn smiles and allows her helper to guide her through the words, pointing at each phrase with the newly sharpened tip of her pencil. Evelyn likes to keep her pencils sharp; she has found it so very useful in the past.

Chapter 8

25 April 1943

My darling, darling man,

I am perfectly well aware that you are no longer here, I am not deluded, but I have no other way of venting my feelings and my fury, other than scribbling so hard on this notepaper that it is practically torn to ribbons. Yes, fury, anger, call it what you will, that you should survive so many missions and then perish. How could they have been so reckless with you, after all you had endured, how could they push their luck so carelessly? I want to scream and throw my maddened self at those responsible for being so careless with your life.

My grief is so bitter, so furious, I am sick with tears of rage. Firstly, I am livid with you for even joining that wretched unit and secondly, I'm absolutely incensed with them for not keeping you safe. I know you could never tell me exactly what you were doing out there (though I can jolly well guess) and that there are losses in all branches of the services, but you simply had to choose one of the riskiest, didn't you? And how dare you say it was because it meant you could practise your French! You foolish, dear man. You were so proud of your linguistic skills, weren't you? So delighted that all those long summer holidays on the Côte d'Azur and skiing in the Alps had helped you brush up your French.

I wish now that you had never learnt a single word of that wretched language, not even the words you whispered to me so sweetly on our honeymoon. All I can think is that your love of French took you away from me and into the most dreadful trouble and now you will never come back, never hold me again, never kiss me again. The country house we planned to have, with stables and gardens, will never happen, the children we longed for will never be born. The life we thought was promised to us for fighting this wretched war cannot be and now I cannot think what kind of a future I can have without you.

I know that you had near misses on previous missions and I cried buckets when I thought you were missing last year, but by a miracle you came back and I never thought I should cry so much ever again. But I was wrong, you foolish, reckless man. I've cried torrents, rivers, cloudbursts of tears since I received official confirmation of your death. Yes, I know you felt you had to go on doing your duty, but I always thought you would be more careful after such a lucky escape. But you loved tempting fate, didn't you? Laughing at fate, relishing the risk. And now there is no one but my parents and our friends to restrain me. I can smoke cigarettes, drink gin to my heart's content and do whatever I like. I can also carry on pouring my heart out to you on paper as it has become a habit I can't break, even though you are no longer here to read my letters.

Your loving wife, Evie xxx
    Ps I love you

Chapter 9

Mrs T-C, 3 November 2016

Smile for the Camera

Pat is here again. Really, she was here only a couple of days ago. Can't she just get on with it, without coming back every five minutes, fussing and asking questions?

'I've found a great stack of old photos,' she says, rummaging in her grubby hessian shopping bag and holding out a biscuit tin decorated with a picture of a thatched country cottage, its garden full of lupins and hollyhocks. 'I thought it would be fun for us to look through them together today. I haven't the faintest idea who all these people are and they won't mean anything to the rest of the family unless you help me write some names and dates on the back.'

'Huntley and Palmers' biscuits,' Evelyn says, staring at the tin. 'I always liked their ginger nuts best. And Mama did so love those pink wafers.'

'Well, the tin's full of old photos now,' says Pat, settling into an armchair and shrugging off her jacket. 'The biscuits were all eaten up long ago. So, let's see if you can remember who's here in these pictures.'

'Oh, I'm really not sure I'll be able to help,' Evelyn says, 'but I'll have a go.' She does remember, of course. She remembers very well, but she's not sure whose picture Pat might come across among the higgledy-piggledy pile of tiny black and white snaps heaped in the tin. This is how it is to be, from now on: Pat unfettered, rummaging through the life of Kingsley and asking questions, rifling through the past, which has never been properly buried and laid to rest. Evelyn can but hope that her secrets will not make themselves known while she is still alive to hear the questions.

'Let me borrow your pencil,' Pat says, picking it up from the side table, next to the newspaper with its completed crossword. 'Ooh, it's lovely and sharp!' She opens the tin and thrusts a clutch of pictures into Evelyn's lap.

The first batch is of a long-ago summer: 1935 was it or '36? No, it was definitely the heatwave of '35, and Evelyn gazes at the group of men in cricket whites, the women in pale dresses, sitting on picnic rugs in the shade, with plates of triangular sandwiches and bowls of strawberries spread before them. 'Straw helmets,' she says. 'That was the year the London policemen were given straw helmets to keep them cool. Everyone said it was like being back in India, when Papa was still out there. I was sixteen that year.' She points to a young woman with bobbed hair at the back of the group.

'See what a good idea this was! You're managing to remember so much by seeing these pictures.' Pat smiles. 'Now, what about these? Is this one of Uncle Hugh?'

She holds out a portrait of a handsome young man, posing for the camera. Evelyn takes the little picture and smiles at her dear, long-departed husband. 'He was so good-looking then. All the girls thought so. I was very lucky to get him. They all set their caps at Hugh.'

'Would you like to keep that one?'

'No, dear, I've got a better one in my room. You keep it and show it to your boys.'

'And what about this one? Who is this little girl? I don't think I've ever seen her before. Is she one of the family?' She is holding an image of a child of about four years old, with braided blonde hair, laughing as she plays with a ball in a garden.

Yes, thinks Evelyn, *she is a relative, but not one you're ever going to meet. You will never see her, not even once, and I will never see her again.*

Pat turns the photo over and reads the faint pencilled words scribbled on the back. 'It doesn't say much. Just Liese, 1951. That's a couple of years after I was born.'

'Liese,' murmurs Evelyn. 'I've no idea who that is.' She gazes at the little snap as if she is trying hard to remember. *How can I ever forget you, my darling? That day you were happy.*

She doesn't take the picture, one of several taken surreptitiously many years ago, in her hand; she doesn't need to. She has one hidden in a drawer in her room and she kisses it every night before she goes to sleep, whispering 'Gute Nacht, liebchen,' after she's kissed the framed photograph of her young husband, Hugh.

'And look at this one,' says Pat. 'This is you as well, isn't it? In uniform? I say, don't you look smart?'

Evelyn accepts the photo from her niece. Her young self smiles back at her, confident with red lipstick and curled hair. 'That wasn't my regulation uniform. I had a suit tailored for me in Savile Row. Not to wear when I was on duty, mind you, but just for when I was going out to dinner. The uniform they issued was simply ghastly, especially the horrible thick brown stockings.'

'Well, you've always liked to look smart, Aunt. Oh, and look, here's another one. It's a group of you and you're all in uniform. That's you again, isn't it?' She points to the young woman in the picture. Her hair is tucked under her cap and she stares uncertainly at the camera. 'And who are the other people with you?' She turns it over. 'There's nothing written on the back.'

Evelyn studies the photograph. She hasn't seen it for many years. She must have enclosed a copy when she wrote home to Mama. Her letters were frequent at first, before everything happened. Two men and two women in formal poses, barely smiling, all in uniform, shoulders back, stiff arms by their sides, standing in front of the doors to a large building. Eva, Colonel Robinson and two others. Would anyone recognise him from this picture? He barely changed over the years. It's very like the image issued when he went missing, thirty years later. But who would remember now that she had known him once?

'Where was that photograph taken?' Pat is still rifling through the remaining snaps in the tin.

'Out in Germany, I think. Just after the end of the war.'

'You've never told me anything about what you were doing out there. It must have been pretty awful, so soon after the war was all over.'

'I don't think I did anything very important, dear. I was the lowest of the low.' *Don't say too much, Evelyn. Don't let her think you remember.*

'It must have been terrible, though. You must have seen and heard some dreadful stories.'

Oh, I did dear, but I can't tell you. Evelyn shakes her head as if lost in thought and mutters, 'I don't really remember much. I know it was a sad time.'

'Mum never talked about it very much. I know she lost her first husband when she was young. Only twenty-two, she said, and then she married Dad, your brother Charles. Poor Mum. She didn't have him very long either, just long enough to have me.' Pat stares at the picture of the uniformed group again, as if trying to imagine the post-war chaos of that time. 'Can you remember who these other people are?'

'Oh dear, it's all such a long time ago.' Evelyn closes her eyes as if she is tired of trying to search her memory, but really she doesn't want Pat to detect her unease at the surfacing of this old image that ties her to Robinson.

'Well, why don't you keep that one, anyway? And can I show my boys the one of you on your own in your smart uniform?'

'That's a good idea. You keep that one. I'd like them to know I wasn't always such a doddery old thing.' Evelyn laughs and slips the photo of the group of four into her cardigan pocket. It won't stay there long. When she is back in her room, she will decide what to do.

'Right,' says Pat. 'And now I've got to get back. I've got a chap from the auction house coming to Kingsley this afternoon to give me some estimates. By the way, I found some old inventories when I was going through the piles of paper in the bureau. You must have had them done quite a while ago though, so I thought I'd better get up-to-date ones done. Were you thinking of selling some of the contents at some point?'

Evelyn tries to look vague, then says, 'I expect it was probably for insurance. Kingsley was always such a responsibility.'

Pat pulls on her coat. 'Tell me about it, Aunt. And I still haven't found those keys, you know.' She bends to kiss Evelyn on her powdery cheek. 'Mmm, you smell lovely. And are you sure you don't want to keep any more of these?' She holds out the tin of photographs. 'Here, why don't you hang on to them anyway and have a good look through? You might manage to identify a few more faces for me.'

Evelyn accepts the collection, saying, 'Oh, very well, dear. I'll try hard to remember some more names for you and the children.' *Or find some more pictures I have to destroy.*

Chapter 10

29 October 1943

My darling man,

I think you would be terribly proud of me! Your little
wife is now a qualified ATS driver and authorised to
drive various officers to meetings hither and thither in an
awfully nice black Humber. I must say it is a much better
car than I have ever driven before, although the greatest
drawback is that we girls are expected to maintain the
vehicles ourselves. I've been down in an inspection pit
covered in grease for the last two days! Still, I suppose
that is going to be something to add to my list of meagre
talents, isn't it, darling?

Although I had already learnt to drive around at
Kingsley (Papa let me drive his old Austin up the drive
and into the level field in summer, and oh, how I am
missing dear Kingsley), that wasn't good enough for the
ATS, so I had to attend a proper driving course near the
barracks in Camberley. I certainly got rapped over the
knuckles for some of my bad habits (probably acquired
from observing you, darling), such as forgetting to look
in my mirror before driving off.

Anyway, one of my first missions is to get to know
my way around London. My billet is right behind Peter
Jones, which is awfully handy and even Mama approves,
as she thinks I will be able to dash in any moment she is

in need of buttons or silks. I've told her several times that I haven't joined up to simply to run her little errands like that, but she seems to think that this is the only advantage of my signing on. She also doesn't understand that I can't use my Humber to nip down to see her whenever she feels lonely. She has no concept of petrol rationing whatsoever, even though whenever I'm missing Kingsley's gardens and countryside I have to go there by train.

The girls in the billet here are awfully nice and although it is jolly cold (it's an old Victorian house), we are determined to keep our spirits up. And at least we get plenty to eat, as I suppose they don't want us 'gels' fainting when we are driving our generals hither and thither. And my first proper assignment will be driving down to Portsmouth, so I'm going to study a map now, to make sure I know how to get there and back.

Wish me luck, darling,
    Your Evie xxxx
    P.S I love you

Chapter 11

Mrs T-C, 3 November 2016

That's Torn It

Evelyn is inspecting the snowdrop bulbs, individually planted in pots for the Forest Lawns Christmas fair. Tips of green have just begun to emerge, poking through the dark brown compost. 'They're coming on quite nicely, aren't they?' she tells Sarah, who organises gardening among many other social activities for the residents. 'I told you that putting the bulbs in the fridge for a few weeks would fool them into thinking it was winter.'

'You were absolutely right, Mrs T-C. Do you think they might even be in flower by the time we put them on sale?'

'It's doubtful, but we can live in hope.' Evelyn checks another of the pots, then shivers. The greenhouse is sheltered and there's a watery sun glimmering on the glass, but there's no heat. 'They're only common snowdrops, *Galanthus nivalis*,' she announces with some pride, 'but they'll still spread once they're planted outside. I had wonderful carpets of snowdrops at Kingsley. Such an encouraging sight in the depths of winter. And some very rare specimens among them too. I was quite the galanthophile, you know.'

'The what, Mrs T-C?'

'Galanthophile, dear. People who are knowledgeable snowdrop enthusiasts and collectors. The rarest flowers can often change hands for more than a hundred pounds a bulb. But it's always best to plant them in the green, while they still have their leaves, if you want to be sure of good results.'

'Well, I never knew that, Mrs T-C. It's just like tulip fever, isn't it? I remember we had that in History at my school. You're a real mine of information, really you are.'

Evelyn smiles to herself. If only the girl knew how much information was buried deep inside her head, beneath her silvery-grey hair. But she must be careful not to tell her so much another time. She must remember to forget.

'Well, I ought to be going in now, dear. Will you be able to manage on your own?' Sarah slides the greenhouse door aside and Evelyn shuffles outside to where her trusty walking frame is waiting for her. As she walks away in her halting fashion, she frets. Did I offer too much detail about the snowdrops? So hard to bury all this knowledge, so much harder than burying all the secrets.

Minutes later, she sits in her armchair in her room, sorting through the collection of old photographs in the biscuit tin. There are several of Mama in furs, silk dresses and large ornate hats at weddings, county shows and village fetes. Dear Mama, so elegant. And look, here are quite a few of Papa and dear Charles, standing proudly with other members of a shooting party. Don't they look grand, all in tweeds and caps, guns cradled in their arms, alert and eager dogs looking up at them and several brace of pheasant at their feet?

There are also more of Evelyn in uniform, laughing with other girls in similar attire and sometimes with young airmen squinting at the camera in sunshine. Such young men, no more than twenty years old or so, soon to be gone, grasping kisses and beauty while they still had life. But there are no more of that awkwardly posed group of four and none at all of Robinson on his own.

It isn't hard to remember how and when that picture of the four of them was taken and she pulls it out of her pocket to look at it more closely. They are standing outside the entrance to Bad Nenndorf, the former health spa adapted to provide facilities for the interrogation centre. It was in the early days, soon after she'd first arrived, when the place had only just begun operating, before she realised exactly what would happen there and before she saw Robinson's true nature for herself. In the photograph this short man of slight build looks stern. He holds his chin high, his lips thin beneath a straight pencil moustache, while the other three people alongside him all bear uncomfortable slight smiles, as if they are unsure why they have been made to stand together in false comradeship, squinting in the bright sun.

Evelyn stares hard at the scene from long ago. His face had looked cruel from the time she first met him, but she hadn't fully understood that was what it was then. He had just seemed cold and efficient, like so many of the commanding officers she had encountered in the service. And although his reputation had preceded him, she had not realised just how calculating he could be until she had seen it for herself.

She begins to tear the photo in half, then stops and peels off just the right-hand quarter, the section that contains the figure of Robinson, standing on the edge of the group, slightly separated from the other three figures. She places this strip on top of her folded newspaper, then picks up her pencil. She tests the tip with her finger, then sharpens it to a needle-like point and then, with the pencil clenched in her fist, she stabs Robinson's face. Into both the eyes she goes, into that nose and into that hard, unsmiling mouth, until the fragment is tattered and unrecognisable. Satisfied with the destruction of his features, she tears the image into tiny pieces and, clutching them in her hand, shuffles into her bathroom and flushes the scraps away in the toilet.

Then she hobbles back to her chair and picks out the single picture of the blonde child from the tin. She compares it with the one she kisses every night, the one hidden in her bedside table drawer beneath the Bible. She holds both the tiny snaps side by side, trying to decide which is the better picture.

She had often walked past the garden, trying to get a glimpse of the child, and before she finally left Germany, she had decided to take some snapshots around the village. If anyone asked, she could say she was returning home shortly and wanted to remember the years she had spent at Wildflecken. She didn't really care about recording the houses, the oxen ploughing the fields or the church; she only wanted to keep the ones of the child.

'Lieselotte,' she whispers. 'They called you Lotte, but you were always Liese to me.' She kisses both of the little photos and puts one back in the biscuit tin with all the other old family pictures. Pat can wonder all she likes, but she will never tell her.

Part Two

Clever and good-looking (6,3,9)

Chapter 12

20 November 1943

My dearest, darling Hugh,

This letter will never leave this country, let alone my possession, so I can say whatever I like without fear of reprisals or censure. All this time, ever since that terrible day when I was told you had gone for ever, I've been blaming **you** for taking risks, cursed **you** for not making it back home to me, but now I know that it was not your fault. Today, I found out that you and the others were terribly betrayed.

He didn't want to 'spill the beans', as he put it, but your friend Tim McNeil came to see me this afternoon. He said he'd promised you that if he managed to get back home and you didn't make it through, then he would call on me. He's such a sweetie and it's a great comfort to know that you were good friends and supported each other. I told him the only thing I'm grateful for in this whole sorry business is that you weren't captured like the others. It's a mercy of a kind that you were shot trying to escape and were never tortured.

Tim and I met for tea at the Coventry Street Corner House. You must remember it, darling, we went there soon after they opened the Old Vienna café and we were both unsure whether we would like the *Aufschnitt* or other foreign delicacies on the menu, so we ordered the special salad, full of prawns, egg and ham. That was four years ago, before the war even started. I wasn't sure if I could manage to go back to where we had once been so happy but I decided to make an effort and wore my tailored uniform, the one Mama insisted I should have made. I think she thought I'd let the family down in my regulation kit. I'm not sure what she'd think if she knew I'm down to my last pair of stockings. If I wreck these, it'll be Bisto seams for me like everyone else!

Tim was very kind when he arrived and I told him he should eat as he appeared awfully thin and pale. I tried the Spam fritters and he had a Welsh rarebit, which looked dreadful. The cheese we're getting now is ghastly and I think they'd mixed it with powdered egg and tried to make it more palatable with mustard.

Then things got even more ghastly when our order came, as Tim suddenly told me he believes you and the others were betrayed. I couldn't believe what I was hearing. I'd just been waffling on about how I kept trying to console myself with the thought that you were doing important work. I said I liked to think that you and your fellows really did 'set Europe ablaze' as Churchill directed and that though I knew you couldn't tell me much about your work, I knew you were excited to be really doing your bit for the war. Then I said I knew you and Tim were sent out on special missions, so he didn't need to worry about what he might let slip.

And that was when I noticed that Tim wasn't eating his food. He was stirring his tea, but his spoon just kept going round and round as if he was never going to stop. He looked awful, so I asked if something was wrong with his meal and suggested perhaps he should order something else and then he looked straight at me and said you and the others never got the opportunity to set Europe ablaze. He said that he and some other chaps were convinced that your last mission had been set up to fail deliberately, to mislead the Germans.

I tried to stay calm, but I couldn't help myself. I dropped my knife and fork on my plate and made a terrible din. I felt sick and had to hold my napkin over my mouth. I couldn't believe what he was saying. But eventually I forced myself to speak and asked him why on earth would they want a mission to fail? He said he wasn't exactly sure, but he believes that some clever double-double-cross agent manoeuvring was going on. He said it's lost them a dozen or so men and women, plus networks.

It was such a shock, I tell you. I closed my eyes and half-thought I'd have to excuse myself and run to the ladies' cloakroom. But what good would that have done? I'd have locked myself in a cubicle and howled the place down for hours. So I decided I simply had to pull myself together, grit my teeth and learn more. I was desperate to hear what Tim knew, so I breathed deeply, folded my napkin on my lap and said I couldn't believe it. After hand-picking recruits with special skills and languages, after all that training, did he mean all of you were considered to be disposable? I was trembling and I know my voice was a bit shaky, but I simply had to know.

Tim took a moment to answer then said it wasn't quite like that, it was more a game, where the risks were unreasonably high. And I said did he mean it was a gamble and he agreed. I was still feeling dreadfully shaky and Tim looked even more uncomfortable, then he suggested we should get the bill and we go somewhere quieter, so we left the restaurant without finishing our food and started walking along Piccadilly, towards Fortnum & Mason and Green Park. Neither of us said much for a bit, then, it was silly of me, I know, I was suddenly reminded of that night you and I had dinner at Quaglino's, the same night that the Café de Paris was hit. I think it was the way the setting sun was glinting on tiny shards of glass in the gutters as we passed the turning into Bury Street. So I told Tim about our lucky escape and how we caught what must have been the only taxicab out in the West End that terrible night, because you had to catch the train to Edinburgh from King's Cross. I said I hadn't realised it at the time, but maybe that was when you first started your special training.

Tim gave me a funny look, then said he was so sorry you didn't make it back and that he thought you were a fine chap. And I asked him again about his earlier remarks about lives being risked in that mission. And then, gosh, I can hardly believe this even now, he said your lives weren't just risked, he believed they were sacrificed. He stopped walking and said he shouldn't be telling me anything, but the head of the whole operation is a chap who firmly believes the end justifies the means. Tim said this chap knew jolly well that our men were highly unlikely to make it back.

Honestly, darling, I felt sick all over again. I could feel those awful fritters I'd tried to eat heaving in my stomach. I must have looked ghastly and I remember slumping against the window of Fortnum's. Goodness knows what people must have thought of me. But I was determined not to be sick in public, so I breathed slowly, till I felt a bit better, then asked Tim if he was quite certain. And Tim said he was utterly serious and that if this fellow had played his hand differently, he was quite sure you and the others wouldn't have died.

Can you imagine what a shock it was for me hearing this? But when I recovered (and I wasn't sick, I just took breaths of cold air), I had to ask Tim who this man was. I looked him straight in the eye and demanded to know his name. I was pretty dramatic, I tell you – I think I said I wanted to know who had gambled with my husband's life.

Tim was reluctant to tell me at first, I suppose because it's drummed into all of you that you can't say a word about the operations. But after a few seconds, he said he owed it to you and to me and said it was Colonel Stephen Robinson.

I reassured Tim that you'd had your suspicions too and that you had almost told me just as much before you finally went that last time. He looked quite relieved after I'd said that and he looked so drained and famished that I felt I had to make it up to him for being so honest with me. And I thought we both needed cheering up, so I said we should run down to Horse Guards Parade to see the German Tiger tank that was captured in Tunisia. It's just gone on display there and it's been in all the papers and everyone's so thrilled to get one over on Jerry. So, we headed off and had some decent fish and chips after we'd had our 'gloat' to make up for that awful tea.

And now I'm back in my billet, wondering what to make of all that Tim told me today. If what he said is true, then I can never forgive this Robinson man. I was just about coming to terms with the death of my darling husband as a consequence of conflict, but I cannot ever accept that your life was deliberately sacrificed.

I'm unlikely ever to meet this chap, I suppose, and there's little chance I could ever tell him how I feel, but I shall do my damnedest to see if I can meet him face to face. I want to curse him to Hell and back for ever for the pain his orders have brought me. In fact, if I can ever meet him, he shall go to Hell.

All my love, darling,
    Your Evie xxx
    Ps I love you

Chapter 13

Mrs T-C, 7 November 2016

Keys and Cases

'I can't possibly talk to you in here,' Pat says when she bustles into the drawing room in the middle of the morning. Her mackintosh is stained, it's missing a button and the loose belt is dangling down the back. She is holding a bulging carrier bag, which has split down one side and appears to be filled with paperwork. 'We'll have to go upstairs to your room or find somewhere else to sit. Somewhere quiet, where we won't be disturbed.'

'Nobody's going to hear us in here if we talk quietly,' says Evelyn. 'They're all quite deaf, you know. Anyway, the coffee and biscuits will be coming in soon.'

'Then they'll just have to come and find us,' says Pat. 'I need a word with you in private, right this minute. Now are we going to move or not?'

Evelyn grumbles and totters to her feet, steadying herself by gripping her walking frame. 'Oh, very well then. There's a little sitting room down the corridor. People hardly ever go in there.'

As they leave the drawing room, Evelyn sees the trolley laden with cups and flasks and calls to the carer on her rounds. 'Mary, could you be a dear and bring us our coffee in the morning room? Thank you so much.'

Pat steers her aunt by the elbow into the quiet, empty room and shuts the door. Once Evelyn has settled herself in an armchair, after fussing over the whereabouts of her hankie and her pencils,

Pat starts talking. 'Auntie, I'm really trying to do my best sorting out the house, you know I am. But yesterday, I found some things I'm really not sure you'd like people to know about and I need to ask you some very important questions.'

Evelyn considers her flustered niece. *Careful now, this is how it starts. From now on, choose your words and gestures with the greatest of care.* And then she says, 'Of course, dear. I'm happy to help if I can. But in the end, you know that everything at Kingsley is yours anyway. You really don't have to ask my opinion about every little thing.'

'Yes, well, that's half the trouble. I'm not sure we're going to want some of the things I've just found, unfortunately.'

'Like what, dear?' Evelyn studies Pat. Her cheeks are flushed and her hair could do with a wash and a good brush. 'You do seem to be in an awful tizz today. Are you sure you're not coming down with something? Are the boys well? And what about your lovely husband? How is dear Humphrey? I haven't seen him in ages.'

'Everyone's fine, thank you. And I'm fine too. I'm just… well, just disturbed.' This last word is practically spat out and Evelyn tries not to smile. She has been anticipating this moment ever since she came to live at Forest Lawn.

'Well, take a deep breath, dear, and tell me what the problem is. I'm all ears.'

Pat does as she is told and takes a breath, then her words spill out in a rapid jumble of gabble. 'I found some keys in the kitchen drawer, like you said, and I tried to unlock the bookcase, which I still haven't been able to unlock, by the way, and which is still a problem, because it's such a valuable piece of furniture and the keys I found, well, I suddenly realised that on this bunch of keys were a couple of small keys, which I thought might be for the suitcases I found in one of the spare bedrooms. There was one on top of the wardrobe and one on the floor, so I took the keys upstairs and opened these heavy cases and was horrified by what was inside, absolutely horrified, I tell you. I couldn't believe my eyes.'

'Really, dear? Why don't you slow down and tell me properly? I don't remember any cases. I probably hadn't been in that room for years. I've absolutely no idea what was in them.' *So why don't you tell me what you think you've found and then we'll see whether I should be worried?*

'Guns, Aunt, guns! And I think there was ammunition in there as well.'

'Really, dear? But at Kingsley, we always kept the guns locked in the gun cupboard. Papa was always very particular about it. We never allowed guns anywhere else in the house.'

'Well, that's exactly what I thought. But then I looked at these guns and realised these aren't the sort of guns that the family always used for shooting. And I don't know anything about guns, you know I don't. I hate blood sports. And I never got involved in any of the shoots you used to have at Kingsley years ago when I was young, but even I can see that these are not sporting guns for shooting pheasant or ducks.'

'Aren't they, dear? What sort of guns are they then?' *Ooh, I am enjoying this. I didn't realise it would be such fun.*

'I think they might be army-issue guns.' Pat heaves an exasperated sigh. 'Guns, uniform, papers and there's other stuff in there as well. Where has it all come from?'

'Well, I wonder who put it there?' Evelyn's head turns at the sound of a light knock on the door and Mary appears with a tray laid with cups of coffee and a plate of biscuits. 'Thank you so much, Mary. Ooh, you've brought us some Jammie Dodgers. Yummy, my favourite.' She smiles and takes a biscuit.

Pat waits until they are alone again, then says, 'But what am I supposed to do with all these guns? I can't exactly send them off to house clearance or the charity shop, can I?'

'Can't you just throw them all away, dear? There's that awfully useful council refuse dump in Milford. I always took all my unwanted things over there when I could still drive my old Volvo estate.' Evelyn looks wistful, then says, 'I do miss driving. It was so nice being able to pop down to the shops whenever I needed something.'

'I'm sure you miss it, Aunt, but that's not the point. These guns and all the other things I've found… I don't even know what they all are… they must be illegal. I'm pretty sure I've got to take them to the police or somewhere and explain how they got there in the first place.'

'Oh, what a nuisance for you, dear. Here, do have a biscuit.'

'So, what am I supposed to tell them? They will want to know how these weapons came into your possession.'

'My possession?'

'Yes, yours. Until you shuffle off this mortal coil, everything at Kingsley is deemed to be part of your estate. I know it's held in trust, but legally, it's all yours so the police are bound to ask me where these guns came from.'

Evelyn frowns, then says, 'I think Father might have had a gun. And I wonder if perhaps Charles brought one back with him from his time out in Africa?'

Pat sits back with her arms folded and sighs. 'But all of this stuff must be yours, not theirs. I'm absolutely sure of it, because there's even a uniform, just like the one in that photograph we found in the tin the other day, and there's personal correspondence with your name on it in the cases as well. Look…' She leans forward and fishes around in her tattered carrier bag, then pulls out some papers. 'How else do we explain these?' She holds out the first piece of paper, a letterhead with some typed wording. 'It's addressed to you, isn't it?'

Evelyn looks at it and adjusts her glasses. It's her transfer to the interrogation centre at Bad Nenndorf. *But it means nothing, unless someone finds out who else was there at the same time.*

'And look, there's an old passport in your name.' Pat shows her the out-of-date passport with her young face, so young, so innocent. 'And there's another one here as well and that's also got your picture, though I don't understand why it's got a different name. Eve Kucha or something.'

'Eva Kuscheck,' murmurs Evelyn.

'Oh, whatever! It's all yours, I tell you. So, I'm betting the guns belong to you as well.' Pat purses her lips and frowns.

Evelyn shakes her head, then says, 'Well, I'm very sorry, dear, but I don't remember any of this. Maybe it wasn't me who put all these things away in the cases.'

'Maybe you didn't. But all these papers, the gun licence, letters and so on are addressed to you. This is all your stuff, yet you're telling me you had no idea what was in the suitcases.'

Evelyn looks at Pat with a smile, then says, 'I really do wish I could help you, dear, but my memory isn't what it was.'

She looks down at the tray. 'You haven't drunk your coffee, dear. Don't let it go cold.' Then she takes another biscuit, looks at it, wrinkles her nose and says, 'I don't know why Mary's given me Jammie Dodgers. She knows I don't like them. I want chocolate digestives.'

Chapter 14

27 January 1944

Dearest darling one,

I know if you were here, you would tell me I am far too flighty and impatient and I should wait a bit, but I am seriously thinking of giving up my chauffeuring with the ATS and following in your footsteps.

I feel sure I can do something much more useful than just sit around waiting for high and mighty officers. It looks at last as if we might soon finish this blessed war and we've heard that the poor people of Leningrad are finally free, now that blasted siege has ended.

It was all right for a bit, getting used to my lovely Humber and so on, but on New Year's Eve, when I would much rather have been letting my hair down, I had to drive a pair of officers to Portsmouth again. I knew the route quite well by then, but would you believe, they let me sit there all night without a word and what's more, without anything to eat or drink to celebrate the New Year? And when they finally came back to the car in the morning, all they said was, 'Oh, driver, we forgot all about you,' and then I had to drive them all the way back to London, feeling wretchedly tired and annoyed. I feel so taken for granted and badly misused that I am quite fed up and feel like a change, as well as being frustrated that I have come no nearer to taking your nemesis to task.

What kind of a change could there be? You might well ask. Well, today, on our company noticeboard, I saw a poster asking for volunteers with secretarial skills and languages, so I am going to offer my services and see where that gets me. My French is pretty good, though I think my German is much better. Driving has been fun and at least I am now a far better driver than I was, but waiting around for inconsiderate, selfish officers isn't enjoyable or worthwhile and I do so want to do something useful, just as you did, my darling. And if that means I end up taking risks just like you, then I know I shall be in good company. Who knows, I may meet you again sooner than I'd thought and then we'd have such fun. I miss you so much, my darling.

All my love,
    Your Evie xxxx
    Ps I love you

Chapter 15

Mrs T-C, 9 November 2016

Ask Nicely

'You can't pretend you don't know anything about the guns,' hisses Pat. 'I've looked all through those cases. They're full of your stuff. There's clothes, documents and passports. You've got to tell the police where the guns came from.'

'Well, dear, I would if I could remember.'

Pat's hair is damp and she is wearing a tracksuit. She looks as if she's just come back from a sports club. What is it they do these days? In Evelyn's day golf and gardening, maybe a seasonal game of tennis were considered to be adequate exercise, but now, people seem to think they have to run everywhere and go to gyms to keep fit.

'You jolly well try and remember! I had no idea there was going to be such a palaver when I took them down to the station. Honestly, you'd think I was a criminal. You should have seen their faces when I went up to the front desk. They said I should never have taken the guns down there in the car. They said I should have left them right where I found them. Could have gone off at any time, they said.'

Evelyn tries not to smile, but the corners of her mouth are twitching. 'I hardly think so, Pat. Papa taught us never to leave guns loaded, especially in the house. He was most particular about that.'

'I'm sure he was, but the police weren't to know that, were they? Anyway, there was an awful lot of fuss down there at the station and then they even wanted to take my fingerprints. Can you believe that? Said they had to do that to eliminate me. See what a lot of trouble you're causing?'

'Well, why would they want your fingerprints? You haven't done anything wrong, have you, Pat?'

'Of course I haven't. They'll be wanting yours next, I expect.'

Evelyn inspects her spotted veiny hands with their neat oval nails. Mary had applied two coats of No7 Dusky Rose varnish the previous day. So important to maintain appearances and well-manicured nails are a mark of one's standards. Evelyn glances at Pat's hands. The nails are unpolished and uneven; the skin looks dry and rough. 'I've never had my fingerprints taken before. What fun! Just like on television.'

'No, it isn't fun, Aunt. They have to do it, to check against their records. It was because I'd handled the guns and the other stuff. And they said they not only had to make the guns safe, but they had to check the serial numbers in case the guns have ever been used for criminal purposes, as they put it.'

'Well, they haven't, have they? Oh, I do hope you've been careful to lock up properly at Kingsley, Pat. Nobody's been able to borrow any of our guns, have they? We only kept guns for the pheasants and sometimes Papa and Charles went duck shooting, but nothing else…' Evelyn pauses and frowns. 'Oh, I might have put down the odd deer a couple of times. Do you think that's what they're worried about?'

'No, I don't, Aunt. They wanted to know all about you and the family and said they will have to check their records.' She gives a great gust of a sigh. 'Honestly, I could do without all this. I'm meant to be sorting out bric-a-brac for the church Christmas fair. But, oh no, I have to stay here with you, because you're a vulnerable adult, apparently.' She adds these last words with a roll of her eyes and Evelyn coughs to disguise her laughter.

'A policeman is coming here today.' Pat looks at her watch. 'They should be here very soon. I said I'd meet him in the home.'

But it isn't a him, it's a her. A petite uniformed officer, WPC Thomas, with dark hair neatly tied into a tight bun at the nape of her neck, is ushered into the morning room by Mary, whose offer of coffee is declined, much to Evelyn's evident disappointment.

'Can you please explain to my aunt why you have to do this,' Pat says. 'She really hasn't grasped why it's necessary.'

WPC Thomas smiles and shakes hands with Evelyn. 'Hello, Mrs Taylor-Clarke, I just need to ask you a few questions. It shouldn't take too long.'

'Oh good, because I'm going out soon for a hair appointment later this morning.' Pat catches the policewoman's eye and shakes her head from side to side, mouthing, 'No, she isn't really.'

WPC Thomas smiles at this, but only says, 'If you don't mind, I just need to take your fingerprints first.' She sets out her inkpad and forms and Evelyn holds out first her left, then her right hand, then sits staring at her inky fingertips, palms uppermost.

When the WPC has finished filling in her paperwork, she says, 'Can you remember the two locked suitcases that were kept in one of the bedrooms at Kingsley Manor?' She sits with notepad poised, eyes alert, watching Evelyn. 'And can you tell me anything about the guns that were found in the cases?'

Evelyn is quiet for a moment, then says, 'We always kept guns in the gun cupboard. That was the rule. Guns were never kept anywhere else.'

'I see.' WPC Thomas makes a note. 'We've taken a look at the firearms in the gun cupboard. Their licences have expired, but those aren't the guns we're interested in.'

'Oh, but you should be. Papa only ever bought very good guns for the shoots. And he always made sure they were safe. And he insisted they were kept locked up, out of harm's way.'

'I'm sure he did. But that must have been a very long time ago. Do you ever remember seeing any other guns at Kingsley Manor?'

'Of course I do. In the shooting season we had at least a dozen or more guns on the estate on several occasions.'

'More than a dozen? You mean you acquired extra guns?'

'No, dear. We invited friends over to shoot the pheasants. It was such fun. Very jolly going out on a frosty day with all the dogs. Papa had a dear working spaniel – Milo, he called him. And Mrs Glazier would send out a hamper with delicious consommé. I think she used to add a dash of sherry. It makes all the difference, you know. So, some years we had several brace hanging in the cellar. Do you like pheasant?'

'I'm not sure. I don't think I've ever eaten it.' WPC Thomas stops taking notes and frowns at Evelyn.

'Oh, it's marvellous. But you must let it hang for a few days; no more than a week, though, or it will get a bit too high. The flavour is vastly improved with hanging and that makes the meat more tender too. You must check, mind, that none of the shot is left in the bird. That can make them taste a bit off, you know, and you don't want to go biting on a bit of lead. That won't do your teeth any good. Our cook used to roast them and sometimes she made the most superb game pie, with a mixture of rabbit, pheasant and pigeon. Absolutely delicious.'

'It sounds wonderful. Now, these guns—'

Evelyn waves at her niece. 'Pat, I want you to check the freezer at Kingsley. I'm certain I left a couple of brace there and this young lady would like to try pheasant, I'm sure.' Evelyn beams at the young officer. 'You're in for quite a treat, dear.'

'The freezer is totally empty, Aunt.' Pat is rolling her eyes again. 'In fact, it's not even there any more.'

'Not there? Why ever not? It was a perfectly good freezer. Served me well for the last twenty years.' Evelyn turns to pat WPC Thomas's hand. 'I bought the pheasants from that excellent butcher in Petworth. I used to shoot them myself when I was younger too, but in later years, I bought them in, ready dressed.'

'Aunt, there are no pheasants at Kingsley. You're getting confused again.'

'What nonsense, Pat. Of course there are pheasants at Kingsley. Our gamekeeper saw to it. Papa would have had words if he hadn't done his job properly. There were always plenty of birds for the shoots. You can't invite people along to a shoot and not give them a decent day's shooting. Whatever would they think? Of course there are still pheasants.'

'But not in any freezer, there aren't.' Pat shakes her head in exasperation. 'Not any more.'

WPC Thomas closes her notebook and turns to Pat. 'I think that's all I need. I'll have to write a crime report, just for the record, but I don't think you'll have any more trouble. The firearms people will have to take a look at the guns and the serial numbers, just to be sure, but I shouldn't think you'll have to come down to the station again.'

'Thank goodness for that. I've got more than enough to cope with, as you can see from today's performance. But do you think they were her guns? And were they still working?'

'I really couldn't say. It's not something I know much about. If the guns are still usable, they'll eventually be decommissioned, put out of action, once the firearms boys are satisfied.' She looks down at the forms in her file. 'But I'll include some information in the report about all the other items that were found in the cases, just in case that's relevant.'

As WPC Thomas starts to leave, Evelyn calls out, 'Goodbye, dear. Do come again, won't you? I've so enjoyed our little chat.'

Chapter 16

10 February 1944

My darling,

This will be quite short, as I am so excited to be starting in a new, and, I hope, much more rewarding role, both for me and for the nation. I was sent to an address in Broadway Street, opposite St James's Park Underground station. While I was waiting in the corridor, I could hear a man and a woman saying, 'She should be all right. She's got the right background.' I think they meant me, but I don't know who had been telling them about me. Maybe they knew Charles. Then, after a short interview, I was told they would like me to join a unit that interviews evaders and escapees who have managed to return to this country from enemy occupied territory.

I said I didn't really want to just sit safely in an office, when others, like you, are out there risking their lives. I said I would rather be playing an active part in the war. They said they might review my position in due course, but at least I feel I will now be used properly and be close to the action!

I believe evaders are those service personnel who have avoided capture after being involved in action of some kind. I am well aware that some of their reports will be full of ghastly harrowing details, so I know it will remind me of that awful business that finished you off, darling, but I am determined to be calm and strong for your sake.

I was so excited by my success at last that I celebrated by walking through the park to Fortnum's for tea and before I left, I bought a chocolate bar they have produced specially for serving military personnel. I'm going to send it out to Charles, assuming his influence helped me get this position. I'd have bought some for you as well, of course, darling, if you were still here, as I know you would have loved such a treat.

I'd better keep news of my little shopping trip from Mama next time I visit, as she will be rather miffed that I didn't buy any delights for her from Fortnum's. She still seems to think having me in central London is for her benefit and is always thinking I can run her errands. Poor Mama. She can't quite fathom the mysteries of rationing and leaves it all to Mrs Glazier, who seems to manage awfully well. Perhaps they are both in cahoots with a local black-marketeer? I find the idea of the two of them dealing surreptitiously in illegal goods frightfully amusing! I shall definitely feel the need to check their stockings next time I am there!

With love,
    Evie xxxx
    Ps I love you

Chapter 17

Mrs T-C, 11 November 2016

A Few More Questions

'Her memory isn't too good these days, I'm afraid,' Pat is saying to the suited man who follows her into the morning room. He's not Humphrey, Pat's husband, and he's surely too old to be one of her two sons. He has brought a large file with him and a sweet smell of aftershave.

'Auntie,' Pat says, 'this nice man is Inspector Williams. He just wants to ask you a few questions. It won't take very long.'

Evelyn gives him her best smile. She has been expecting such a visit ever since Pat left the other day in a flurry of dishevelled impatience, after that little policewoman had been. *Bad Nenndorf. It's a link I can't avoid. Once I'm placed there, the connection is obvious, but then anyone digging into service records could easily find out where I had been stationed during those years.*

Evelyn shakes the Inspector's hand. 'How nice to meet one of Pat's young men. Would you like to stay for coffee?' She presses the buzzer hanging on a long ribbon round her neck and Mary immediately appears in the doorway, looking very concerned, as if it's an emergency.

'Mary, dear, we have visitors today. Can we have coffee in here this morning?' Evelyn waves her out, then calls out after her, 'And bring a nice selection of biscuits for the young man too, won't you?'

'Really, Aunt,' Pat says, 'you treat everyone just as if this was a hotel.'

'Don't be silly, Pat, of course I know my home's not a hotel.' Evelyn looks around the bright morning room, with gold brocade curtains and a Regency stripe of burgundy and cream on the walls. 'Do you like the way I've had this room decorated? I chose the wallpaper myself.'

Pat leans across to the Inspector and whispers, 'Don't take any notice of her. She does this sometimes. She forgets where she is and starts thinking it's her own house. I don't know whether you're going to get anything useful out of her today.'

'Don't worry, it's just a formality,' he says. 'For the record.' Then he turns to Evelyn. 'Mrs Taylor-Clarke, I'd like to ask you a few questions about the weapons that were found at your previous address, Kingsley Manor. Firstly, can I confirm that you are the legal owner of the property and were the sole resident there until you came to live here, at Forest Lawns?'

'My parents lived at Kingsley,' Evelyn says. 'Such beautiful gardens. Have you been there? Did you go to see the snowdrops?'

'They aren't out now,' Pat says. 'It's the wrong time of year. It's November, not spring.'

'What a pity,' Evelyn says. 'Then you simply must go back in January or February. The snowdrops are wonderful at that time of year.' She waves her hand in a sweeping gesture. 'Great carpets of them. The Kingsley gardens are quite famous for their snowdrops.'

'I may well do that,' says the Inspector. 'But what I want to know now is this – did you pack items into these suitcases that were found in one of the bedrooms? There was one on the floor and another on top of the wardrobe.' He holds out a photograph of the two cases.

Evelyn stares at the picture. 'Those cases look awfully heavy. You must be very careful lifting heavy cases, young man.'

'Of course, madam, I'll bear that in mind. But do you recognise these suitcases?'

She glances at the picture again and shrugs. 'Should I?' Then, at the sound of the tea trolley, she looks towards the door. 'Oh goodie, coffee's on its way.' Mary enters, bearing a tray, and Evelyn peers at the plate of assorted biscuits. 'Aren't there any Bourbons today, Mary? I do rather like Bourbons. I'm not too keen on these Garibaldi – the currants stick in one's teeth awfully.'

'I'll see what I can find,' Mary says. 'And if we're in luck, I'll be back in just a tick.'

The three of them stir their cups and Inspector Williams dunks a digestive biscuit in his coffee. He leaves it rather too long and a sodden segment plops into the cup with a little splash that spatters his shirt. Evelyn doesn't approve of dunking and nibbles a custard cream. 'Can you tell me what was stored in these suitcases?' he says, brushing at his shirt with a crumpled handkerchief he has found in his pocket.

Evelyn pauses in her nibbling, then says, 'Oh, I don't know. Could it be clothes? Old clothes? Mama never threw anything away. She always said good-quality clothes should never be wasted, they can always be remodelled. She had some lovely dresses and coats and a marvellous dressmaker. I must give you her address, Pat. You could do with some good outfits.'

Pat is wearing a creased sweater and dark slacks strewn with dog hair. She glares at her aunt and sips her coffee.

'We did find some items of clothing in the cases, madam, but that's not all there was. Take a look at these pictures.' Inspector Williams holds out two more photographs. 'This is what we found inside.' One picture shows a tailored uniform and some papers; the other is a Sten gun, its leather strap coiled in a loop, alongside a handgun and ammunition. 'Do you recognise any of these items?'

I'm so annoyed I couldn't clear out those cases, Evelyn thinks. *But I did try, tottering on top of that rickety chair in the bedroom, stretching up to the top of the wardrobe, nearly grabbing the handle and then falling. That's when I knew I couldn't hide away any longer, when I knew I could no longer cover my tracks. I should never have put the cases up there in the first place. Under the bed would have been much more sensible. Why didn't I think of that?*

But all she says is, 'What a big gun, Inspector! However did it get there?'

'Exactly. That's what we'd like to know, madam. It would be most helpful to us if you could throw any light on the ownership.'

Evelyn is silent. The Inspector takes a picture of an old passport from his file. 'We found this in the case as well,' he says. 'Your niece has told us that the photo in this is you when you were younger. But the passport is in the name of Eva Kuscheck. Can you tell me why you appear to have a passport in that name?'

Evelyn continues staring, then looks at the tea tray on the side table and says, 'How disappointing. The Bourbons have all gone. Pat, have you eaten them all?'

Pat heaves a sigh. 'No, I haven't, but I'll go and see if they've got any in the kitchen. Mary said she'd find some ages ago.'

Evelyn watches her go. 'She always was a greedy child. Just like her father, Charles. He was my brother, you know. So sad that she never really knew him.' She twists her handkerchief in her hands and wonders if this would be a good moment to dab at her eyes. But perhaps she should save teary distress for now, save it for when the questions get uncomfortably close to the truth.

Inspector Williams shuffles through his file again, then holds out a copy of a letter, inviting her to visit the Kaiserhof Hotel. 'Perhaps this will jog your memory.'

Evelyn holds the photographed letter, remembering so clearly how daring she had felt driving to her assignation, how relieved she had been to have this opportunity to escape and how intimidated she had been by his imperious gaze, his arrogance and his assumption that she would never speak about his methods. All pleasure she had taken in the interview and the civilised coffee and cake had been eradicated under his stern, dismissive disdain.

'I understand from your niece that you were stationed in Germany soon after the end of the war. Can you tell me anything about that time?'

Evelyn continues to stare at the invitation, deciding how best to reply. *About that time. That time of horror and uncertainty, immediately after all the horror that had gone before.* After a minute, she speaks, looking at the Inspector with a bright smile. 'Apfelküchen,' she says. 'There were still shortages of supplies everywhere at that time, but we had wonderful Apfelküchen. I brought the recipe back with me and often made it at home.'

'I see. This, this Apfelküchen or whatever… was it served at the Kaiserhof Hotel?'

'Apple cake, Inspector. It's apple cake. We ate it with Schlagsahne, when we could get it. Sugar was in short supply in those days, but when I came home in later years, I made it with a sprinkling of brown sugar on top. So delicious. Shall I ask the kitchen here to make some for you?'

'That's very kind of you, Mrs Taylor-Clarke…'

'Oh, Mrs T-C will do, Inspector. Everyone here calls me Mrs T-C.' Evelyn cocks her head to one side, looking at the baffled man, his pencil poised over his pad.

'Your pencil isn't very sharp,' she says, 'Would you like me to sharpen it for you?'

He looks down at the blunt stub of pencil, then hands it to her. Evelyn delves into her capacious handbag and pulls out a small silver pencil sharpener. Curls fall onto the coffee tray and when she has finished, she hands it back to him. 'There, that's better. You'll find your writing is much clearer now.'

He looks at some notes in his file, then says, 'We've been doing some background checks and believe you worked for a time at the Combined Services Detailed Interrogation Centre at Bad Nenndorf in Germany. Is that correct?'

'Oh, I don't know. Is that where I went?'

'Service records would indicate that you did. Can you tell me anything about the work you were involved in there?' He sits, pencil poised over his pad, waiting for an answer, as Pat returns with another plate of biscuits.

'You're in luck. Danielle managed to find a new packet in the kitchen. Perhaps you'll be satisfied now.'

'I had to help this nice gentleman sharpen his pencil,' says Evelyn. 'Fancy coming to work without a sharp pencil.' She smiles at the two of them, Pat sipping her almost cold cup of coffee and Inspector Williams, still waiting for an answer to his question. Evelyn stretches her hand across to the fresh plate of biscuits and takes a Bourbon.

The Inspector clears his throat, then says, 'We've been able to confirm from service records that you were based at the centre at the same time as Colonel Stephen Robinson. Do you recall a gentleman of that name? I believe he would have been your superior officer in those days.'

'Robin,' says Evelyn. 'Was there a Robin?' She nibbles her biscuit, then begins to hum, which develops into singing in a wavering voice, 'When the red, red robin comes bob-bob, bobbin' along—'

Pat slams her cup down on its saucer, rattling the whole tray. 'Do you see what I mean? It's hopeless. I don't know how we're ever going to find out what's been going on.'

'Not to worry,' says Inspector Williams. 'I can pop back another day. Sometimes, when people have had a chance to reflect, they remember things after a while.'

Oh, I do remember. I remember it all most distinctly. There's no doubt about that. But all Evelyn says is, 'Oh dear, are you all going now? Do come again soon, won't you? I'll ask Cook to make us a special apple cake.'

Part Three

Animals have strange cuter ears (9)

Chapter 18

12 July 1945

My dearest darling,

Such a thrill! At last my language skills are finally going to be useful. I always thought they would be eventually, although during the months when I was training and they were making me crawl through woods in Scotland and I was brushing up my French, I wasn't sure if I would ever be able to make good use of my German, which as you know is really quite fluent.

But now the war in Europe is finally over and we have to ensure it stays that way, so I am finally going out to Germany after all. When we first heard the news of the surrender, of course I was thrilled, just like everyone else, but I'm ashamed to say that, even as we were all celebrating, a little part of me was just the teeniest bit disappointed, thinking I would no longer be useful and actually joining in with the real action and following in my brave husband's footsteps. I had been so looking forward to my new identity, to being called Eva. It quite suits me, don't you think?

The division I'm joining is setting up a new base to interview German military personnel and others, not far from Hanover. I am really quite excited, but also a little apprehensive, now that we know how dreadfully so many people were treated out there. I'm hoping it won't be too ghastly, but I do so want to help. I know I will encounter some awful people, I'm sure, but some of their strategic information will be jolly useful. Thank goodness I have not let my German get rusty or *aus der Übung*, should I say. I had to keep it up to scratch while I was training, just in case.

But, and this a very big but, my darling, and I think you would be rather cross with me if you were here and knew this: I believe the unit is under the command of your 'he who cannot be named', Colonel Stephen Robinson. I know, I know, you're thinking how on earth is she going to keep her feelings under control and will she be sent back home in disgrace? Well, to tell the truth, I am wondering how I'll feel when I see his face for the first time, as my hatred for the man who caused your death has not declined one tiny bit. But I've decided I'm going to absolutely do the best job I possibly can and while I'm doing it, if I see any glimpse of a chink in his armour or find any opportunity to make him pay dearly for his dreadful errors of judgement, I will do so, just you wait and see.

Our operation will be based in Bad Nenndorf, which I understand is a spa town somewhere near Hanover. Apparently one of the spa resorts there is being equipped for use as the centre of our operations, so I expect it will all be very clean and up to the minute.

The Germans call the spa facilities the *Schlammbad*, which literally means mud bath! Sounds quite exotic, doesn't it, but I'm sure I shan't be getting my hands dirty or having any wonderful spa treatments, as I expect I shall be scribbling away, trying to get every word of the interviews down on paper. I hope I will be able to do the job justice and that you will be proud of me.

Much love darling,
    Your Evie xxx
    Ps I love you

Chapter 19

Eva, 15 August 1945

Glorious Mud

Eva Kuscheck, Evelyn Taylor-Clarke as was, walked from her guesthouse to the interrogation centre. Her scratchy khaki was stifling in the hot sunshine of late summer and she was sure her uniform carried a faint odour of the cabbage that her sullen German landlady was continually steaming into damp submission.

It was Eva's first day of duty at the Winckler-Bath spa in Bad Nenndorf, but there were no rows of athletic bronzed maidens in swimsuits, bending to touch their toes at the foot of sunbeds by the edge of a glittering pool; there was nothing at all that corresponded to her idea of a luxurious health resort. The sweeping brown walls of the complex reminded her of the mud treatments available in the *Schlammbad* for which the town was famous. Perhaps the mud was ubiquitous and used for everything here: the spas, the bricks of the buildings, even the rendering of the exterior. She imagined mud puddling around her feet in their sturdy polished shoes, as she sat writing reports at her desk inside the former clinic.

A tiring combination of boat, train and trucks had conveyed her across the war-battered landscape of Europe. She'd passed towns reduced to piles of rubble, where tired ragged women and shaven-headed children piled bricks in the streets, and shattered stations where emaciated refugees held out their hands as the trains trundled by. At last she had arrived at this famous spa town in Lower Saxony, about twenty miles from Hanover, where people had been coming for the acclaimed healing powers of the waters for nearly two centuries. As the final lorry carried her to the clean but sparse guesthouse where she and some of the other clerks were billeted, she glimpsed the extensive landscaped gardens of the spa town's *Kurpark*, now unmown and weed-strewn from neglect during the years of war.

The town's buildings were undamaged though not well maintained, the people were thin but not starving, her landlady was curt but not hostile. *I've tried to make her smile, but she resents us*, Eva realised. *We're the enemy now, here to tell them how to manage their country and looking at every citizen and wondering how much they really knew and whether they too were complicit in that horrific regime.*

And now she was reporting for duty, ready to record in shorthand and longhand, in English and in German, the interviews with prisoners for the Combined Services Detailed Interrogation Centre, which had now established its headquarters in the former baths. She paused and took a deep breath as she approached the glazed entrance doors. She'd been determined to obtain this posting. Her discreet questions had told her where she'd find him and now her efforts would bring her face to face with the officer she held responsible for Hugh's death. But now she was here, she felt nervous. This would be her first encounter with him. Would she know it was him? Would she be able to tell straight away from his steely eyes that he was the ruthless man who had condemned Hugh and the others?

And this was going to be very different to the work she had been hoping to do if the war hadn't ended. She'd prepared herself to follow in Hugh's footsteps, training for armed and unarmed combat, crawling through Scottish woods and operating radios. In the stately 'omes of England, as the SOE recruits all joked, they had undergone mock interrogations as well as lessons in coding and silent killing. *I thought I might be a heroine and die a vainglorious death just so I could meet you again, my darling.*

After her time as an ATS driver and a brief period translating interviews with returning agents and prisoners, she had been ready to sacrifice herself as a special agent like Hugh, if necessary. And then suddenly it was all over and yet not over. There was joy and jubilation, but there was also chaos, and the devastation across Europe required order, restoration and investigation and so she was here, with her secretarial skills, her keen ear and her talent for interpretation, here to listen and report and maybe to put the record straight too.

'Hello. You're new here, aren't you?'

A cheery question, from a red-cheeked sergeant who had walked up behind her, interrupted her thoughts. His razor obviously hadn't been sharp enough that morning for a smooth shave, but was keen enough to nick his jaw, where a wisp of tissue still clung with a dark stain to his skin.

'Just arrived. Evelyn Taylor-Clarke. At least I think I am still. For quite a while I thought I was going to be Eva Kuscheck. If the war hadn't finished when it did, I might have been able to put all that crawling around in Scottish forests to good use.'

'Well, you can call yourself Eva while you're here, if you like. Training for SOE, were you?'

Eva didn't answer, but saw the lift of his eyebrow. 'Count yourself lucky the show finished early. Hardly any of those chaps ever made it back.' He offered his hand. 'James McGregor – Jimmy. Welcome to the Bad Nenndorf Spa.' He glanced up at the austere building. 'Doesn't look like the healthiest of places, does it?'

Eva smiled. 'I had expected a spa would be a bit more salubrious than this. What's it like to work here?'

'It's pretty strict, but not bad. At least we're getting decent rations now and the town was never a target, so we're fairly comfortable. How's your billet?'

'Spotless, but it reeks of caraway and cabbage. At least I won't have to eat there!' She laughed. 'Still, it's slightly better than the ones back home – they all smelt of carbolic and onions.' She looked around at the grounds, the park and the forests beyond. 'Is there anything around here to help pass the time when we're off-duty?'

'Afraid not. It's a pretty dead town and I suspect it always was. After all, you can't expect much of a lively nightlife in a place that's supposed to make you fit and healthy, can you?'

'I suppose not. Then I'll just have to make do with walks in the fresh air when I get some free time.'

At that moment they both turned at the sound of an army truck pulling up nearby. Two guards positioned themselves either side of the tailgate and yanked the handcuffed occupants out. Some were still in uniform, others were just in shirt and trousers; more than one stumbled as they jumped to the ground. And one young man caught Eva's eye and smiled at her. He was about the same age as Charles, her brother. Despite his capture he had clean, neatly combed blond hair, and as he was marched past her and into the centre, he smiled again.

'Looks like we'd better get started,' Jimmy said, once the procession had disappeared inside.

'I'll follow you then. I haven't been briefed yet. Any tips you want to give me now, or do I just jump in at the deep end?'

He turned and looked at her with a grave expression. 'Just follow orders, particularly those from Robinson. Wouldn't do to get on the wrong side of him.' Then he opened the door for her. 'Abandon hope all ye who enter here,' he said, as he waved her through.

Robinson. She felt a tingle on the back of her neck at the mention of his name and she remembered Tim McNeil's words: 'He's a little terrier of a man. Sinks his teeth in and won't let go.' *We'll see who won't let go*, she told herself. *I've come this far and now we'll meet at last.*

Chapter 20

Eva, 16 August 1945

Smile for the Camera

'Can you tell me why we have to have our picture taken today?' Eva grumbled as she tucked a few stray hairs under her cap. She had reapplied her lipstick but was determined not to smile in the photograph.

'The Chief likes to keep a record of everyone. Maybe he hasn't got a good memory for faces. Don't worry, you'll get your own copy for old times' sake.' Jimmy had come to collect her from the little office where she was going to be typing up her interview notes. 'Come on, don't want to keep the gang waiting.'

Eva followed him along the corridor. It was her second day and she'd done nothing so far, apart from equip her typewriter with a new ribbon, file some reports and sharpen her pencils. But maybe this would be the day she finally met the man she had come here hoping to confront.

Another new female clerk joined them as they neared the entrance and they all stepped outside into the hot sunshine. Squinting in the brightness, Eva said, 'How long is this going to take? I haven't even started on any real work yet.'

'Don't worry about it. I should make the most of the peace and quiet while you can. You'll soon be hard at it.' Jimmy felt inside his jacket, then offered both girls a cigarette. When they declined, he said, 'Well, if you're not going to smoke your ration, best save it and sell it on later. Keep it quiet, mind, but the locals are desperate for fags so you'll get a good rate for them.'

'The people here are luckier than most,' murmured Eva. 'So many cities have been devastated. I saw such terrible destruction on my way here – people begging, digging through rubble, desperate for anything we could spare. And I know we're not supposed to give the Germans anything, but we're getting more than enough to eat, so surely it wouldn't hurt to share some of the rations coming in now?'

'Nasty business, war,' muttered Jimmy, wafting his smoke away from them and taking off his cap to wipe his brow with a crumpled grubby handkerchief. 'But you'll be in trouble if you try to help them. One of the chaps said their German cook was caught taking home scraps of food from the barracks and now he's been sent to prison. He was only doing it to feed his family.'

'But do you honestly think all the Germans are guilty? You can't blame everyone, surely?'

'You'll soon see for yourself. They can all say, oh, I wasn't that sort of a Nazi, as much as they like, but I can't believe they didn't really know what was going on in the concentration camps.'

After another five minutes, Eva said, 'How much longer will we have to wait around here?' She peered inside the entrance to the building, but still couldn't see anyone else coming. 'I'd just like to settle down to some proper work.'

'Oh, you won't be doing anything for a day or two, I bet. That new consignment's only just come in. They won't be ready for us yet.' Jimmy ground the cigarette end under his heel, then strolled up and down, flexing his shoulders.

Eva watched him, trying to work out what he meant, then heard brisk steps marching down the hallway, accompanied by curt, clipped words, and out stepped a small, dapper man with a tidy moustache, wearing a sharply pressed uniform.

'Right, line up. Let's get this over with,' he snapped, waving at the three of them with his swagger stick. The photographer who'd followed him fussed with his camera and waved his hands backwards and forwards to position the group till the Colonel spat, 'Just take it, man. Take it as we are and have done with it.' And then the camera clicked two or three times as he stood in front of the entrance doors, with his lesser colleagues arranged to his right.

So this was Robinson. This slightly built, brusque little man was the 'terrier' Tim had described. Eva tried to look at him while they all stood side by side, heads up, shoulders back, but the cameraman urged them to stay quite still and look straight ahead. She caught a glimpse of uncertain half-smiles on the faces of her two companions and thin, tightly pressed lips on the Colonel, who jerked his chin as if his starched collar was constricting his throat. And after the shutter had clicked, she heard him bark, 'Right, as you were. Back to it, chaps.' Then he marched back inside the building, the footsteps from his highly polished shoes echoing on the flagstones of the entrance hall.

'We can relax now,' Jimmy said, lighting another cigarette. 'You can take your time if you want. There's nothing much doing today.'

'Why not? We should be getting on with the debriefings, shouldn't we? Not hanging about, twiddling our thumbs.'

Jimmy shrugged. 'You'll be busy soon enough, once he gives the signal, don't you worry. I tell you, if he had work for us, he wouldn't be out here taking beauty shots. Once he gets going in there, he doesn't stop.'

'Bit of a taskmaster, is he?'

'I wouldn't say that exactly. It's more that...' He paused, as if trying to find the right words, '...once he's picked up the scent, he follows it to the end. There's no stopping him then.'

'Am I right in thinking that was Colonel Robinson?' *Please let it be him. That's the reason I'm here. I've come all this way, but I have to be sure.*

'That's him.' Jimmy leant close to Eva and, in a lowered voice, said, 'Ruthie, we call him.'

'Ruthie? Isn't that a girl's name?'

Jimmy laughed. 'Short for Ruthless. He got the name in his previous position, running agents on special ops. End justifies the means, he always says.'

Eva watched Jimmy disappear through the heavy swing doors with the other clerk. The words he had uttered just before he left had made her shiver, with their echo of all she had heard about Robinson from Hugh and Tim McNeil. She was relieved that all her efforts had brought her to the right place, but how was she going to work under this man? How could she come to terms with what he had done to Hugh? She could feel a knot in her stomach and a hard lump of bile rising in her throat. He didn't look like the type to succumb to the charms of blonde hair and lipstick. But at least she now knew what he looked like, and soon she'd have her own copy of the group photograph to keep, so she would never be able to forget him.

Chapter 21

Eva, 10 October 1945

The Promise

'Bitte, helfen Sie mich.' The words were half croaked, half whispered through the cracked and bloodied lips of the German prisoner, who had been dragged into the interrogation room and strapped to the metal chair. He was alone in the room, half mumbling, half sobbing to himself. His head slumped to his chest, his lank, dirty hair fell over his eyes and she could barely hear his words. 'Ich habe nichts falsch gemacht.'

Eva had just arrived for that morning's interview. The door to the room was open and she glanced over her shoulder along the corridor. It was quiet for the moment and she couldn't hear those brisk clipped footsteps, but she knew Colonel Robinson would come back to the interrogation room very soon, accompanied by Arnold Miller, the brutal thickset sergeant who did his dirty work.

'You poor man. I'm sure you're innocent,' she whispered, closing the door a little. 'I believe you. I'm so sorry they're treating you so badly.'

'Jede nacht,' he said, lifting his head so she could see his face, 'they take away our clothes, we have nothing…'

Eva gave a sharp intake of breath. She realised she had seen him before. She recognised him, despite the bruises and the layers of grime. Kurt Becker. She knew from his file that he'd been a teacher before the war started and that he was planning to return to teaching in Frankfurt, but it also noted that he had links to Communist sympathisers. She remembered him arriving at the centre and greeting her cheerily with a comment about the wonderful weather and saying, 'Ach, sehr gut. Ich habe Schlammbad sehr gern', as if he was here for a spa treatment and a holiday, not imprisonment and deprivation.

At his first interview, six weeks previously, his blond hair had still been relatively clean and neat, his shirt unstained, his skin clear and healthy. He had smiled at her and politely introduced himself in a formal manner before the questions began. Now he was hollow-eyed, his face grey, his once-strong body skeletal, and Eva could smell the sour odours of vomit and urine from his filthy clothes.

'Kurt – I can call you Kurt, can't I?' Then she stopped and listened. Steps were coming nearer. 'I promise you,' she whispered. 'This is all so wrong. I promise I will do whatever I can to stop this. They shouldn't be treating you like this.'

And then the door was flung wide open with a crash, making both her and the prisoner flinch, and it started all over again. She kept her eyes on her notepad, her hand shaking as she recorded the interview with her sharp pencil, trying hard to be indifferent to the Colonel's curt questions and the prisoner's faltering replies.

'Come along now,' Robinson said in his crisp, clipped tones. 'You may as well admit it. We know you meet with your so-called friends.' Kurt's head slumped forwards. If he hadn't been strapped to the narrow metal chair, he would have fallen onto the concrete floor.

'Miller,' Robinson snapped. 'Sit him up.' With a passive face, his sergeant grabbed a handful of Kurt's hair in his huge fist and wrenched him back into an upright position. Kurt moaned and as his battered mouth fell open, Eva could see broken and missing teeth.

'Good. That's more like it,' Robinson said with a tight smile on his face. 'Now look me in the eye and tell me where you have these meetings.' And all the time he probed with his insistent, repetitive questions, he stared with cold, unkind eyes, smiling at every blow, every slap from the guard. When Miller pulled him up by his ears or his hair, whenever his head fell forward, Robinson gave a little murmur of approval or said, 'That's it, Miller. Remind him why we're here.' And every time those fists lashed out, Robinson smirked.

Was that how Robinson had looked when he planned and executed that fatal mission, that final operation that meant the end for Hugh? And did he nod with smug satisfaction when he reported that while the loss of a handful of agents might be considered unfortunate, it was necessary collateral to hoodwink the Germans?

Eva bit the inside of her cheek, tasting blood, feeling her heart pounding, trying to control her anger and concentrate on taking notes. Hugh and his men were merely pawns for Robinson, that's all he was thinking when he sent them on their last disastrous journey. And as the questioning continued, Eva noticed blond hairs glinting on Sergeant Miller's khaki uniform, a scattering of hairs torn from Kurt's scalp.

She never saw Colonel Robinson ill-treat the prisoners himself; she never saw anything happen directly in front of her, she never saw the crushing blows to the head or the tightening of the leg-irons that broke the skin and left ulcerating sores; nor had she seen the damp cells chilled by icy winds blowing through unglazed windows. No, they were too clever for that. But she could guess why the prisoners who began their weeks of interrogation in a relatively healthy condition soon became bruised, emaciated, shivering shadows of their former selves.

Chapter 22

Eva, October 1945

Slammed Up

Jimmy confirmed her fears when they took a stroll around the grounds of the spa one afternoon, a couple of days later. It was good to take deep breaths of the clean cold air after another gruelling morning under the harsh lights of the interrogation room. They walked for a while in silence, Jimmy smoking, Eva's polished shoes crunching the crisp fallen leaves. Behind some trees she saw one of the resort's old sign boards: *Gesund und Geheilung*. 'Healthy and healing,' she translated, pointing to the fading words. 'Not any more, it isn't. It's a slammer, not a Schlammbad.'

'They had to take another one of the Germans down to the hospital last night. He was in a really bad way. And it sounds like he's not going to make it,' Jimmy told her. 'I reckon if this happens too often, we could be in a spot of bother here. I've heard that the fellow last night told the doctor he didn't want to come back here because of his treatment. I kept telling them they were pushing their luck.'

'Who was it? Do you know?'

'Kurt something or other. Youngish chap.'

'I know the one.' She hung her head and took a deep breath before speaking. 'I'm sure I remember seeing him when he first arrived. He wasn't in bad shape at the start. Now all the prisoners are in terrible condition after only a short stay at this so-called health resort. They practically had to carry one poor chap in this morning. I saw him when he arrived as well, so I know he was fit and healthy only a few weeks ago. And now they're all weak and filthy. What on earth are they doing to them down there?'

Jimmy took a long drag on his cigarette, then said, 'Well, I've not actually seen it with my own eyes, but I reckon they're not exactly tucking them up in bed in their pyjamas with hot cocoa every night, are they?'

Eva's face was white and she bit her lip. 'I think I know what you mean. It's brutal. They shouldn't be doing this. They're deliberately mistreating them. They must be stripping them when they go back to those freezing cells, as well as starving and beating them.'

'Reckon so. Doesn't look too good, does it?'

'I've tried saying this can't be right, but I just get told to keep quiet, as they're getting results.'

'End justifies the means,' he murmured.

Eva shuddered at hearing those words again. 'It goes against all the rules, Jimmy. You know it does. We've got to stop it.'

'Try telling old Ruthie and the others that. While they're getting the results they want, or so they say, then I guess they'll keep on doing it.'

'But they're going to end up killing them.'

'Between you and me, I don't think they care if they do.' Jimmy finished his cigarette and threw it down, grinding the glowing stub with the toe of his boot into the gravel path. 'Anyway, I heard Ruthie Robinson stirred all the guards up good and proper before the prisoners first started arriving. His way of giving them all an induction course before he really got cracking here.'

'Why, what did he do exactly?'

'He gave all the boys a nice little day out. A special outing, just for them. Arranged a personal tour of Bergen-Belsen and then told them they'd be guarding the men responsible. I reckon that got them all fired up.'

Eva gasped. 'He did that deliberately? But he knows full well that's not true. None of the prisoners here were concentration camp guards.'

'Exactly. He pretty much lit the blue touch paper, didn't he? And now the trials have started at Lünenburg, everyone knows what horrors went on in the camps, so our boys certainly aren't going to hold back.'

Eva stared into the distance, taking more deep breaths of the fresh air, renowned for its health-giving properties. 'I've seen the way he looks at those poor men during the interviews. I can't bear looking at him or the prisoners. I try to keep my head down and just do my job, but whenever I catch a glimpse of his face I get the feeling he's really enjoying himself. He gloats and smirks while they're suffering. Especially when that brute Miller has his way with them.' She shook her head, frowning in disgust. 'And these wretched men have had nothing to do with those ghastly camps. That's not why they're here, that's not what he's after. He's quizzing them about their affiliations.'

'Commies,' said Jimmy. 'He's looking for Commies.'

'I understand that and I know it's important, but does it have to be so brutal?'

Jimmy shrugged. 'He's only interested in the end result. You know he chose this place deliberately? Bad Nenndorf was known as a stately old spa town before the war and before he got this set-up running. Quite the holiday resort, it was.'

'This was one of the spas, wasn't it?'

'That's right. He inspected this place, saw the tiled bathrooms and said they'd make ideal cells. So they weren't exactly cosy in the first place. No wall-to-wall carpet to rip out, just bare floors and cold tiles. Perfect for him.'

Jimmy lit another cigarette and drew on it, making the tip glow red. 'You know what the locals are calling this town now, don't you?'

Eva turned to him, her eyes puzzled. 'No, what? Tell me.'

'Das Verbotene Dorf,' Jimmy said, pronouncing the words with a slight rise of his eyebrows to underline its significance.

'The Forbidden Village,' Eva murmured. 'No wonder. We came over here to put things right, but we're making it worse. We're almost as bad as they were.'

Chapter 23

Eva, 1 November 1945

The Kaiserhof Hotel

Eva let the gleaming black Horch V8 slow to a crawl as she entered the wrought-iron gates of the Kaiserhof Hotel. The former Wehrmacht car, which had been requisitioned by the interrogation centre for the use of staff on rare days of leave, purred down the long gravelled drive towards the grand baroque establishment. The tall elm trees on either side of the avenue were bare and the formal flower beds, once alive with colour all summer long, were now empty, but this wintry scene was a welcome relief for Eva after the hypocrisy and horror of the work she was enduring at Bad Nenndorf.

'They're recruiting at the Kaiserhof in Bad Pyrmont,' Jimmy had whispered to her three days previously, during a brief break from the intense questioning. 'Get yourself down there. You can't take much more of this.'

Eva was shaking after that morning's ordeal. The female prisoner, bruised and filthy, had fainted after struggling to answer a series of stern questions. Robinson hadn't looked pleased this time. He was impatient at this waste of his time and told Miller to take her away for a cold bath.

Jimmy was right. She couldn't take much more, it was killing her. She didn't know who was recruiting at the hotel or what they were recruiting for, but she had to take her chance and try to get away before it broke her as well as the prisoners. She had wanted to stay as long as possible to find an opportunity to undermine Robinson, but he was so thorough, so efficient, she could not see how she could ever defeat him or call him to account.

With its sculpted Dutch gable roof, the hotel reminded her of the blue and white ceramic houses filled with kirsch that she had brought back as innocent souvenirs from her trip to Germany before the war, before she married Hugh, before all the horror of the years of combat and after. A number of other cars were parked outside and Eva hoped there would not be a lot of applicants for whatever posts were on offer.

Inside, fires crackled in the stone fireplaces on either side of the grand entrance hall and chandeliers twinkled overhead from gilded ceilings, in utter contrast to the stark interview rooms and the cold, squalid cells of the interrogation centre. As she crossed the hall, she caught sight of a group of men ascending the imposing stone staircase and heard what sounded like American voices.

The receptionist directed Eva to the *Salon*, a side room where buttoned leather and walnut armchairs were paired with pedestal tables, inviting intimate conversation. A man in a tweed suit was sitting in the furthest corner and lowered his newspaper, peering over half-moon spectacles, which he removed as Eva entered.

She held out the headed letter she'd received that had directed her to the hotel. 'I hope I've come to the right place. I heard there might be some openings here.'

'Could be,' he said. 'If you don't mind hearing a few sob stories.' He waved at the unoccupied chair opposite him. 'Brian Joliffe. Very pleased to meet you.' He looked kind, his eyes crinkling at the corners as he smiled, so unlike the icy features of Colonel Robinson. She glanced down at the newspaper and noticed he'd half-completed the crossword, something the cold Colonel would consider a frivolous waste of time.

'Eva Kuscheck,' she said as they shook hands. 'I've been hearing a lot of sad stories lately. Trouble is, I don't like the way they're being told. Or rather, the way they're being dragged out of the subjects concerned.'

'Where's that then?' Joliffe beckoned to the waiter, who had appeared in the doorway, a tray tucked under his arm. 'Kaffe und Küchen, bitte.' Then he glanced at Eva and said, 'We'll see what they can rustle up, shall we? There's not much variety with all the shortages, but the food is gradually getting better.'

'I'm happy with anything, thank you, although I haven't had much appetite lately, because of my present job.'

'So where are you now?'

'Bad Nenndorf.'

His expression changed immediately and he reached for the silver cigarette case on the table, offered it to Eva, who shook her head, then took one out for himself. Tapping the cigarette on the little table, he said, 'I'm not surprised you want to leave. Rumours are circulating that Bad Nenndorf is a bad, bad operation. Remind me who's the chap in charge there?'

'Colonel Stephen Robinson. Do you know him?'

'Heard of him. I'm told he knows how to get results.' He looked at Eva and fumbled in his jacket pocket for a lighter.

Eva hung her head. 'I suppose you could say he makes absolutely sure nothing gets in the way of him getting the results he wants. Doesn't mean to say those results are the truth, though.'

'That's pretty much what I've heard too. He could come unstuck eventually, but for now, he'll be giving the Allies exactly what they want.'

'I've tried my best,' Eva said, biting her lower lip. 'I've told him and the others, but no one will listen to me. And now one of the prisoners has died and others are likely to follow, given how they're being treated. I can't stay there much longer, I've got to get out as soon as I can.'

'When did you sign up?'

'I joined the ATS in '43. August, actually.'

'So you haven't done your three years yet.' He drew on his cigarette and paused. 'But you could get out early on medical grounds. Fake it, keep going off sick. Or pretend you're pregnant. That'll scare them, they'll have you out on your ear in no time then.' He winked at her. 'Think you could do that?'

Eva was shocked for a second, then she laughed. 'I'd do anything to get away, but won't that mean seeing a doctor? How will I get them to believe me?'

Brian smiled. 'You needn't worry about that. Let me know when you're ready to move on and I'll arrange the medical for you.'

As their food and drink arrived, each slice of cake topped with whipped cream, she said, 'But why are you recruiting here? You haven't told me what I would be letting myself in for. Though it can hardly be worse than where I am right now.'

Brian was distracted by the food, thanking the waiter, then saying, 'I guessed they'd give us apple cake again. I think they must have had a good crop this autumn, it's apple this and apple that everywhere I go. Still, it's jolly good.' He passed one of the scalloped porcelain plates to Eva. 'Now, where were we?'

'The job, the position you're recruiting for. What is it?'

'Ah, yes. It's a newish outfit. You probably won't have heard of it.' He slid a forkful of cake piled with cream into his mouth, then wiped his lips with the napkin as he munched. After a second, he said, 'What do you think is desperately needed here in this country right now?'

Eva stared at him, her cake untouched. 'Rebuilding? Restoration of agriculture and industry? I saw how damaged the stations and railways were when I was travelling across Germany. And I know the people are short of food. A driver at our centre told me he and his wife are only getting four pieces of bread a day each.'

Brian shook his head slowly, then said, 'All of that's important, yes, but what we also need now is humanity and dignity. In fact, relief and rehabilitation. It's the most gigantic problem ever seen.

Can you believe there's currently something like eleven million people in this country who didn't ask to be here? All those poor beggars who survived those ghastly camps and the factories that ran on slave labour.'

'I had absolutely no idea it was so many.'

'Poor devils can't go home without our help. Many have lost their whole family, while others are desperately trying to trace their relatives. Some of them will never get back home, some will choose to emigrate and get away to start a new life. All we can do is feed them, help them get healthy, if that's ever going to be possible, and sort out their paperwork.'

'It sounds like it needs a lot of administration and interpretation, as well as supplies and medicine. I can do that. I came to Germany wanting to do my bit and this could be my chance to really help at last.'

'Good girl! But it won't be an easy job. These people have suffered terribly. But at least they've survived this far and with the right kind of help they may be able to go on to rebuild their lives. But it's only the displaced people we're helping, not the Germans themselves.' He put down his plate with a thump, making the little cake fork jump and clatter. 'They got themselves into this mess, they don't deserve our sympathy or our food.'

For a second Eva remembered the ragged children, the women with scarves knotted over their heads, the men in tattered army uniforms. She told herself to stifle her compassion for them and said, 'Will there be a uniform?'

He laughed. 'Not particularly. Come as you are. Anyone asks why you're still in ATS kit, blame it on me.' Then he gave her his card and told her to phone him once she'd reported sick.

Eva never forgot that interview, nor the disturbing encounter that occurred just as she was leaving the hotel. After agreeing details with Joliffe and thanking him for his hospitality, she walked through the mirrored reception area, smiling properly for the first time in weeks and congratulating herself on using her accumulated cigarette ration to pay one of the regular drivers for the use of the car.

It was going to happen, she would escape Bad Nenndorf. She would call in sick in the morning and adopt a phantom pregnancy, as suggested, to spirit her away from that ghastly place. She was nearly at the entrance with its large glazed doors when she heard a brittle but familiar voice, which sent a piercing chill into her heart: 'Kuscheck! What the hell are you doing here?'

She turned. To her horror, Colonel Robinson was coming down the sweeping staircase, ahead of the group of men she'd spotted earlier. He strode towards her, heels clicking on the polished stone floor. 'Well, well, well… What have you been up to? Having a little private assignation, eh?'

'No, sir. Just tea. I mean coffee. And cake.'

'Just so long as you're not talking about our operation.' His eyes narrowed and he jerked his chin. 'Insubordination is punishable, you know.'

'I was just leaving, sir.'

'Mind how you drive then. Wouldn't want you having an unfortunate accident now, would we?' He tapped his swagger stick several times on the palm of his left hand. 'There are penalties for that too, you know.'

Chapter 24

Eva, 10 November 1945

Morning Sickness

It wasn't hard to fake nausea when every day of witnessing the interrogations brought a new wave of revulsion. Eva closed her eyes, covered her mouth with her hand and pretended to retch in plain sight. She created pallor with a lighter face powder and hollow eyes with smudged eyebrow pencil.

After three or four days in which she only picked at dry, bland foods at mealtimes and sipped plain water, Jimmy cornered her: 'You feeling all right? You're looking a bit peaky, if you don't mind me saying.'

She looked around the canteen, checking no one was listening. 'I took your advice about the hotel. I hope to be leaving very soon.' She rested her hand on his arm. 'Whatever you hear next, just don't believe a word of it.'

'Right you are. Just so long as you're sure.'

Eva was sure. She had to stop herself smiling and concentrate on her act, knowing that she must carry it off with utter conviction. But she wasn't looking forward to the next step.

The following morning, she decided she would make sure there could be no doubt. After collecting her bowl of breakfast porridge in the mess, she sat where she knew she could be seen clearly by Robinson and his closest cohorts. She stirred the sticky grey sludge with her spoon, toying with the food but not eating it. After pressing her hand to her stomach a couple of times, she sat back, taking deep breaths with her eyes closed. Odours of cooking fat, fried bread, Brylcreem and stale sweat filled her nostrils. It wasn't hard pretending to be nauseous.

'I say, are you feeling okay?' a girl at the next table asked. And that was Eva's curtain call. She stood abruptly, knocking her dish to the floor as she rose, and then let her knees weaken and she fell down into the swill of porridge and broken crockery.

When she opened her eyes, she was being helped onto her chair by two members of staff, who were wiping breakfast off her uniform and placing a glass of water in front of her. She lifted her head a little as she sipped and looked across the room. It appeared to have worked. Robinson had noticed her and he was frowning. 'I think I'd better report sick,' she said.

Later that day, while she was lying down in her room, waiting for a response to her star performance and her report to the centre's medical officer, armed with the note provided by Joliffe's contact, one of the other girls knocked on her door. 'The Colonel's asked to see you right away. Do you feel well enough to go on your own?'

Eva swung her legs off the bed and stood up, brushing her skirt and reaching for her jacket. 'I'm ready to face the music.'

Robinson didn't look at her when she entered his office. He continued to stare at the documents before him, crossing out a line here, adding a word there. She stood before him, her face impassive, arms stiff by her side.

Eventually he murmured, 'Sit down, before you fall down.'

So she sat upright on a hard chair on the other side of his desk, till he deigned to lift his head and acknowledge her. He leant back in his seat, staring at her, hands bridged together, fingertips tapping his lips. And then he finally spoke. 'Kuscheck, I'm disappointed in you. Wouldn't have thought you were the type to get yourself up the duff. Though after seeing you sneaking out of that hotel the other week, I suppose I shouldn't be surprised.' He paused, still in his prayerful pose. 'Damned annoying, though. You're a good interpreter. You know you'll have to go, don't you?'

'Yes, sir.' She hung her head, as if contrite.

'If there wasn't a shortage of interpreters I'd never agree to recruit women. You're to leave immediately, you hear?'

'Yes, sir.' She bit her lip to stop herself laughing. She didn't care what he or anyone else thought of her, she had achieved her objective and would soon be free.

'A driver will take you to the station in one hour. And you can forget all about what goes on here. Keep your damned mouth shut, you hear?'

He dismissed her without further questions about her plans for the future or her welfare. He didn't care whether she was sick or pregnant. She was of no consequence to him; her departure was just an inconvenience. Outside in the corridor she muttered under her breath, 'I damn well won't forget what goes on and I won't forgive, either. Humiliate me, disgrace me all you like. I'm free of you and I'll make sure you get what you deserve one day.'

She packed her case quickly, eager to leave. Brian Joliffe had given her instructions when she phoned him and soon she would be leaving one kind of hell and entering another, where those who had been to hell and back could at least be helped and even saved.

Chapter 25

Germany
15 November 1945

Darling,

I rather feel that if you were still here you would tell me I'd been foolish and naive to ever think I could cope with that posting. What a fool I was, not to see what was coming. The very title of the division should have alerted me in advance – Combined Services Detailed Interrogation Centre.

I know that it is important to find the most guilty people after all the terrible things that have been discovered and I know too that useful information about military and scientific developments can be gained from questioning, but what I can't stomach is man's inhumanity to man. I thought our country was on the side of the angels and now I feel that all men are capable of being equally ruthless and cruel.

To sit there, in those interrogations, day after day, translating as I wrote, seeing those poor wretches being brutally abused, starved and frozen, well, I just couldn't stomach it any more. I want to do my bit, you know I do, but I can't do it this way. I tried to make my views known, but I was told in no uncertain terms that the information gained this way was of national interest and their methods were permitted. I was even threatened with a court martial if I didn't keep quiet.

I wish I could have stuck it out for your sake, darling. I so wanted to catch Robinson out if I could, but I simply couldn't stay there any longer. Please forgive me, darling, for not getting even with him for you. I will try to think of some way in which I can seek revenge one day, you see if I don't. Not only will I be making amends for your demise, but I shall do it for the sake of those other poor wretches too. That odious man shall not get away with it.

And I hope you will also be able to forgive me for pretending to be 'in the club' just to get out of that awful place. I felt a little guilty, because I'd only ever wanted children with you, darling, but as it was the most effective and quickest way to get myself out of that hellhole, I had to do it. I rather think you might have found it a little amusing. You would certainly have enjoyed my play-acting!

So now I'm moving on again. Please don't think I'm being inconstant and capricious, I'm really not. I'm desperate to do some good but I can't do it here, so I'm transferring to an organisation that is helping to resettle the thousands of displaced people lost in this country. It's called the United Nations Relief and Rehabilitation Administration – UNRRA for short – and I'm going to a place near Frankfurt in a few days' time.

I had an interview with a very nice ex-colonel in the organisation at the Kaiserhof Hotel in Bad Pyrmont, not far away from here. It nearly went very badly as Robinson was also there for some reason and caught me as I was leaving. He tried to intimidate me but I managed to get away from him and shall be going to Frankfurt shortly. I shall be so relieved to leave Bad Nenndorf – the locals call it *Das Verbotene Dorf*, the Forbidden Village, and I think that just about sums it up.

Your loving Evie XXX
   Ps I love you

Four

Grand tea cooked in mall.

Different size portions (5,3,5)

Chapter 26

Evelyn, 22 July 1970

London

Evelyn settled herself on the park bench in the sun. West Square wasn't as pleasant a spot for lunch as St James's Park, which she could walk to in just minutes when the office was based in Broadway, but London had many pockets of green, which gave her the air and space she craved during a working day. Dear Broadway, right at the heart of government yet so near to that lovely park with its water birds and magnificent displays of bedding plants throughout the summer. And the elegant St Ermin's Hotel, so conveniently near for special meetings and the occasional afternoon tea for celebratory occasions. What fun she'd had years before, learning to dodge her trail around the back streets and taking photos surreptitiously in the park. That was such a lovely time, although she'd failed to take any snaps of the lake, the pelicans and ducks as she'd forgotten to remove the lens cap.

Century House, where the service was now located, wasn't nearly as attractive a location, but it was nearer Waterloo station and although she did rather miss her end-of-day stroll across Westminster Bridge (such a beautiful view of the Thames at all times of year), she appreciated the chance to catch an earlier train home, especially in summer, when there was so much to enjoy in the gardens at Kingsley. If she left her desk on the dot of five, why, with luck she could be home a little after six.

No, life was not so bad, she told herself as she unwrapped the egg and cress sandwich she had bought, just as she did every morning, from the little café run by such friendly Italians, Arturo and Maria, near the office. They knew her order off by heart now and she could nip in on her way to work and out again, in less than five minutes, with a lovely hot frothy coffee in a plastic cup too. Such a pleasant start to her day before the first of many dreary meetings.

Evelyn relished these quiet lunch hours when she could read and think in peace while other members of staff disappeared to smoke and drink pints with cheese and pickle sandwiches in local pubs or stroll along the river with their lunches packed in cloudy Tupperware or, the more senior ones, headed for clubs where they could claim to be discussing policy. She opened *The Times*, then folded the pages to fit her lap – she could read while she ate. She didn't enjoy its crossword nearly as much as the *Telegraph*, which she read on the way to work, but *The Times* was one of a selection of daily newspapers delivered to the office and, anyway, she preferred doing her puzzle when she caught the train at the end of the day. Concentrating on the cryptic clues always took her mind off the crush of commuters with their winter coughs and sniffles and their summer hay fever sneezes.

After a tedious morning of report reading, with no exciting conclusions to be drawn, Evelyn was glad to be outside, even though she could hear the drone of traffic and the occasional screech of a motorbike above the cooing of the pigeons gathering near her feet. But there was freshly mown grass, there were bright red geraniums and blue salvias planted in rows, heads up to the sun, just like her, and this quiet little square did not appear to have been discovered by any of her colleagues, nor was it a haunt for comatose tramps at this time of day.

She had just started to glance at the paper and taken the first bite of her sandwich when she read his name. It jumped right out of the columns of print, slapping her across the face. At first she wasn't too sure it was him, so she scanned the lists a line at a time. The bread felt like wet cardboard in her mouth and she struggled to swallow. And there it was, right there in the list of Birthday Honours, the name she could never forget: Stephen Robinson. It had been bad enough when he had been awarded an OBE a couple of years back, but for him to receive another distinction was simply too much. Order of Merit indeed. He must be swelling with pride and primping his prissy little moustache. 'Awarded for merit,' it said. Merit indeed. What merit was there in his brand of inhumane treatment?

Over the years, since leaving Bad Nenndorf under the cover of her phantom pregnancy, she had followed his career as best she could, but most of the time he had been abroad, where she could well imagine he had exercised his particular talents for extracting information. He'd been in Kenya in the 1950s, then Egypt and Aden, as far as she could tell. She'd often thought that their paths must eventually cross, at one or other official event, but he spent so little time in London and she'd never once seen him since the day she had left the interrogation centre under a cloud.

Evelyn forced herself to swallow her mouthful, then returned her now unappetising sandwich to its paper bag. Sometimes I almost forget, she thought, and then it all comes back again to taunt me, like a nasty buzzing fly that can't be swatted. Hugh should be the one getting the honours, not men like Robinson. They should be giving them to genuine heroes, men who've shown humanity and courage, not heartless cowards who hide behind stiff authority and punishment.

She turned the page, hoping to find some good news to give her hope that there was still sense in the world, but to her horror there was another bleak story to make her feel that decent honourable men would never receive the recognition they deserved. Karl-Friedrich Höcker, sentenced to seven years' imprisonment at the Frankfurt Auschwitz trial in 1965, for aiding and abetting a thousand murders in that terrible place, had been freed. 'He's only served five years,' she muttered aloud, almost choking with rage. Five years for his dreadful crime, him and others like him. *It's just not right.*

At the time of the Frankfurt trials she had been relieved that more war criminals had been traced and sentenced, even though in her opinion, and that of many other righteous people, the sentences were far too lenient for the terrible crimes they had committed. *But at least they've been named,* she'd thought. *At least everyone will know what they did. And how can they ever lead a normal life again once they've been singled out as monsters?* But she'd read and heard, one by one, that normal life was still theirs to claim. *That monstrous dentist, Willi Schatz, didn't even go to prison,* she'd thought, fuming. He was arrested at his private practice in Hanover and they tried him, but couldn't make the charge of selecting prisoners stick. And Dr Franz Lucas, convicted for gas chamber selection, only served just over three years. *These sentences are nothing for what they did.*

Evelyn sat with the folded newspaper and her wrapped sandwich on her lap. She had no appetite now. She couldn't eat after reading this terrible news, reminding her that she had never been able to make amends, taunting her with the thought that whatever she had done to live well and do good could never atone for the evil that had been perpetrated. *We had such hopes of Nuremberg,* she thought, having followed the trial closely. Such great hopes. But was the task simply too great? There were nearly four thousand cases, but most were dropped and fewer than five hundred went to trial. Of those, about two hundred were executed and nearly three hundred received life sentences, but a few years later, nearly all of them had been released. How could that be fair?

She stood up and brushed down her skirt, although no crumbs from the barely touched sandwich had fallen on her crisp, striped shirtdress, then began slowly to walk across the little park. She felt so sick, so disheartened, but then she remembered the face of the distressed prisoner who had pleaded for her help. *Pull yourself together, Evelyn. You must try harder,* she told herself, *you must find a way. You might not be able to deal with the Germans, but he will return to London. He is nearby. He may be only one of many who do not deserve to live, but he is the one you can deal with. You must find out more about him. Where does he go, what does he do in his spare time? Does he like music, theatre or opera? You'll have your chance one day if you really try.*

She came to a halt by the park waste bin and was about to throw her sandwich away, but then she stopped. She tore the offending pages from the newspaper, folded them and tucked them into her handbag. Then she emptied the paper bag onto the grass and a pigeon stepped forward and began pecking at the bread.

You don't need it, she thought. *You can manage with an extra couple of Rich Tea this afternoon when the tea trolley comes round.* She bent down to pick up a crisp packet that had been dropped on the path and popped it in the bin with her sandwich bag, then she lifted her head and walked briskly back to the office.

Chapter 27

Kingsley
22 July 1970

My dearest,

Sometimes I wonder if we will ever be able to make this cruel world a better place. All the sacrifices we have made seem to me to have been for nothing when there is still so much injustice. Why you had to die, when the worst of mankind is getting off scot-free, I simply can't understand. Surely, once convicted, they should serve the full custodial sentence and be reminded every day for the rest of their lives of their monstrous crimes? Early release only implies that their deeds weren't so terrible after all. They leave prison and return to normal society, some of them to the positions they even held previously. It makes me so angry, darling, I just want to strangle them myself.

Oh, listen to me, ranting as if there's the slightest chance I could nip over to Germany and track some of these bastards down! I may have been athletic in my youth and I may have earnt the praise of my sergeant when I was creeping up on him with my garrotte in our training, but I'm not so nimble now and am thinking that if and when I do find an opportunity to get even on your behalf, I shall have to be very careful how I proceed. I think subtlety and deviousness will be the best tactics. You always said I was a cunning little vixen, didn't you, darling? How we loved that music! I shall be cunning, darling. And I shall make him pay one of these days.

All my love as ever,
Your Evie xxx
Ps love you

Chapter 28

Evelyn, 21 February 1985

At Last

Evelyn finally knew for certain that it was him, the second time she saw him there. She could see the same sneer on his lips and the way he kept stretching his neck, as if his tie was too tight. She had seen him make that gesture many times as he asked question after question of his trembling prisoner, while she sat in the background, trying not to look at their bruised faces and ulcerated legs, making notes of the entire interrogation with a trembling hand.

Colonel Stephen Robinson, a name and a man she could never forget, sat two rows in front of her in the concert hall of St John's Smith Square in London. She had seen him attend a previous Thursday lunchtime concert and at first had wondered if she was mistaken, but this time she had arrived early and had been able to observe him removing his dark blue overcoat before slipping into his seat.

Sleety rain had been falling that morning and the department stores and the concert hall were full of stifling heat and the smell of damp winter wool. Evelyn's coat lay across her lap and over it she clutched her handbag and that morning's bargains of furnishing fabric remnants from Peter Jones. She had planned, if she didn't spot the Colonel again, to walk to the Tate before catching the train home, but now she thought she might make other plans.

Thursday was a good day to come into town. Sometimes she stayed on into the evening for the late-night shopping, but recently, she was more inclined to leave before the rush hour, before the trains were crammed with large men in suits spreading their legs and their papers wide. But perhaps she would risk the crush tonight, if it meant she could find out more about her old colleague.

At last, forty years since his arrogant dismissal of her concerns at the Bad Nenndorf interrogation centre in Germany, four decades since he ordered her to leave immediately, he was here, almost within touching distance. She had known he was still alive, unlike a number of his prisoners, whose end had come all too soon, but she had not come close to him once since that time. He had spent the rest of his career travelling to wherever his interrogative powers were required: London, Cairo, Berlin and other cities had all experienced his talent for extracting the so-called truth. His name had cropped up from time to time on overseas reports, which she quickly read, noted and filed. Most of the intelligence work was humdrum, but the station summaries were always worth a glance for snippets like that.

He was retired now, of course, like her. Robinson had received an honour shortly after his retirement, not the greatest of honours but an OBE, in recognition of his 'services to his country'. A second honour had followed. Evelyn had choked on her breakfast porridge when she had read that first announcement in the list of birthday honours in the *Telegraph*; she always read them and the entries in *Who's Who*, checking his progress, checking there was no one close to him who would miss him, hoping that she would be the one who could swat the man she despised now more than ever. His write-up had mentioned his love of classical music, particularly Mozart and Bach, which he said he enjoyed hearing at 'lunchtime concerts in London' and that had set Evelyn on his trail.

And now, at last, there he was, here right in front of her, looking fit and spry, and she might finally have a chance to fulfil her promise. He wouldn't be much of a challenge, even though she could tell from the way he moved that he was still in good physical condition. He had never been a large man; more of a Monty, she thought, especially with his neat moustache, just as she remembered it. How often she had imagined meeting him again, stabbing his heartless soul, shooting his cold brain, with the hatred that had fermented in her core all these years.

After Mozart's *Rondo in A Minor*, a melancholy piece that always made Evelyn reflective, the pianist played the sonata Schumann had dedicated to his beloved Clara. Such a favourite for Evelyn, with its hidden messages and references to his love's own compositions, like a romantic musical code. Then, in the brief interval, Evelyn was surprised to see Robinson stand up in his seat. She realised he must be leaving, not just stretching his legs or heading for the cloakroom, because he was wearing his coat and doing up the buttons.

For a minute or two, Evelyn hesitated. She really wanted to stay for the second half and hear the lovely Albéniz pieces with their Andalusian rhythms, but what if he didn't come to another concert? This might be her only opportunity. So she promptly left the hall, coat over her arm, and followed him. As he neared the steps down to the entrance, before he could disappear into the street, Evelyn let the Peter Jones bag fall. Folded packages of velvet and chintz slapped the stairs and reels of cotton bounced. He turned at the noise and, as she had guessed, was far too much of an old-school gentleman not to stop and help her.

As he bent to gather up her shopping, she said, 'Excuse me, but I rather think we've met before, a long time back.'

He stared at her and she knew that she had changed much more than him. Then she had been in her twenties, in uniform, blonde hair, and now, though she was still elegant and trim and her blue eyes still sparkled, her hair was grey. But her voice, her clear, enunciated voice, was recognisable and he seemed to register that.

'Have we? I'm not sure I can recall.'

'Bad Nenndorf?' Evelyn smiled. He would surely be familiar with her engaging smile, but she hoped he didn't remember the circumstances of her departure. 'I know it was an awfully long time ago, but I remember it very clearly. You were the officer in charge and I was there to record the interviews.'

He did that strange jerking gesture with his chin and coughed. 'Ah, right, Miss…'

'Mrs. Mrs Taylor-Clarke – Evelyn.' She held out her hand, forcing him to accept.

'Of course. I think I remember.'

'I was just about to go for some coffee. Would you like to join me? I'd so like to know if you have any news of our colleagues from that time.'

He glanced at his watch. 'Well, perhaps just a quick one.'

The restaurant in the vaulted crypt was nearly empty as concertgoers returned to the music. Evelyn headed for a quiet corner table and as she sat down, she said, 'I always wondered how long the centre continued. I left in the winter of '45.'

His left eyebrow lifted as he said, 'We'd barely started then. The workload was simply enormous.'

Evelyn shook her head in agreement. 'I know. Those times were utterly chaotic. People just don't realise how important the work was. One war was over, but we were desperately trying to make sure there wasn't another one.'

'Exactly. We had to make sure the war stayed won.'

'So were you there very much longer?'

'The centre was dismantled in the summer of '47. There was a bit of a kerfuffle afterwards, but those in the know recognised that security work isn't always clean and easy and it has to continue.' He smiled a tight, cold smile, his teeth hardly visible.

'And after that, did you come back to London?'

'For a bit. I'm multilingual, so I went wherever I was needed.'

Evelyn smiled as well, but her smile was real and warm. 'It was languages that got me out there too. Well, not multiple languages, just German mostly.'

Stephen's chin rose again. 'I've got Urdu and Arabic as well as the European languages.'

'So you've been a valuable asset then.'

'You could say that.' At last his face creased into what would normally be called a faint smile. He drained the last of his coffee, then rose. 'Well, Mrs Taylor-Clarke, it has been a pleasure. I don't often meet former colleagues now I'm retired.'

She shook his hand and as it extended, she noticed that the edge of his shirt cuff was frayed. A small but sure sign of impoverishment, despite his tailored suit and the crisp pressed handkerchief displayed in his breast pocket.

'Me neither,' she said. 'But perhaps I'll see you here again soon. Maybe we could have lunch first next time?'

'It would be a pleasure,' he said, patting his coat pocket and then fumbling inside his jacket to produce a card. 'You can get me on this number. I'm planning to come back for the Bach on the seventeenth.'

'I'll make a point of being here,' Evelyn said.

And he turned on his heel with a military air and almost saluted as he left.

She waited for a couple of minutes, slipping into her raincoat to change her appearance, then followed. Another hour of music would have been lovely, but this was more important. He walked briskly, but she kept up, halting at corners, hovering at pedestrian crossings, watching his reflection in windows, taking refuge in crowds. She'd always been good at tailing her mark. Top of the class during her training.

He clearly didn't suspect he was being followed. Not once did he dodge into a shop, slip into the Underground and out again, browse in a bookshop, look back over his shoulder or do anything to suggest he knew she was following him. Finally he came to a mansion block overlooking a garden square and disappeared into the main entrance. Evelyn checked the card he had given her. It tallied. This was indeed his home address. Reassured, she allowed herself the luxury of hailing a taxi to Waterloo, knowing that if she was never able to tempt him away from London, she at least now knew where he lived.

Chapter 29

Evelyn, 21 March 1985

Slowly, Slowly, Catchee

After her meeting with Stephen Robinson, Evelyn checked the forthcoming programme of concerts at St John's. She wanted to be sure she could attend the Bach performance if he was going to be there. It was a month away; plenty of time to prepare.

Ever since she had finally inherited the Kingsley Manor estate, Evelyn had enjoyed assuming control of the house and gardens. And since her retirement from what she always told everyone was a dull section of the Civil Service five years previously, she had enjoyed it even more. Mama's choice of stiff and garish bedding plants, reminiscent of public parks, had gone, usurped by spires of lush delphiniums and full-blown scented peonies; the drab brocade hangings in the library and dining room replaced by the sheen of bright velvets and glowing florals. And when local friends from the Garden Club, the Conservative Association or the Women's Institute asked if she missed going to work, she always replied, 'Oh, not a bit! I never did anything very interesting or useful there. I mostly did the filing.' She never mentioned the agent reports or the steaming kettle that deciphered incoming messages in the diplomatic bags.

But now she was going to do something really useful; something beneficial, if she could think about the details carefully. Colonel Stephen Robinson had been responsible not only for the deaths of Hugh and his brothers in arms, but also for selecting the location for the interrogation centre and for its mode of operation. He was not the only one who was guilty of misconduct at Bad Nenndorf, but he and he alone had been instrumental in directing and encouraging the inhuman methods employed there. And he was the one who took pride and pleasure in the administration of abuse. Not for nothing was it known as the Forbidden Village.

I won't phone him, she thought, looking at the card he had given her. *I must be sure my next move buys his trust.* The card was slightly scuffed and dog-eared; he obviously didn't have much need for calling cards any more. It bore the London address of the mansion block near the river to where she'd followed him; probably a place he'd had all the time he was posted abroad. Not a safe house exactly, but somewhere he could scuttle back to hide and gloat after whatever distasteful mission he had been deployed on. She knew what those places were like. The carpeted stairs and creaking lifts with iron grilles, the smell of Pledge polish and Brasso. An on-site caretaker to add to the security of the entry system and the locked mailboxes. The furnishings were always plain and no more personal than a third-rate seaside hotel. It almost made her pity him, as she glanced at the glowing patina of her Georgian sideboard and polished dining table.

And she could guess how miserably reduced his life was now that he was retired, how insignificant he now felt, as her investigations showed no sign of him ever having had wives, children or mistresses. He was neither a husband, father, grandfather nor a lover; he was just another lonely pensioner, whose achievements were all in the past, living on a reduced income. All he had now after his years of duty was a barren life, shrunk to an austere routine, taking advantage of London's many free and inexpensive diversions, keeping trim by walking to his club to read their papers, then eating a meagre supper on his own in his sparse flat. He was not the sort to retire to thrifty solitude in the sticks, rearing bantams and growing dahlias, he was too dependent on his status-conscious London habits for that, so he might well be tempted by a rather more sumptuous country residence, befitting a man of his self-perceived stature.

'Dear Colonel Robinson,' she wrote, 'I have checked my diary and find I am indeed going to be in London for the Bach next month. If you would still like to join me for lunch (we'll go Dutch, I insist), that would be most agreeable.'

Of course it was the address on the headed notepaper that tempted him, even more than the offer of splitting the bill, as she knew it would. The title of Kingsley Manor looks so impressive printed in raised black script at the top of a sheet of watermarked cream Croxley Bond stationery. She guessed he would not be able to resist phoning her to confirm. 'I'll make a reservation for twelve noon,' he said, in his brisk officer tones. 'That suit you?'

It suited Evelyn very well. She could catch the ten o'clock train, then pause for coffee at Waterloo station, where the ladies' cloakroom was perfectly respectable. She decided it was important she did not stir any memories he might have of her all those years ago, shamefaced in her khaki uniform. So after checking her hair and touching up her lipstick, she would not walk to the Tate nor browse the fabric remnants in Peter Jones; she would travel to the concert by taxi, arriving chic and elegant in her pale blue mock-Chanel suit, Mama's largest diamond and sapphire brooch pinned in clear view to one side, her hair set in place, with a raincoat over her arm just in case the weather was unpredictable.

He was ready for her, waiting in the restaurant, gallant, waving her to the spare seat. As she shook his hand, she said, 'This is quite delightful, Colonel.'

'Stephen, please.'

She smiled at him. 'Then you must call me Evelyn.'

'You're looking very spring-like,' he said, casting an eye over her clothes and the brilliant, sparkling brooch.

'It certainly feels like spring out in the country,' she said, 'but even the London parks have a lovely spread of daffodils.'

'I know. I was walking through St James's Park only the other day. Tons of daffs. What was it Wordsworth called them?'

'A host. A host of golden daffodils. Actually, it was his sister who came up with the phrase, apparently.'

'Really?' He sniffed in a somewhat disapproving way. 'Lot of other stuff out on the trees too, I see.'

'It's a bit early for cherry blossom. Might it have been magnolias? They're earlier in London. I always pray mine will wait till the frosts are over.'

'You certainly seem to be well up on your horticulture.' He peered at her over his half-moon spectacles as he studied the menu.

'Just a little. I suppose I grew up with it, having gardens and grounds to care for.'

They ordered and then he said, 'Tell me about your place, Kingsley Manor. It sounds awfully grand.'

She laughed. 'Not at all! Well, not to me, anyway. It's where I grew up, so for me it's just always been home. And since my parents went, I've been able to run it how I like. I'm a widow, so there's no one to tell me what I can and can't do.'

'Sounds splendid. And here am I, a stuffy old bachelor, with nothing to do but cricket matches in summer and concerts the rest of the year.'

'Well, that would seem lovely too, for a lot of people. But I like the contrast. I've got livestock and gardens at home, but the pleasures of London are only ever a short train journey away. Of course, there's a lot of work involved in managing an old house. Bit like the Forth Bridge, I sometimes think. Tiles slip in storms, trees fall, gutters block and so on and so on.'

'How old is the house?'

'Part mid-fourteenth century, modernised in the seventeenth century with twentieth-century additions.' Evelyn laughed. 'I know, I've got it off pat. But that's the easiest way to describe it. Every family that's ever lived there has made their mark with alterations of one kind or another. And as far as I know, most of them lived there quite happily all their lives.'

'And how long has your family been there?'

'Since around the beginning of the century. It was a wedding present for my parents from my mother's family. It was rented out during their time in India and then when they came back, my parents added the library and converted some stables into a staff wing.'

She shook her head, then laughed. 'No, it's really not all that grand. There's no staff now, just me and a cleaner and a gardener once a week.'

'It still sounds very impressive, all the same. I get by very simply in my little apartment and it's very convenient, I admit, but I do envy you the grounds and the space.'

'Then you must definitely come and see it one day,' she said. 'Come soon and see me while the magnolias are in flower. They're quite magnificent. I'll ask the frost to stay away if I know you are coming.'

Chapter 30

21 March 1985

My dearest darling,

I can't tell you how his eyes lit up when he saw Mama's brooch! I think he would have loved to snatch it off my suit and pawn it then and there. He paid his half of lunch, of course, as I'd already suggested it. But a true gentleman, like you, my darling, would have tried to settle the bill in full or at least gone through the motions. I can't wait to have him here on home territory, but I know I shall have to move slowly and carefully if I am to get him where I can manage the situation best.

Oh, what fun, darling! All that training wasn't wasted after all. My time has come at last.

All my love,
Your Evie xxx
Ps I love you

Chapter 31

Evelyn, 15 April 1985

A Web is Spun

Evelyn had been watching the pale pink and white cups of blossom unfurl for nearly a week. She prayed that the weather would hold and the flowers would not burn with frost overnight. It was not the most important aspect of Stephen Robinson's visit, but it justi-fied the timing. Many gardens have a burst of magnolia flowers in spring, but few could offer blooms quite as magnificent as the *Magnolia grandiflora* at Kingsley Manor. Some years an early warm spring encouraged the neighbouring cherry to flower in unison, but this year the sculpted flowers were the sole star of this corner of the walled garden, where primroses and violas were scattered beneath the gnarled trees.

'They're perfect this year,' she said, pointing as she led Stephen through the gardens. 'My parents must have planted them the year they moved in here and I think now they are better than ever.'

He gave the trees, heavy with their large, cupped blooms, a quick glance, then looked across the lawns to the fields and woods. 'Mmm, marvellous,' he said, 'and is all this yours as well?'

She'd expected this. Of course he would be more enthusiastic about the extent of her valuable property than her beloved flowers. She shaded her eyes as she joined him in looking into the distance. 'Our land goes as far as the road and the lane on each side.' She turned round and pointed in the opposite direction, 'Then over this way, we go all the way down to the river.' She saw the glint in his eye, assessing the value of the acreage. She was tempted to act swiftly, to swat this acquisitive parasite, but she calmed herself. She knew she should be patient: she had to wait for the shooting season.

He turned with her to look across the fields. 'Good fishing there on the river?'

'The occasional trout. I'm told it could be greatly improved with some clearing of the river, dead branches and so on, and the bank on this side is all ours, right along the boundary. It's a good spot for swimming. I still take a dip there when it's not too fast.'

'Must be damn cold.' He repeated that peculiar jerking gesture with his chin. 'So how much land have you got altogether?'

'Around a hundred and fifty acres, plus a few more if you count the gardens and grounds.'

'Very nice.' He nodded. 'Very nice little estate you've got here.'

She smiled. 'We've always loved the place.'

'What do you do with all the land?'

'Let's walk around and I'll show you.' She led the way across the formal lawns to the rougher grass of the paddocks and the meadows beyond. They stood by the fence and she waved a hand, taking in an expanse of acreage. 'These fields are currently let for grazing sheep. I love seeing them with their lambs in spring. Look, there's a little group of them playing with each other now.' A gang of lambs was skipping across a corner of the field, taking turns to jump onto a tree stump and down again, just like small children playing a game of chase. 'And over there,' she pointed towards the river meadows, 'that's used by a local farmer for his cattle in the summer. The grass is too rich for sheep because it's floodplain land.'

'Is that economical? I mean, do you get much income from letting it out for grazing?'

Evelyn shrugged. 'No, not much, but I've never really thought it was about the money. It's just a good way of managing the land. Grazing keeps down the scrub and the ragwort and the tenants maintain the fences and give us some extra security. It's more a matter of quid pro quo.'

'I see.' His chin jerked again and he appeared to be thinking for a moment. 'I wouldn't like to interfere in your affairs, Evelyn, it's entirely up to you, but I do hope you are receiving good financial advice.'

Evelyn smiled inside. This was so terribly easy. Were all men this simple when they saw a situation they thought they could turn to their advantage? But she just said, 'I haven't really thought about it, you know. I've just carried on the way my parents did. Do you think I'm making a terrible mistake?'

'My dear.' He turned and held her hand. 'This is all quite charming and very quaint, but you have to think about planning for the future. None of us is getting any younger. I don't suppose you have more than your pension to support you and all this property?'

'That's true.' She shook her head and averted her eyes. 'The house is certainly becoming expensive to run. Utilities these days are a frightful burden. But I couldn't possibly sell – Kingsley means so much to me.'

'Of course it does, I can see that. But you might want to examine your options. You are what they call asset-rich but cash-poor.'

Over tea that afternoon in the drawing room, with a fire crackling despite the spring sunshine outside, he continued to explore ideas for Kingsley Manor, not forcefully, he was far too clever for that, but gently and persistently. 'This house presents huge possibilities. Have you ever thought about developing it as a hotel or a conference centre? Or what about weddings? I believe there's an awful lot of money to be made in wedding venues.'

She sipped her Earl Grey tea and nibbled a slice of Madeira cake while she listened to him, occasionally interjecting with, 'Oh, Stephen, that's such a good idea,' or, 'I suppose that could be made to work,' while he continued to make suggestions.

Then finally he said, 'And then of course, there's the land itself. If you're not even getting the benefit of a substantial rent from your tenants and don't want to raise livestock yourself, then you should think about the value of the land.'

'You mean I should sell it?'

He drained his porcelain cup and it made a delicate clink as he replaced it on the saucer. 'It's a thought. There's always a demand for land, particularly around desirable villages such as yours. Could be a very easy way of acquiring some instant capital. I'm sure it would be handy to have a nest egg for next time the roof needs repairs.'

'Do you really think so?' Evelyn dabbed at the cake crumbs on her plate with the tip of her finger, but she didn't eat them, she just brushed them to one side. 'I do like looking out across the fields at the sheep. Houses wouldn't be same really.'

He leant across the table and patted her hand. 'But you could sell as much or as little as you liked. And anyway, these things don't happen instantly. If you read the financial pages, as I do, you'd know that companies sit on land sometimes for years before they finally develop it. Land banks, they call them. And in the meantime, you'd be enjoying all the rewards.'

Evelyn gave him her best smile, enjoying the smug expression that had been growing over his mean features. 'Gosh, Stephen, you're such a revelation! Really you are. I haven't been very clever in my thinking, have I? Perhaps I'll arrange a valuation, just so I know where I stand.'

He gave her that little thin smile, which was the best he could manage. 'You're a very capable woman, Evelyn. But sometimes a bit of analytical thinking is called for.'

Chapter 32

Evelyn, 19 September 1985

Greedy Eyes

When Stephen first offered to speak to the land agents for her, Evelyn demurred. 'Oh dear, I don't know if you should. My family and Kingsley are very well known around here. I wouldn't want anyone to get the wrong message if you appeared to be acting for me. People do talk so. I know, why don't I meet the agents first and then discuss their valuations with you later?'

He didn't press any further. Why should he? She was already giving him access to reams of information about the property and could see his eyes greedily totting up her worth. She had let him look at the land registry documents and read copies of the estate agents' valuation reports after they'd met her, but she didn't want him to know that the property was held in trust and she certainly didn't want him being seen by any neighbours.

On his visits she kept her distance from Neil, her shepherd, if he was out in the fields, and made sure Stephen only came on days when Sharon, her cleaner, and Jim the gardener were not around. She discouraged the few friends she still had from calling these days, but on the odd occasion when someone delivered the parish magazine or a flyer for the Garden Club Annual Show, no one would think there was anything odd in seeing a middle-aged man looking through a pile of papers on the kitchen table, or wandering deep in thought around the grounds, even if he was totting up her worth rather than admiring the herbaceous borders.

Watching him reading the reports and making suggestions, she sometimes found it hard to believe he was the same man she had known in Bad Nenndorf. Certain aspects of Stephen's old character were still evident, of course: the precision, the skilful manipulation, the eye for weakness and, most importantly, the isolation. But she remembered all too clearly his cold disregard for the pathetic men and women he had questioned as they shivered, flinched and fainted in front of him, while he probed their memories. *And when I kiss your photograph goodnight each evening, my darling, I remind myself I'm doing this for you too.*

'These summaries are very interesting and the valuations are most encouraging,' he said when he had finished reading the estate agents' reports. 'But they make it quite clear there's absolutely no point in selling off land for its agricultural value. Far better to deal with the land acquisition people, that's where the real profits lie. What do you think?'

Evelyn thought she'd like to chuck the whole lot of files on the fire, blazing away in the inglenook, and see them burst into flames, but she said, 'I rather liked the Knightley people. If I did decide to go ahead, I'd like to deal with them. I thought some of the others were rather brash with their big shiny cars, but the Knightleys came over in a Land Rover. I felt they were more sympathetic and had a better understanding of the management and importance of a small country estate.'

He nodded. 'Good to know who you're dealing with, I agree. But what's more relevant is how do you feel about actually selling the land, or part of it?'

Sunday lunch was nearly over. Stephen had started coming over for regular Sunday lunches these days. The first few times he'd visited he had driven, but now when he came, Evelyn picked him up at the station, or more often he walked, so he could enjoy a few glasses of wine with the roast beef. He had brought a meagre bunch of daffodils with him on his first visit, but nothing since then, miserly old sod, not even a cheap box of chocolates.

Evelyn toyed with the rind of the piece of Stilton she'd served after the apple pie with cream. 'I still need time to think about the land,' she said. 'It's such a big decision. I don't have to decide now, do I?'

'Of course you don't. In fact, I think the market might pick up next year and you could do better for waiting.' He sipped the vintage port she'd poured from Papa's decanter, then added, 'And the house? What about that? Did you give it any more thought?'

'I did rather like the idea of weddings,' she said. 'We have got such a beautiful space out there on the lawns for a marquee. I can just see a beautiful bride posing beneath the rose arch for photographs. Making people happy would be rather nice.'

'No one goes into business to make people happy.'

'Don't they?'

'And you'd probably have to provide the marquee yourself, I think. I'm pretty certain brides and grooms don't bring their own kit and they are damned expensive to erect and maintain. You have to get heaters for the ruddy things too.'

'Oh, really?' She pretended to look downcast as she cracked a water biscuit between her fingers. 'And of course I would be a little concerned about the furniture and the paintings. It would be such a worry having a lot of strangers here, running about and looking through one's possessions.'

Stephen glanced around the panelled dining room with its George IV oak sideboard and Chinese famille rose urns. 'You're right to be worried – you've got a lot of valuable stuff here. Have you had any of the contents checked over in recent years, for insurance?'

'For insurance? I haven't had to claim anything on insurance.'

He gave a queer scoffing laugh and said, 'No, I don't mean a claim. I meant insurance valuation. Please tell me you have got contents insurance.'

'I'm not sure what you mean by valuation. I know I pay insurance every year for the house and the contents.'

He peered at her. 'You mean you haven't checked whether you're fully covered recently? You've just carried on, year after year?'

'Yes, I suppose I have. Isn't that what everyone does?'

'Evelyn, with an extraordinary house like this and valuable antiques like the ones you've got here, you have to review and update your insurance from time to time. You are probably vastly underinsured.'

'So you don't think weddings would be a good idea then?'

'Not without a full risk assessment. And if you did want to go ahead as a wedding venue, your insurers would certainly impose new conditions, as the place would then be classified as a business and that would mean your premium would increase.'

'Oh dear, it all sounds awfully complicated.' Evelyn sighed, then looked across the room at the large oil painting of ruined temples under dark, thunderous clouds. 'Perhaps I should just sell a few things.' She pointed to the picture. 'I've never liked that gloomy thing for a start, reminds me of a bombed-out city.'

He glanced at the picture too, the oil darkened by years of smoke from cigars and open fires, relieved only by its curling gilded frame. 'You'd be better off talking to a good auction house, for a start. Getting their advice on the kind of prices you might get. In fact, that would be a sensible move altogether. They're always interested in finding good pieces for their sales and they'll give you an idea of value both for selling and for insurance. Do you want me to fix that up for you?'

She waited a moment before replying, pretending to be unsure, but then said, 'Oh, I couldn't possibly trouble you any further. I'll arrange for some people to come round and then we can have another nice chat when they've given me some figures. Would you like to do that?'

He eased himself back in his chair, his balding head lit by the glow of the fire. 'I think that's a very good idea. We'll talk about it together. You don't want to be pressurised by some pushy know-it-all auctioneer.'

Chapter 33

Evelyn, 11 November 1985

What a Lot You've Got

Evelyn polished the wine glasses with a clean linen tea towel and glanced at Stephen. He was hunched over the auction house valuations spread across the scrubbed kitchen table. A mug of coffee steamed in his hand and the overhead light shone on his bare pink scalp. Now and then he scribbled some figures on a notepad. He was totting up her valuables, figuratively rubbing his hands with delight at the thought of sharing in her good fortune. Evelyn stopped polishing – she felt like throwing the glasses at his head.

Even now, after forty years, Evelyn remembered exactly when she had made the promise. It had been piercingly cold that day, with the first hint of winter snow, but it was even colder in the cells, where there was no glazing in the windows, no blankets, and the walls and floors were slick with the chill of ice.

She had already decided she could not tolerate the work much longer, sitting at a desk, translating as the prisoners whispered their hoarse confessions, scribbling their incoherent words as Stephen ranted. But she had not known at first that she would one day try to make amends on their behalf as well as Hugh's. All she knew then was that she wanted the brutality to stop. She had tried talking to the others, even tried speaking to Stephen, as he was the colonel in charge, but all they ever said, almost with one voice, was, 'If they have any useful information, we have to get it out of them.'

I should have realised sooner, she reflected. I was so naive. I could see how deprived they all were. Their clothes were filthy, they were bruised and beaten, with sores on their legs from those damn leg-irons. I should have known what was happening. None of the conventions of prisoner treatment were being observed and the abuse led to deaths. Why I took so long to understand, I don't know, but when I recognised Kurt that day, I knew I had to help. I'd seen him arrive, healthy, wearing a clean shirt, and within weeks, he was barely alive.

And that's when I made my promise. I leant forward at my desk, listening out for the steps that would warn me of his return, and said, 'I promise, I will do whatever I can to stop this.'

But I didn't do anything then. I took the cowardly way out and left. The Colonel tried to intimidate me when I bumped into him after my interview at the Kaiserhof Hotel and later when he dismissed me, but I never stopped him. I know I was able to do some good after I left, when I went to Wildflecken, but I never stopped the ill treatment in that godforsaken centre. It went on for another couple of years, by which time there had been more deaths and a trial. Yet the man who was responsible for all that horror still believes he was right; he believed then and believes now that he acted for the good of his country. Look at him, sitting there so pompous and self-satisfied, looking forward to a good lunch, a couple of glasses of wine and port with his Stilton. He doesn't deserve it.

As usual, he had walked to the house from the station along empty lanes in bright wintry sun, meeting no one. 'Don't you ever feel nervous, living here all alone?' he had said on arrival, his thin, dry lips giving her a brush on her cheek in what had become his customary greeting and farewell. 'I didn't see a single soul on my way here.' He patted her shoulder as well, underlining a growing feeling of intimacy, and it occurred to her that he might be thinking of making a proposal of marriage, now that he had a clearer idea of her worth. The very idea made her shudder.

'Oh, I feel quite safe in this house,' she said, walking past him to the dining room, where she placed the glasses on the table set for lunch with white napkins and the silver she had inherited from her parents. During the week she ate in the kitchen with what she thought of as the 'cook's cutlery', often having an end of cheese and a heel of bread for her lunch. But today was Sunday, the day when Stephen came to ogle her wealth. Sunday was a day to display her riches and possessions, so she made a point of showing him the best that Kingsley could offer. The more she showed him, the more he wanted.

Of course she had always expected him to relish the chance to size up her value, but what she hadn't anticipated was his impatience; he couldn't resist helping himself to a little of her wealth immediately. She had thought he might wish to handle her investments or perhaps even propose marriage, but it came as a surprise to her to find that he couldn't resist taking a little something now and then. Was he really so hard up? Was he pawning or selling the souvenirs he spirited away? Or was it his way of thumbing his nose at her? Yes, that was more likely. And the more she tried to understand why he was doing it, the more she realised that he assumed that she was so careless with her inherited good fortune she would never notice the loss and he disdained both her and her way of life.

She first realised that he was pilfering after his second or was it his third visit, when she noticed that one of the Georgian silver napkin rings was missing. For a moment she thought it might have rolled off the table when she removed the cloth or that she might have put it aside for polishing, but she noted its absence and when, after a further visit, she realised that the sweet little owl pincushion Mama had always used for her needlepoint had disappeared from its usual place on the marquetry work table, she began to wonder. Then she smiled to herself. *I can play that game too. But I won't let him have the best pieces.*

She tucked her most valuable pieces of jewellery under the floorboards in the long cupboard beside the bedroom fireplace and Papa's netsuke collection remained locked in a cabinet. The silver cow creamers she hid at the back of the sideboard, but she didn't concern herself with the silver cutlery; he saw her count the knives and forks out and count them back in again into their boxwood canteen. If he took a silver teaspoon or two, or maybe a little piece of Staffordshire, she didn't care. She'd note it, add it to her list of his misdemeanours, and it would strengthen her resolve to deal with him when the time was right.

'Weren't there any cyclists or horse riders around today?' she said as she walked back to the oven to check the temperature for her Yorkshire puddings. 'There's usually a few of them around on a fine Sunday morning like this.'

'No, not a single one today. I was the only human being out and about.'

He put his cup down, then tapped the reports in their glossy folders. 'I had no idea you had so many antiques and valuables stowed away here. Are you sure you feel quite safe here, all on your own?'

'I always have done, so far. Don't you think I should be?'

'Look, I'm not trying to make you feel unsettled, but I'm very concerned for you being here alone all the time, with so much in the house.' He picked up one of the reports, turned the pages and said, 'Your jewellery alone is worth thousands. You'd be such an easy target. You should at least have a safe for that.'

What, store all my valuables in one place, just so you could take your pick? She stood with her back to him, whipping the batter. 'I'm very careful about locking up the house at night, and when I go out too. And I do have a burglar alarm.'

'Just as well. That should put off the casual intruders at least, but if anyone really wanted to break in, that's not going to stop them. They can see there's no one within earshot around here. They'd be long gone before the police ever turned up.'

'But I do have a gun, as well.'

He laughed, not joyfully, but in a short derisive burst, and said, 'Well, that's all right then! Might get you into hot water though if you go firing it off at all and sundry. There have been a couple of cases of owners being charged for assault on burglars.'

'Oh, I would be very careful. I was trained properly in the ATS and anyway, I've handled a gun since I was very young, for pheasants and that sort of thing.'

'Pheasants and people are a whole different kettle of fish.' He sipped his coffee, looking at her over the top of his cup, then said, 'I have a vague memory of you now. I didn't at first, but some of it is gradually come back to me. You were that timid little thing at Bad Nenndorf, weren't you? I couldn't quite place you at first, but now I think I remember. You didn't stay very long, did you?'

'I moved on after a short while. It didn't really suit me. I could see I'd be more use elsewhere.' *And I've been wondering when you'd remember and how much.* Evelyn glanced at the knife rack next to the Aga. All the blades were freshly sharpened. She didn't want to have to abandon the plan she'd laid so carefully, but she'd have to see how this conversation developed.

He pointed at her. 'Yes, I've got it now. You were... what was it now?' He clicked his fingers. 'Eva something or other, not Evelyn. That's who you were then. You were the little blonde who asked questions about our whole operation out there.'

'I may have done.'

'You left under a bit of a cloud, didn't you?'

So he didn't remember the exact details then. 'No, I wasn't well. I was given a medical discharge,' she said, pouring boiling water over the potatoes.

'Yes, it's sort of coming back to me.' He gave her a pitying look. 'Well, we can't all be the right type to handle those difficult kinds of assignments. You just weren't cut out for that particular posting.'

'No, I suppose I wasn't.' She turned away and looked out of the window at the oak trees finally starting to lose their leaves, then said, 'I might get some pheasant next time you're here. It would make a change from beef.'

'Marvellous,' he said, 'Now tell me, have you had a good look at these figures yet?' He tapped the papers spread before him.

She sat down beside him. 'I tried, but I got a bit lost. There's so much to think about.'

'I know, my dear. But I'll help you. Why don't we start by listing the things you feel you don't need or care about any more?' He smiled that tight smile and patted her hand, confident she would agree.

'Yes, please. Let's do that.' She smiled too. 'What would I do without you, Stephen?'

Chapter 34

Kingsley Manor
25 January 1986

My darling,

I have no way of knowing whether you would act as I am going to do, but I feel you would sympathise with me. You always displayed such integrity and had such a clear sense of justice. I'm sure you would believe in 'an eye for an eye' and would not be clinging to 'love thy neighbour'. I may be rash, but it is something I have considered for many, many years and just never have had the chance until now.

At last I have an opportunity to avenge not only your death, my darling (a pointless sacrifice in my view) but also to make amends for the ill treatment and deaths of those poor, innocent men. It might not be right in the eyes of God (and believe me, I have often prayed to Him on the subject) but as long as it is right in your eyes, I will feel justified. I believe that if I am ever to find any peace in this life, I must fulfil this mission, which has taken me so long to complete. I never got the chance to go out there and do my duty as you did. I could have been engaged in mortal combat in wartime and now that my enemy is here in peacetime, does not, in my eyes, make him any less guilty of your demise and that of many others.

Please forgive me if you cannot condone my actions. I am only doing what I believe is right. He is arrogant and cruel and has never paid the price, but now he will.

Your ever-loving Evie, xxxx
Ps I love you

Chapter 35

Evelyn, 4 February 1986

Bang, Bang

'There are still quite a few pheasant out there,' Evelyn said. 'I thought we could bag a couple today before the season is finally over.' *In time for the foxes to start feeding their hungry young and before anyone thinks to question the sound of unseasonal gunshot.*

'The ones you've cooked for me so far have all been jolly good,' Stephen said. 'Were they from the estate?'

'No, I got all those from an excellent butcher in Petworth and stuck them in the freezer at the start of the season. It's always such a bore plucking and drawing them, I prefer buying them ready dressed for the oven. But there are so many still roaming around out there and they can be an awful nuisance in the garden, come springtime, pecking at the primroses and so on. I thought I'd have a go at them this morning. It's a dry day and we've plenty of time before lunch. Would you like to join me? I can sort out a gun for you.'

He jerked his chin in that characteristic manner, saying, 'No, that's okay. It's not my thing, actually – I don't much like killing animals for sport. No, you carry on. But I'll come out with you, stretch my legs for a bit.'

But you don't mind torturing and killing human beings, do you? That's your thing, your cursed speciality. 'Fair enough,' she said. 'Wear the wellies you used last time. It's a bit muddy out there from the rain during the week.' She looked at her watch. 'Lunch won't be ready for at least another hour or so. I've done a casserole for a change.' *Because it won't spoil if this takes a while*, she told herself.

'Jolly good,' he said, pulling on his padded jacket and cap. 'All this country air gives a chap a keen appetite.'

They set out through the gardens, Evelyn pointing out the scattering of snowdrops beneath the bare oaks and the white hellebores flowering beneath the scented mahonia. 'Those are known as Christmas roses,' she said. 'Such a sign of hope, and there are some rare species among the snowdrops over there. I'm quite a galanthophile these days.'

He barely acknowledged any of the flowers, but returned to his favourite topic. 'Perhaps we should discuss the potential of the land again soon. The sheep have all gone now, I see.'

'Yes, Neil has moved them over to Churt.' *Because I asked him to leave, because it was time to remove all witnesses.* 'He said this last damp winter has been terribly bad for their feet and some of them have had a touch of liver fluke as well. I don't think he'll be coming back here again. Shame really, as I've always enjoyed having the sheep and their lambs.'

'Well, you didn't stand to gain anything from it, if you ask me. And if the land stays vacant, then you're all set to negotiate when the time is right. The last thing you'd need would be a sitting tenant.'

Evelyn didn't respond. She'd spotted a cock pheasant pecking at some snowdrops near the rhododendrons and took aim. He toppled with hardly a feather out of place.

Stephen jumped at the sound, then recovered himself. 'I say, good shot! I was wondering whether you'd still got your eye in. And you certainly have.'

'Oh, I don't do much shooting nowadays, just the odd magpie pestering the chicks, and the pheasants now and then, of course. But my father always said I was a natural shot.'

Stephen stepped towards the bird, but Evelyn said, 'No, you can leave it there. We'll pick it up on our way back to the house and I'll let it hang for a few days. Or do you want to take it home with you later?'

'Might look a bit odd on the train, don't you think? Chap with a brace of pheasants under his arm. No, thanks, I'll stick to the *Sunday Times* if it's all the same to you.'

'Up to you.' She laughed. 'Would be funny though if you hopped on the train with tail feathers hanging out of your pockets. But better to keep them here and hang them for a bit. I can't see you doing that, up in your London flat.'

'No, maybe not. Bit too countrified for Dolphin Court.'

They walked slowly round the grounds, then through a five-bar gate into one of the fields that faced the river. Stephen waved towards the furthest point. 'You know, the proximity of the river has got to add enormous value to your land. I mean, the fishing rights alone are worth something, especially if we can clean the river up enough to encourage the trout. I wonder if it wouldn't be better for us to reconsider the whole estate as a package. Why don't I look at those figures again when we're back indoors?'

'That would be lovely. You can amuse yourself with some intricate calculations while I'm boiling the potatoes. You're such a great help to me.' Us, we; his use of those collective words indicated just how much he was beginning to feel entitled to share in her estate. The other week he had grasped her hand and said, 'You and I could make a good team.' It wasn't quite a proposal of marriage, though she felt that might yet come from his thin, dry lips, but it demonstrated how secure, how unsuspecting, he now felt with her. Evelyn loathed him. She looked at him, gazing across the fields as if he already owned every single blade of grass, every tree and every acre of her land. He was so unbearably smug, so sure of himself. Today was the perfect day to do it.

'I think if I'm going to make it a brace we need to head back towards some cover. We're not going to find many pheasants out in the open here.' She steered him towards the copse known as

Marley's End, where fir trees grew thick and tall amidst a fringe of hawthorn, alder and brambles. 'These dense clumps of woodland are where the pheasants like to hide and roost at night. We should flush some more out very soon.'

He followed her obediently, this hunter of imprisoned men, not wild game, walking alongside her as she carried her gun. As they neared the woods, a small roe deer suddenly broke out of the bushes and darted away across the fields, soon merging into the brown fronds of last year's bracken and long grass. He watched it bound away, its white tail bobbing as it leaped, and said, 'Do you ever shoot the deer as well?'

'Not normally. Only if the numbers increase to nuisance level,' she said, leading him further into the wood to the thicket she had in mind. 'Or if I have to put an injured one down. I've had the odd one tangle itself up in fencing before now. If they're badly hurt, they're unlikely to recover so that's when I have to deal with them. I don't like leaving an injured animal to the mercy of foxes and crows.' *And I'll finish you off properly too, don't you worry. Wouldn't want you crawling away from the perfect hiding place.*

He glanced around the thicket of trees. 'And then what happens to the body? Don't tell me you come out with your hacksaw and carve all that up for your freezer as well.'

She laughed. 'No, I don't have to lift a finger. That's when the foxes are welcome to help themselves.' *My friends the foxes will come soon, don't you worry.*

He stood there in a proprietorial manner, hands in pockets, surveying the woods and the glimpses of the fields, the grounds and gardens and the old house through the trees, then said, 'Are you sure you're going to find another damn pheasant soon? My feet are bloody freezing in these damp boots!'

This is it. The moment has come. But first he has to know why. 'Freezing?' she said. 'You don't know what freezing is.'

'What are you talking about?' He turned towards her with a frown. 'I should have worn an extra pair of socks. My feet are getting really cold.'

'Nowhere near as cold as all the prisoners you mistreated at the interrogation centre. You really enjoyed yourself there, all those years ago, didn't you?'

He shook his head in confusion. 'What are you going on about?'

'I haven't forgotten what you did. You didn't care whether the prisoners lived or died. There was no need to make them all suffer so harshly. And you also had no regard for my dear, brave husband's life.'

'Now look here…' He took a step forward, but she took a step back and raised her gun slightly.

'Stay right there. I've waited years for this. Don't move. You don't even remember his name, do you? My husband, my darling Hugh?'

'Hang on a minute, Evelyn. Put that thing down.'

'I saw how you behaved in Bad Nenndorf. You were in your element. You've never valued life, just the end result.'

'This is ridiculous.' He took another step towards her, but she raised the gun again and he put up his hands and stopped. 'Okay, I can see you're upset. But let's be rational about this, shall we? It was a long time ago and we all had a very necessary and sometimes unpleasant – yes, I admit it wasn't pleasant – job to do. I know you can see that.'

'All I saw was the starving wretches you were persecuting, no, torturing for information about Communist links. The ones with military secrets, with knowledge of armament developments – huh! They were let off the hook, no matter what despicable things they'd done during the war. That's what I remember seeing. You were no better than many of the SS and they didn't all get punished either.'

He shook his head and smiled his tight, wry smile. 'I pity you. So deluded. You never could see the bigger picture, could you? Been watching too many Hollywood films I bet, where the baddies are all rounded up and the good guys get the girls. Our work wasn't black and white like the movies. Many of the so-called "bad guys" were useful to us and as far as we were concerned, many of them had been caught up in a system where they'd had to follow orders. In our eyes that didn't make them evil. That's wartime, Evelyn – or should I call you Eva?' He smirked, then said, 'Why did you give yourself that exotic name, I wonder? To add to your romantic notion of what post-war work should be?'

'Be quiet,' Evelyn said. 'I saw you. You tossed Hugh's life away as if it meant nothing. He was merely a pawn as far as you were concerned. You gambled with his life in your game with the Germans. You used my husband in your double-crossing, caring nothing for his existence. And I saw how you enjoyed your work. Humiliating, hurting, punishing. It wasn't just about obtaining the information for you, it was about the power you felt. You loved every revolting second of it.'

'My God, you are so naive! You were then and you are now. You just don't realise what a money pot you're sitting on here. I could have helped you make a fortune. You'd have been comfortable for the rest of your life, if you'd let me help you.'

'Money, land, possessions, they're not important,' Evelyn cried. '*Life* is important. Respecting it, protecting it, caring for the living. You killed people for their beliefs, but colluded with others who had killed hundreds and thousands.'

He laughed and for once it was real laughter, mocking her and her beliefs. 'I just don't believe this. You are so deluded. There were losses on both sides, you stupid woman! The Germans killed thousands in the camps; we killed just as many when we bombed their cities. What's the difference? That's the reality of war. We're all killers in the end.'

'Not cold-blooded killers,' she said. 'I'm doing this for all those you hurt and for all they hurt too. For all those who committed war crimes but were not punished and for all those who were let off lightly.' She raised the gun and fired, hitting him full force in the chest. He staggered back, his hand wavering over his heart, then she fired again at his head. He was right, she was a good shot. He fell and was still.

She stood over him, watching until she was quite sure. Then she looked around. The fields were quite empty; no one called out in alarm at the noise. A pheasant had flown off squawking in alarm when she fired and she could hear a motorbike in the distance, but there were no other unexpected sounds to make her think she had been seen. It wasn't the silent killing she had been taught, but it was accomplished at last.

Evelyn bent down and pulled off his wellington boots. They belonged in the boot room and would be missed if she didn't replace them. She'd deal with his shoes in the house later. She slipped his arms from his jacket and pulled at his trousers, revealing skinny, almost hairless, white legs; she'd need to check all the pockets thoroughly and the fewer the layers the better for the wildlife. Rummaging in her pocket, she found her newly sharpened pruning knife and sliced through his sweater and shirt. Underneath, his grey vest and Y-fronts, worn elastic showing through holes in the waistband, emphasised his pitiful genteel poverty, but did not elicit her sympathy. Grabbing his ankles, she heaved and pulled. Years of hauling dead sheep, hay bales and bags of manure had kept her fit and he wasn't a big man, barely taller than her and of spare build, despite her wholesome Sunday lunches. She dragged him a couple of feet, inches at a time, into the thickest part of the undergrowth, then scooped leaves over his body. It was barely noticeable.

Chapter 36

Evelyn, 4 February 1986

Covering Tracks

Evelyn hung the shot pheasant in the cool of the boot room and put the Hunter boots Stephen had borrowed back in their rightful place. She was fairly certain that every time he'd come to Kingsley, he'd said he hadn't seen anyone on the way. He was naturally observant, with the ingrained habits of one used to surveillance, both as follower and followed. But what if a neighbour had seen him on one of his visits, what if someone else usually caught the same train from Waterloo on a Sunday and often went back around the same time?

Evelyn helped herself to a portion of the beef casserole with dumplings. Such a good idea to have something hot and nourishing waiting for her after her stressful morning. She sat down at the kitchen table and, while she ate, she began to analyse the details as far as she could remember them.

Could he have told a friend about his regular visits to the countryside, about her excellent Sunday lunches, about the financial advice he was so keen to dispense? And did he keep a diary or leave used train tickets in his flat?

Keep a clear head, Evelyn. He was trained to be watchful. Like you, he was a skilled operative. It's second nature for us to notice faces, observe changes in circumstances and commit information to memory. He wouldn't have to write it all down. And like you, he'd have kept his own counsel, worked alone and covered his tracks. Stay calm. He surely wouldn't have left any trace of his movements at home.

But, she wondered, should I visit his flat to double-check? Would there be anything there that could be traced back to Kingsley Manor and therefore to me? Would the little collection of knick-knacks he pinched raise suspicion, or has he already sold them?

On the table in the kitchen, where he had so often analysed the extent of her wealth and the possibility of sharing in her fortune, she laid out the contents of his jacket and trouser pockets: the two halves of his return ticket from Waterloo to Witley; one wallet containing a single bank card, driving licence, some banknotes and a library card; a small bunch of door keys, one plain white handkerchief (thin and fraying, but folded and apparently clean), a handful of coins, a pocket diary, an almost empty cheque book and his passport.

There was no souvenir of his visit in his pockets this time, but then he'd hardly had the opportunity to help himself to a choice treasure before she'd persuaded him to go outside. Lucky he didn't have one of those new phones everyone was talking about and she was sure he'd only phoned her a few times from his flat, so there should be little chance of her number standing out from others.

She considered the bank card and train tickets. If he used the card to authorise cheques to pay for his regular journeys, transactions would show up on his bank statement. Is it possible to determine his destination from the price of the fare alone? Perhaps he always paid in cash and there was no trace of his regular visits.

Flicking through the pages of the diary, she could find nothing that tied him to her. No 'ETC' or 'KM' every Sunday, no address note in the section at the back. Of course, the year had not long started, so would last year's diary still exist? She thought it unlikely. He was a man of tidy, frugal habits, with no room for clutter.

But what else had he told her about his routine? She searched the library of her mind methodically, recalling all the times when she had encouraged him to talk about his life in London. 'Oh, I'm a boring old bachelor now I'm retired,' he'd said. 'I walk everywhere for exercise. Can't stand waiting for buses and cabs are too bloody expensive. Can't stand the Underground either, with all the ruddy tourists.' And his regular activities? 'Rain or shine, I stroll along to the RAC Club in the morning to read the papers. No, I don't have lunch there. Far too pricey for the likes of me, these days. Can't see me keeping the membership on for much longer the way things are going either.'

She weighed his door keys in her hand. The thought of going to Dolphin Court was tempting, but far too risky unless she did it immediately, before his absence was noted and neighbours, the concierge, a cleaner or anyone else there might wonder why she was visiting his flat. No, she had to assume there was nothing in his apartment that could link him to her and that, like her, he was used to committing all his arrangements to memory.

And then there was the matter of the house and contents valuations he'd been so keen on getting. How sure could she be that he'd never taken anything away with him? Every time he'd said, 'Would you like me to arrange that for you?' or 'Shall I contact them?' she'd declined and had made the appointments herself, meeting the agents alone at home. Then she'd let him enjoy looking through the documentation, all the property reports, the insurance reviews and the auction house summaries, greedily totting up his sums, virtually rubbing his hands in anticipation of his share of the riches, right here in the house. She had never made extra copies for him and she had kept all the papers firmly stapled together and had checked after each visit that not a single page had been removed, so she felt certain nothing could have travelled back to London with him.

No, she was fairly sure she'd thought of everything. Or had she? Evelyn looked at the evidence of his life spread out on the table. It wouldn't hurt to create a little diversion, perhaps, and it wouldn't take her very long.

She quickly picked up her coat, bag and car keys. It was a lovely afternoon for a drive. Somewhere quiet, somewhere that might suggest he had gone further afield, she decided as she turned southwards onto the A3. In the summer it was heaving with cars returning from weekends of summer sailing, but at this time of the year there wasn't much traffic. Lymington perhaps, maybe somewhere not far away from the ferry terminal.

*

Just as she had hoped, the town was fairly deserted when she arrived and she pulled up in an almost empty car park. She could have chosen Southampton and disappeared in the crush of vehicles returning from weekends on the Continent, but Lymington was discreet, so unassuming. She strolled, just another middle-aged lady at leisure, enjoying an afternoon walk.

A little way down the road she found just what she was looking for: a bank cash machine on a side wall just off the high street. It was a quiet Sunday afternoon, very few tourists, the pubs were fairly empty, the town was dead; with gloved fingers she slipped Stephen's debit card into the machine and hoped this would work. She tapped in four numbers, then another four, then finally four more, and she breathed a sigh of relief. The card didn't reappear. It had been taken by the machine, and if her understanding was correct (and yes, she did read the financial and money pages of the papers, despite what she had let him think), his account would record an attempted transaction and the bank would eventually assume the card had been stolen. Anyone checking his whereabouts would wonder where he had lost it. In London or in Lymington?

She glanced around her. The street was still almost deserted. The sun had nearly finished setting over the sea and it would have been rather nice to wander down to the water and enjoy the end of the day, but she knew it would be best to head back home. Anyway, there was still some of that lovely casserole left over from lunch.

Chapter 37

Evelyn, 6 February 1986

The Fox Café

After two days she made herself go down to the copse to check. It was still there, looking just the same as when she had dragged his body between the close-grown saplings and brambles. He? It? It wasn't him any more. More leaves had blown over the corpse but his shoulders and head were clearly visible, the thin hair sticking to the scalp, dark with blood, and the skin now grey, greyer than she remembered. Wearing thick gardening gloves, she scooped handfuls of leaves and twigs over him until he was completely covered.

The day it happened had been cold, but the last two days had been mild and wet. If it continued to be mild, they would catch the scent and would soon come, just as they had come before. They are not particular – food is food, though there was a time when a badger took a long time to disappear. 'Oh, foxes don't like 'em,' Neil had said, when she had pointed out that the black and cream pelt was still visible under the hedge that ran alongside his sheep's field. 'None of 'em like a badger's stink.'

So what about a man's stink, thought Evelyn. What if I'm wrong and they don't want him? I've assumed they'll go for him just as they went for the hens, the ducks, the geese and the lambs, but what if I'm wrong? What will I do then?

She walked away from the copse as if it was just one of the checkpoints in her regular casual inspection of the grounds. Wouldn't do to linger too long; better to look as if it was merely one element of her constitutional, her perusal of the boundaries, her survey of her domain. As she walked, hands pushed into the pockets of her old Barbour jacket, still filled with ends of straw and twists of twine from her sheep-keeping days, she tried to remember how long it had taken before.

There was the fallow deer that dropped dead outside the front door one Easter. Lying there, legs out straight, just as if it had been standing upright one second, then fainted and toppled over the next. If Charles had still been around, he'd have been all for gutting it there and then and lobbing the joints into the big chest freezer in the garage. But her brother was long gone and Evelyn had to wait till Jim the gardener arrived after the Bank Holiday was over, by which time she wasn't sure it would be safe to butcher the carcass, so together they lifted it into a wheelbarrow and trundled it across the lawns, through the paddocks and into the nearest copse.

Three days, maybe four, and then there was hardly anything left. They went for the abdomen first, clearing out the cavity and exposing the ribs, then the limbs were torn from the torso and dragged a little way off so each animal or fox family could gorge. She'd heard them that night, shrieking at each other as they fought over the choicest cuts, like squabbling housewives at a cut-price butcher's stall in a noisy street market.

Over the years, sheep and a pig had all gone the same way. Why pay the knacker man to take the bodies for dog food and glue when the foxes could do the job for nothing? Now and then, these scavengers brought their own dinner to Kingsley and Evelyn would discover a reeking corpse or a decomposing fragment of a hind leg in a corner of the grounds, where the grass was allowed to grow long and wild with buttercups and clover during the summer months.

Years ago, when she first returned to Kingsley Manor, after Mama's death, after the fruitless wait for Hugh's return, she had struggled to like the foxes, with their raids on the hens and ducks, killing so many in a frenzied night of slaughterous bloodlust, but taking and eating so little. But gradually she had come to see that they were Nature's dustmen, seizing opportunities, scavenging if they were able, but clearing away every scrap of edible flesh, fur, skin and bone until what little was left was indistinguishable from the humus of mulch and decay beneath the trees. Such useful partners in crime.

And she depended on them now. It had been so long in the planning, so long in the waiting, it couldn't fall apart now, just because the foxes were too well fed or some local farmer had killed a vixen and let her cubs starve to death. Evelyn was sure she had heard their cries recently, so it was surely only a matter of time.

She worried as she walked that she should have removed every shred of clothing, that the garments she'd left on his skinny body were delaying the start. She knew she couldn't risk having anything of his, anything at all, in the house, so she'd burned his clothes immediately. But she was relieved he had followed her into the woods, so trustingly, so tamely. This way was cleaner, further away from her. No one knew he was here. No one else ever came to the house now.

It pained her at first to tell Neil to take the sheep elsewhere, but his girls, 'Those black Welsh bastards,' he called them, were great escape artists and he was always having to jump over fences, waving his crook and sending his two collies to chase them back to their allotted grazing areas. It pained her even more to finally give Jim notice, to know the formal areas of garden would gradually become knotted with mare's tail and ground elder when her knees and elbows could no longer cope, but it was necessary. She would weed as much as she could and still prune the roses up as high as she could reach. It was not such a terrible price to pay for keeping a promise.

Chapter 38

Kingsley Manor
6 February 1986

My dearest darling Hugh,

There's no going back now. I've burned my bridges, as it were. I feel absolutely no remorse in dispatching him – it felt just and right. And he felt no remorse either. I think I made it clear why he had to go, but he didn't even apologise for my losing you. I doubt he even remembered you: lives meant nothing to him.

I had a slight pang of regret that I didn't make him suffer longer. Maybe I should have winged him and left him there for a bit. It would have served him right. But I couldn't take the risk – it had to be finished then and there.

So the deed is done and if there are consequences to be faced, I will face them.

Yours always,
    Evie
    Ps I love you.

Part Five

Eric's partner in Louis's world is both

clever and brilliant (4,3,9)

Chapter 39

Mrs T-C, 13 November 2016

Miss Scarlet

'What I'd like to do this time,' says Inspector Williams on his second visit, 'is ask you a bit about your time in the forces. I believe you joined up after you lost your husband, when he was killed in action. In 1943, wasn't it?'

'Is that when it was? I can't remember dates. Hugh wasn't at all keen for me to join. He wanted me to wait for him, but I so wanted to do something useful.' She looks across the room at Pat, who is sitting with her arms crossed, looking irritated. 'Can you remember, dear? When my poor Hugh was killed?'

'How on earth would I remember? I wasn't even born then.' Pat stands up and addresses the Inspector. 'I can't see you getting anywhere today. I'll go and see if they can bring us some tea.'

When she has gone, Evelyn says, 'I did rather think I'd like to join the Wrens.' She puts her hands to her hair, mimicking a cap. 'They had awfully smart little hats and I rather fancied that would suit me. We all thought their uniform was so much more flattering than the Women's Army Corps, too. All that ghastly khaki, so unbecoming for an English complexion. I don't think any of us ever looked attractive in it.'

Inspector Williams smiles at this admission, then says, 'I wouldn't say that. Your niece has been able to give us a very nice picture of you in uniform.' He selects a photograph from a clear plastic folder and holds out the studio portrait that Pat had found in the biscuit tin, a week or so before. 'That's you in this picture, isn't it?'

Evelyn peers at the photo he is offering for her consideration, but she has also noticed his file contains copies of other pictures, the photos of a rustic village, of gardens with fruit bushes, of laughing children and one child in particular. *Please don't ask me about them, please don't ask if I know that little girl,* she pleads inwardly. But all she says of the studio portrait of herself is, 'That cap isn't nearly as attractive as the one they gave the Wrens. I really should have joined the Wrens, I think, but by then they just wanted women to join the ATS.'

'Well, you look very smart in this photo. Had you had done any of your training when this picture was taken?'

Evelyn manages to look blank for a second or two. 'Training? Well, we all had to learn to drive and I learnt typing and shorthand. You should do shorthand, young man. It would be very useful, as long as you remember to use a sharp pencil.' She sighs. 'Those skills will always be useful, Mama said. And of course I was always very good at languages.'

'You were a linguist, were you?'

'At home we had a governess who taught us French and German. Both were considered suitable for a young lady in my day. Then I continued with those languages at school when my parents were abroad. And my grandmother taught both Charles and me a little Russian. Such fun – we used to send letters in code to each other once we'd learnt their alphabet. Mama could never get the hang of Russian, so she couldn't understand what we were saying or writing. And my parents sent me to Munich when I was older, to be finished, as we called it in those days. I stayed with a lovely Graf and Gräfin in Bavaria.' Evelyn sighs. 'I went there with a couple of other girls. Such fun it was, though we did get into a bit of bother.'

'Bother? You mean in trouble?'

'The National Socialist Party, you'd know them as Nazis. They produced an awful newspaper and pinned it up on public display in the village there. Horribly anti-Semitic. We tore it down several times and then we got caught one day.' She giggles. 'We were all sent home in disgrace, but we didn't regret doing it.'

'Well, I'm sure your German must have been very useful when you were working in the country later on. How long did you stay at Bad Nenndorf?'

'No, it wasn't there. I went to Bavaria, not far from Munich.'

'I meant when you were older, after you'd joined up. You were assigned to the British interrogation centre in Bad Nenndorf, weren't you?'

'Is that where I went?'

'Service records indicate that you were there. Did you take part in any of the interrogations yourself?'

Evelyn pauses and is silent for a while, picturing a bruised and bloodied face, then says, 'I think I might have done some filing and taking notes. Nothing very important, I'm sure.'

'I see. And do you remember working with a Colonel Robinson? He was the commanding officer in charge of the centre.'

'Did I?' Evelyn can't let her amusement show, but she is thoroughly enjoying these interviews. Such a diversion during the long days, which the staff try to fill with interesting activities, but which often leave her longing for more stimulation. Yesterday they made paper chains for Christmas decorations in the activities room, followed by a word search game in the afternoon. Evelyn enjoyed the game and could easily have won the prize of a bar of chocolate if she'd wanted, but she made sure her paper chain didn't link up the way it should and kept writing the word 'blimp' during the game.

Then Pat returns, bearing a tray of tea and little iced cakes. 'I've brought it in myself this time. I didn't want to keep you waiting any longer and the staff are all gossiping in the kitchen.' She glances at the Inspector's notepad. 'Well, have you got anywhere with her yet?'

He clears his throat as she passes round the filled teacups, then says, 'I was just about to ask Mrs T-C another question. Can you recall meeting Colonel Robinson again, after your time in Germany? After you were reassigned?'

'Oh, I don't know. Do you think I could have done?'

'He continued in the service for some time after the war.'

'I think I was in the Civil Service. Is that where he was?' *I wouldn't mind betting he was involved in that odious interrogation centre in London too. I bet he made sure he enjoyed himself there. The London Cage, they called it. Nasty place by all accounts. The Red Cross heard about it and checked it out, but all their dirty washing was bundled away so no one was ever brought to account. How convenient.*

'Colonel Robinson had a flat in London,' Inspector Williams says, 'and he continued to live there after his retirement from active service.'

'Oh, I do miss London,' Evelyn says. 'I used to love shopping at Peter Jones.' She turns to Pat. 'Why don't we go to London soon? Shall I book us tickets for a show? Is there anything you'd like to see? I could treat you.'

'No,' says Pat. 'London's getting packed out with Christmas shoppers already. It's the last place I want to go while I'm still trying to sort out the house for you.'

'Christmas,' repeats Evelyn. 'We could go and see the Christmas lights and the lovely window displays. I took you there when you were quite little, didn't I? We went to Selfridges, to see Father Christmas in his lovely grotto. You screamed the place down and had a tantrum in the toy department, then I took you for a delicious tea and you ate too many cream meringues and were terribly sick on the train on the way home. All down your dark blue coat. Do you remember that dear little coat with the velvet collar?'

'We're not talking about that now. You're meant to be con-centrating and answering Inspector Williams' questions. It's very important that you try and remember everything.'

Evelyn pushes the plate of cakes towards the policeman, who is trying not to smile. 'You'll have an iced fancy, won't you, Inspector?

I'm going to have one.' She picks up a pink cake with a little sugar flower and takes a bite.

'Thank you,' he says. 'I'll have one in a moment. Just one more question, if you don't mind.' Evelyn nods her assent and carries on eating her cake while he talks. 'Colonel Robinson hasn't been seen since the mid-1980s. He was a man of regular habits in his retirement but no one has seen any sign of him since February 1986. When his absence was noted, after a few weeks, other residents at the block of flats where he was living were interviewed, along with former colleagues, but no one had any information on his whereabouts. Do you have any idea what might have happened to him?'

Evelyn dabs her lips with a lace-edged handkerchief with the initials E.M.T.C. embroidered in one corner. 'Gosh, this is such fun, Inspector! It's just like that marvellous programme on television. Oh, what's it called? *Midsomer Murders*, that's it. Now, is it my turn to have a guess?' She pretends to think for a moment, then says, 'Could he have been kidnapped, or knocked down in a road accident? Did he drown in the river? Or maybe he just lost his memory and wandered off?' She shakes her head. 'No, I can't guess. It's beyond me. What do you think happened, Inspector? Do you think you'll ever find him? Are you going to search for clues?'

He smiles. 'I think that was all done a long time ago. We're just tying up loose ends now. I just thought seeing as you appear to have known him in the past, it was worth me asking whether you'd ever seen him again.'

'Oh, what a pity you haven't found him! I was so hoping you'd know where he was. Pat, do you know what happened to this poor man?'

Pat rolls her eyes, 'Of course I don't. I never even knew the man.' She looks at Inspector Williams. 'This is hopeless, isn't it? Do you want to give up?'

He smiles and closes his notebook. 'I think we have to assume we'll never know the full story, but I've enough here to write a report. There shouldn't be any need for me to return, I think.' He collects his papers and, as he stands to leave, lowers his voice for Pat's ears alone. 'And it looks like the guns were just standard-issue. I expect she's not the only one to have kept a souvenir of that time.'

'Cluedo,' calls Evelyn. 'It's just like Cluedo. Colonel Mustard in the drawing room. Shall we have another game? I always loved being Miss Scarlet.'

Chapter 40

Mrs T-C, 18 November 2016

Give Us a Clue

'Can you help me solve ten across, dear?' Evelyn is doing the crossword. More to the point, she is trying to convince Pat she can no longer manage to solve the *Daily Telegraph* cryptic, which has been her daily mental exercise for many years.

'You know I've never been very good at those puzzles,' Pat says. 'But let me see what it says.' She studies the page and reads the clue out loud in a ponderous voice. 'Leave carrying early paper celebrating the past. Three letters, three more, then five and four.' She glances at Evelyn, sitting in her armchair with a slight smile on her face. 'No, I've simply no idea what it means. I've never understood how to do those darned things.'

'Oh, what a shame. I'm finding it a bit of a struggle these days.'

'I don't know why you still bother with it if you can't do it any more. You do have to pay for that newspaper, you know, to be delivered here, and they're not cheap.'

'But it's part of my routine, dear. I've been doing it for years and years. Since the start of the war, I think. I had a friend who was awfully good at crosswords and she taught me all the little tricks. I don't know exactly what happened to her, but she was recruited for something that required that kind of ability. And crosswords helped pass the time when we were in air raid shelters and on duty. You ought to try to have a routine, Pat. It gives one's day structure, dear.'

'I've got plenty of structure in my day, thank you very much. All because of you, Aunt. The police have insisted on searching every wretched part of the house because of the blasted souvenirs you'd kept in those suitcases. I don't know what else they're expecting to find. Cyanide capsules? An unexploded bomb perhaps?'

'Not at Kingsley, dear. They didn't bomb us out there in the country. It was very dull, though sometimes the Germans dumped the odd bomb on their way home. Alton had one, I think, but we didn't. London and the big cities had all the Blitz and the unexploded bombs. There certainly won't be any bombs at our house, you can tell them that from me.'

'Yes, I know. But that's beside the point. Anyway, I came here today to tell you that the policeman who was talking to you the other day is coming back again.' She looks at her watch. 'In fact, he should be here by now. He says he wants to ask you a few more questions.'

'Who dear?'

'The policeman, Inspector Williams, who was here with me the other day, asking you about the guns in the suitcase.'

'Did he, dear? And what did I tell him?'

'He wrote it all down, Aunt. I expect you'll remember everything when you see him.'

Evelyn decides it's time for a dramatic flourish. She pulls a clean hankie from her handbag and lowers her head. Her shoulders shake and she feels Pat putting an arm round her. 'Don't worry, Auntie,' she says. 'I'm sure he won't be here very long. It will all be over soon.'

Evelyn keeps her head lowered and mumbles, 'But I can't remember things any more. It's all so confusing.' She has seen other residents behaving in this way when questions are asked or their half-recalled memories are corrected. She has also seen them closing their eyes several times an hour, appearing to fall asleep in the middle of activities or conversations or asking when it will be lunchtime, when they have only recently eaten a good lunch. It is most educational, observing all these mannerisms and behaviour patterns. It really is most useful indeed.

'Here he is, at last.' Pat stands up as Inspector Williams arrives, bearing his usual folder under his arm.

'Sorry I'm a bit later than I thought I'd be,' he says. 'I've just been to the house to check on the latest.'

'And what is the latest, exactly?' says Pat. 'What have you found?'

'We've conducted a thorough search, but I don't think we're going to find anything else that would concern us. There are other guns there, sporting guns, but they're all legit. The licences have expired, but that's no reason to question them being in the house.'

'So is there anything you still need to check on with us?'

'Well, we'd like a full explanation for the guns in the suitcases, of course, but we're coming round to thinking that these were simply souvenirs from her time in the services. Nothing more than that.'

'And this man you were asking about the other day? Are you still looking into his disappearance as well?'

Inspector Williams takes a picture out of his pocket. 'We'd like to tie that up if we possibly can, so I thought I'd show her this today. Just to see if it might jog her memory.'

'You can try, but I doubt if you'll have much success. Today doesn't seem to be a very good day for her.'

He pulls a chair nearer to Evelyn, then says, in a loud voice, 'Morning, Mrs T-C. I'm going to show you a photograph of a man we're looking for and I want you to tell me if you recognise him, all right?'

Evelyn lifts her head and smiles at him. As he leans forward she can see a delicate scattering of dandruff on the shoulders of his dark suit. She's tempted to brush it away, but she tucks her hankie into the sleeve of her cardigan and looks at the picture held out before her. The face is familiar, of course, that cold stare, those thin lips. It's the same dated picture used in the papers, when his absence was first reported. 'He doesn't look very friendly,' she says. 'Should I know him?'

'That's what I'm asking you. Do you think you may have ever met him?'

Evelyn shakes her head. 'I don't think so. And do you know, I don't think I'd have liked him if I had.'

'He was at the centre where you were stationed in Germany, years ago.'

Pat is bending over her aunt's shoulder, also studying the photograph. Evelyn can smell her scent, failing to mask the stale smells of her unwashed hair and thick sweater. Pat leans in for a closer look and suddenly says, 'That's funny. I think I've seen that face before. Now where was it?'

The Inspector looks up at her. 'It would be most helpful if you can recollect where you saw him.'

Evelyn looks up at her too. This is most interesting, but will Pat remember? She's never had a very analytical retentive mind. She struggled at school, especially with Maths and English. She's very good at needlework and knitting though. Pity she doesn't apply that to herself. She's wearing an awful jumper with a hole in it, scattered with dog hair, and she still hasn't sewn that button back on her raincoat.

Pat is chewing her bottom lip and looking down at her feet while she thinks. Her shoes need polishing too. Then she points at the photo with an eager look and says, 'I've got it! That biscuit tin I found in the house. When we were looking through those old photos the other week, I'm sure we saw him somewhere among all those snaps in the tin.' She jumps up, adding, 'I'll just run up to your room, Aunt, and fetch it.'

'I'd like a biscuit while you're at it,' Evelyn says. 'Don't eat them all yourself before you come back down here.'

'I'm guessing she means it's an old empty tin and there aren't any biscuits in it any more, just photos,' says Inspector Williams.

'Oh, that's a pity. I'm feeling a bit peckish. I'd rather like a biscuit now. Isn't it time yet for morning coffee?'

'Shall I see if a member of staff can bring us some drinks and biscuits then?'

'Oh, that would be nice. You are kind. Ask them to open a new packet, will you? They grow stale so quickly and I really don't like a soft biscuit.'

Evelyn watches him leave and thinks about her next move in this fascinating game. She doesn't really like crying; tears were never her way. Maybe she could pretend to feel unwell. Or she could say she needs to be escorted to the bathroom; that would stall him for a while, but perhaps she can think of something else more amusing.

He soon returns and announces that refreshments are on their way. Then finally, Pat comes back, bearing the infamous biscuit tin. 'I've had a quick look for that photo,' she says, 'but I can't seem to find it. I would have emptied the tin out upstairs and had a proper look, but I didn't want to keep you all waiting. I thought we could sort them out down here instead.' She goes over to the mahogany console table, removes the pile of old issues of *Country Life* and tips out the contents of the tin. Shots of a past life slip and slide on the polished surface, some falling to the carpeted floor.

While Pat is cursing the mess and picking up the little Brownie camera snaps, Inspector Williams hands Evelyn the cup of coffee that has just arrived and offers her a biscuit. She takes a Nice biscuit and holds it up, saying, 'It always amused Mama when I was little, when I said I liked nice biscuits.' He obliges her with a polite restrained laugh.

Pat has been muttering in the background and then she appears at Evelyn's side, thrusting a torn photograph under her nose. 'Look at this. When did this happen?'

Evelyn peers at the black and white picture in Pat's hand. 'What's that, dear? It's very creased. Taken a long time ago, I should think.'

'Yes, I know that. We both know that. But I mean, when did it get torn? It wasn't like this the other day, was it?' She waves the damaged photograph in front of her aunt again and points to the torn edge. 'Look, there are only three people in this picture now. I'm sure there was a fourth the other day when we looked through the tin. There was, wasn't there? I know I'm not imagining it.'

She gives the photo to Inspector Williams, saying, 'I don't know how this has happened, but I'm sure this was a picture of a group of four and that the man you're asking about was one of them. And I definitely don't remember it being torn the other day. It looks like a strip has been ripped off the side of the photo. And look, there's my aunt. In her uniform, just like in that portrait photograph. She's right there, on the left.'

He studies the image, then says, 'This print is quite crumpled and there's another small tear in the middle. Maybe it was already torn and you didn't notice. Mrs T-C, do you remember this picture being taken?'

Evelyn shakes her head and her coffee spills into the saucer, so she puts it down on the little table at her side.

'Take a minute to think about it,' he says. 'Can you remember who else was in the group when this was taken?'

She frowns, then shakes her head again.

Pat says, 'It was him, I'm positive. It's such a distinctive face. I knew I'd seen it somewhere and I know it was in this picture the other day.' She looks cross and folds her arms. 'I should never have left the tin with her. I just thought she'd enjoy looking through it, for old times' sake.'

Evelyn looks up, a big smile across her face. 'Pat dear, that's it. You've just solved the clue. You are a clever girl.'

Pat looks puzzled. 'What on earth are you going on about now?'

'The crossword, dear. Leave carrying early paper celebrating the past. That's the answer. For old times' sake. Well done, dear.'

'Oh, honestly, Aunt! The blessed crossword doesn't matter. What we need to know now is, where is the rest of this photograph?'

'Why don't we sort through the photographs methodically?' says Inspector Williams, getting up. 'Maybe the missing piece is still there.' He goes across to the pile of photos Pat has left strewn on the side table and begins sorting them into neat groups. She joins him and they stand for several minutes shuffling the snaps like playing cards.

Evelyn watches them, then murmurs, 'For old times' sake.' She repeats the phrase several more times, then begins singing 'Auld Lang Syne', quietly at first, but when she can see her voice hasn't been heard, she sings more and more loudly until a nurse enters and says, 'Oh dear, I think Mrs T-C is getting a little overwrought. I'll take her back to her room for a bit of a rest, shall I?'

'Please do,' says Pat. 'We're not getting anywhere with her today.' And she turns back to looking at the photos and shaking her head.

Evelyn can't help smiling as she is helped to her feet and as she leaves the room, guided by her carer, she nods at the Inspector. 'I've so enjoyed our little chat. I hope you can come again soon.'

Chapter 41

Mrs T-C, 1 December 2016

Just a Few More Questions

'Who's this you've brought with you today, Pat?' The police officer is right behind her, with a smile on his face. That doesn't bode well. She thought she had seen the last of him.

'Oh, you remember Inspector Williams, Aunt? The detective who was here before? He just needs to show you a few pictures. You won't mind looking at some pictures, will you?' Pat offers what she thinks is an encouraging smile. It isn't.

He comes forward, pulling a chair across to sit next to Evelyn. 'Good morning, Mrs T-C, I've got a few photos here I'd like you to take a look at.' He spreads some pictures out on the coffee table in front of her: there's the ATS uniform, various documents bearing her name, the passports, the guns and also a cream cabled sweater, now yellow with age, and a pair of light brown cord trousers.

'You may remember I showed you some pictures of things we'd found in those old suitcases the other day, but I'd just like to take you through them again, if I may.'

Is he really asking her permission? But Evelyn simply nods and says, 'Very well then, but don't let's take too long about it. I'm going out on a coach trip this morning. We'll be leaving very soon. We're going to Bognor Regis for fish and chips.'

'No, she isn't,' hisses Pat, leaning towards the policeman. 'I checked. Nothing's happening and she never goes out, anyway.'

Inspector Williams coughs behind his hand, then points out the two photos of the sweater and trousers. 'As I was saying, these are pictures we took of the contents of the old cases that were found in the bedroom at Kingsley Manor.' He pauses for a moment, allowing her time to study the images. 'Now, I'd like to know whether you recognise either of these items.'

There, arranged with its arms outstretched as if inviting her into its embrace to remember that day of icy blue sky, brilliant white snow and harsh brutality, is the Aran sweater with its thick cream cabling, oiled wool and incriminating spatters of blood, no longer crimson, now rusty brown, but still very evident all across the breast and the folded cuffs.

'Is this your sweater?' he asks, holding the photograph closer, so she can almost touch it, almost smell the musty wool of it, remember the scratchy warmth of it clinging to her body.

Evelyn peers at it through her specs, blinks, then says, 'What's that tatty old thing? Pat, it's one of yours, isn't it?' She looks up at her niece, wearing one of the many misshapen, unpressed jumpers she always seems to be wearing when she visits. She looks at the photo again and says, 'Or it might be the one I used to wear for gardening? I never wore my good clothes for working in the garden. You should remember that, Pat.' She looks at her niece again with a critical eye. 'All that manure and rose thorns don't do your clothes any favours, dear.'

'And the trousers? Do you recognise them?' He shows her a photo of the baggy cord trousers she had struggled to secure around her slim waist as she skied and then struggled even more to keep wearing during that terrible attack. They too are laid out; the legs are parted, inviting penetration. The blood spatters, once so evident, have blended over time into the brown of the cord fabric, but must still be present. Evelyn squints at the picture again, adjusting her glasses on the bridge of her nose.

'They look like Jim's old gardening trousers to me.'

'Jim? Who's Jim?'

'My gardener. Pat, you should make sure he gets these trousers back right away, he doesn't want to wear his good clothes to work in the garden at Kingsley.'

'Jim?' Pat gasps. 'You haven't used Jim for years. I wouldn't be at all surprised if he was long dead by now.' She leans towards Inspector Williams and says in a stage whisper, 'I doubt very much if they're his. And I can't think why on earth they'd be in that suitcase, if they were.'

'Dead? Jim's dead? Why ever didn't you tell me? You know how much I've always valued Jim's help. Such a reliable man! He's worked for me for years. Really, Pat, you mustn't hide the facts from me. Now, where's my diary? I must send flowers to his widow, right now.'

Pat reaches out to stop Evelyn rummaging in her handbag. 'Later, Aunt, later. Let the Inspector finish asking his questions first.'

'Oh, very well, but you mustn't keep these things from me, you know, Pat. It's very remiss of you.' She smiles at the detective. 'Now, where were we?'

He gives that polite clearing of the throat again. 'We've noticed stains on both these items of clothing, here, here and here.' He points with his pencil at circled areas on the photos, indicating smudges on both garments. 'Initial tests indicate that these marks are bloodstains. They're old stains, admittedly, but have you any idea how they might have got onto these items?'

Evelyn knows exactly how that spray of blood spattered across her clothes, how he screamed, how she took him by surprise. She feels her fingers twitching for her sharp pencil, but she needs a moment to formulate a response. She gazes at the photos, then turns her attention to first Pat, then the policeman, then back again to the pictures. 'I did once have to rush Jim to A&E at the hospital,' she says. 'There was quite a bit of blood then. I think a branch had sprung back on him when he was pruning the climbing roses. I seem to remember it was the Kiftsgate over that oak tree – you know the one, Pat? It caught him just above the eye and also right on his ear. There was quite a lot of blood everywhere. Could have been very nasty if it had hit him directly in the eye. I knew someone who was blinded by a rose once. Jim had to have stitches that time. Oh, Jim was always shedding blood on my behalf!'

'I see,' Inspector Williams says, reaching to clear away all the photographs, but she leans forward and stops him, pointing at one of the pictures, which shows a labelled bottle standing next to some papers.

'Oh, look! There's a bottle of slivovitz. How did that get there? We used to drink it all the time in Germany. Inspector, you wouldn't mind if I had that, would you? Maybe you can bring it in with you next time? I've completely run out of sherry.'

Chapter 42

Forest Lawns
2 December 2016

My darling,

Sometimes I think I can't tell what is true and what isn't. Yesterday, when I was being asked about the clothing in the suitcase, I talked about Jim. I shouldn't have, should I, if I can't remember anything? Or is that far enough back for it to be all right? People here often remember the past better than the present.

Maybe I'll play just one more game and then I'll stop. This lovely home with its sweet, kind people tries to keep everyone occupied, but really, we're all just sitting in life's last waiting room with very little to do. Most of us can't manage to go on long outings any more, very few can concentrate long enough to read anything more demanding than a page of a newspaper and every day brings another degree of deterioration. A dear man told me yesterday that he'd had a lifetime of achievement but now he could no longer achieve anything and couldn't see the point of life. I'm inclined to agree with him.

This game has kept me occupied and entertained for a time. And it's been such a lot of fun, but I'm not sure how much longer I can keep up this pretence. I'm feeling very tired and sometimes I think I would like to just fall asleep and never wake up again, then I could join you in Heaven and we would be together for ever more.

Your ever-loving Evie,
    XXX
    Ps I love you

Chapter 43

Mrs T-C, 2 December 2016

Talcum and Sherry

This looks serious. Pat has just arrived, all crumpled lambswool sweater and fraying scarf, with a bagful of brochures. Whatever is she going to want now?

Breathless, she says, 'I suddenly thought, ages ago, you told me to look in the bureau. Do you remember?'

'Did I, dear? What did I tell you to look for?'

'Insurance valuations. You said you thought you had some old ones there. Well, you were right. I found them yesterday and they've been very helpful. It's given me a complete inventory of the stuff worth saving at least.' She holds out one of the reports.

Evelyn remembers it very clearly and also remembers why he had wanted the information, as he sat in her house, Sunday after Sunday, scoffing her food and drinking her wine, and calculating how much he would profit from any sales.

'And someone's done some very useful sums as well, totting up all the different amounts involved.' She points to some figures written in ink in the margin. 'That's not your writing, is it?'

Evelyn shakes her head. No, it isn't hers, but she knows whose it is. She had truly forgotten that this scrap of evidence, this proof that he had visited Kingsley Manor, ever existed. How could she have forgotten? Without even trying she can see him sitting at the kitchen table, reports spread out in front of him, pen poised, his greedy mind identifying her choicest valuables, adding up their combined value. He had almost salivated at the prospect of enjoying some of her wealth.

'Auntie, are you feeling all right? You're awfully pale.' Pat puts a hand on her aunt's shoulder. 'Should I fetch someone?'

'No, dear. I'm all right. Just a little tired today, I think.' Evelyn stares again at the tidy handwriting, precise and neat, just like him. If the police saw this and compared it to any documents they might have collected from his flat, they could link it to him and then how could she explain? But how likely is it that they would still have any evidence from there? He disappeared so many years ago and the case should have been closed and forgotten.

She points to the brochure and the scrawl, then says, 'I think it must have been the man from the auction house, dear. I seem to remember he came over to Kingsley in person and explained to me how they calculate these figures. I didn't take him up on it, of course. I didn't want to sell anything at that time, I just did it for insurance purposes.'

'Well, I'm jolly glad you did have him over. It's been most helpful. But I'm having trouble finding everything that's listed here. Like this, for instance, Majolica Palissy ware. Sea creatures and seaweed, it says. I'm not sure what they look like and I can't seem to find anything that fits that description.'

'Let me see.' Evelyn pretends to think. She knows exactly what happened: she sold the ugly plates at a country auction and the handsome profit paid for an airfare to Frankfurt. Just one last visit, before it was too late, for old times' sake. She had driven out to the village and found the little house with its fence, its hedge and its fruit trees, looking much the same as they had all those years ago. There was no one there and even if there had been, how would she have recognised her?

'They may have got broken,' she says. 'Those grotesque platters, with all those curling hideous creatures, were terrible dust traps. We only took them off the wall once a year for a good wash. But

Sharon always had a lot of trouble trying to clean them properly. Yes, I think that's what happened.'

'Well, it's a pity. They were worth a few bob and it all adds up, you know. Every little bit helps to keep you in comfort here in this lovely home.'

'It's not home,' Evelyn says. 'It's very nice, but it's not like home.' She decides it is time for a little drama and grasps her niece's wrist. 'I want to go home, Pat. Are you taking me home today?'

'No, Aunt. Not today. You're staying here, it's much better for you. And safer.'

'But I don't want to stay here, I want to go home, I want to go back to Kingsley. If you won't take me there, I'll call for a taxi. I'd drive myself, but I can't seem to remember where I parked the car.'

'Auntie, you haven't driven in ages. You sold the car years ago. Don't you remember?' Pat is looking round for a member of staff. When Evelyn behaves like this, she usually makes a swift departure.

'I didn't say you could sell my car. How could you?'

'You sold it yourself, Auntie. You decided it wasn't safe for you to be driving any more. I think you did it straight after one of your accidents. You drove through a red light, remember?'

'Well, I've changed my mind. I want my car back again now. I'd find it very useful for getting to the shops.'

'You don't need to get to the shops, Aunt. Everything you need is here.'

'How do you know what I need? I shall go to Waitrose and get my shopping myself.'

'That happens on Thursdays, doesn't it? A group of you go shopping? And if you need anything urgently, you know I can get it for you or one of the staff will pick it up for you when they go out.'

Evelyn adopts a calmer tone of voice. 'Talcum powder. I need talcum powder.'

'Again, already? I'm sure I brought some in for you only a couple of weeks ago.'

Yes, you did, but you don't know how useful that powder is and how much I use every day. 'For my feet,' she says. 'The nurses say I have to have it for my feet.'

'Oh, very well then. I'm going into Sainsbury's on my way home. I'll get some there and bring it in next time for you.'

'Thank you, dear. Make sure it's Coty, won't you? I do like powder with a nice scent.'

'Yes, all right, I'll get you Coty. Anything else while I'm at it?'

'Sherry,' says Evelyn, looking bright and mischievous. 'I'd like a bottle of sherry to keep in my room. Then when I have a visitor sometimes, I can offer them a nice glass of sherry.'

Pat sighs as she gets up from her chair. 'I suppose you'll be wanting more sherry glasses next.'

'That's a very good idea. I wasn't going to mention it, but now I think of it, we had some very nice ones at Kingsley. I think there was a set with twisted stems.' She makes a spiralling gesture with her index finger. 'Could you bring those in with you as well next time, dear?'

'Whatever happened to the ruby ones we picked up on your last visit to Kingsley? Have they gone? Oh well, I suppose I can get you some more. Given that I'm sorting out all the contents anyway. It won't scratch the surface, mind, there's so much junk there.'

Junk indeed. Beloved possessions of mine, you mean. Now it's time for the final stroke of genius. 'And why don't you leave those old valuations with me, dear? I'd like to take a look through to remind me of all the lovely things we had at home. You don't need them any more, do you?'

'Oh, all right then. I've got to get up-to-date valuations organised anyway. There you go.' She drops the pile of reports on the little side table.

'Thank you, dear. And do make sure it's dry sherry, by the way. Mama always liked a cream sherry, but I've always been partial to a manzanilla. I'm sure you'll find it easily in Waitrose.'

'I'm sure I will. Now if that really is all for one day, I simply must be going.'

Pat leans down and kisses her aunt's cheek, then leaves, while Evelyn recites, 'Amontillado, oloroso, fino, manzanilla... any of those will do.' And then she drops her voice because she can hear Pat talking just outside the door to Mary, saying, 'She seems a bit more with it today. I almost had a proper conversation with her.' And Mary replies, 'Oh, they're like that. One day on and one day off. Like an out-of-tune radio some days. Still, if today's a good day, we must count our blessings.'

And Evelyn turns the pages of the reports on her lap, counts the figures written in that rigidly controlled handwriting and tries to think if there are any other traces of his presence that she might have forgotten.

Chapter 44

Mrs T-C, 11 December 2016

At Last

Those who can, knit. Evelyn never did learn to knit well, despite her younger self's desire to keep Hugh's feet dry and warm. Other pairs of hands are clicking needles and rolling wool as far as their swollen arthritic knuckles permit. Evelyn resigns herself to checking the pots of snowdrops, now almost in bud and likely to flower when they are brought indoors from the cold greenhouse.

The care home is preparing for its Christmas fair when relatives and neighbours will come to buy knitted toys, strips of tombola tickets and jars of mincemeat prepared by Foffle, the Friends of Forest Lawns. There is a festive atmosphere about the place even though the actual day is still three weeks away. Some residents will be able to leave for a couple of days to stay with daughters and sons who can cope with an elderly parent, but others will remain at Forest Lawns, which will be filled with the sounds of snapping crackers, music for Pass the Parcel, the Queen's speech and the gentle snores of those who have dined well on turkey and Christmas pudding.

Evelyn is not looking forward to the festivities. Until she broke her hip, she had spent the Christmas Days of recent years at church, followed by lunch in the local pub, where she was well known and was warmly greeted by other villagers. There were one or two years when she had joined Pat and her family for lunch, but it was always served very late and she couldn't bear the extravagant presents, the bickering and the drive home in the lonely dark.

And now she is looking forward to a new tradition: Secret Santa. She's never heard of it before, but Sarah, who coordinates the home's activities, says it is quite the thing nowadays. 'You'll see, Mrs T-C. This way, everyone gets a surprise present. Just like when you were a little girl, waiting for Father Christmas to come and fill your stocking with goodies.'

'We hung Papa's fishing socks on the beam over the inglenook fireplace,' Evelyn says. 'Long cream woollen socks they were. They seemed enormous to me, when I was a child. But they were never completely filled, even though I wished they could be, year after year. But I remember a grey rabbit one time. Not a real one, of course. A little Peter Rabbit type of rabbit, but without the waistcoat.'

'Well, who knows what you'll get this year. Won't it be fun, having a surprise?' Sarah is smiling and laughing, as if she thinks Evelyn hasn't realised that most of the secret gifts will have been chosen from the selection Sarah has bought herself and offered to each resident to wrap as they can't all leave the home for Christmas shopping. And some even think they will be receiving the scented soap or chocolates they've chosen themselves, although they will of course be labelled for another resident.

Oh, but there will be secrets, Evelyn thinks, and there will be surprises too, though not ones I'm sharing with you. Now, which shall be first? She smiles to herself as Sarah does her round of the drawing room, the dining room and the morning room, chatting to the knitters and the ones rolling wool. I think it has to be Pat first. Pat and then that nice police detective. They both deserve a surprise for Christmas. I'll ask them each to visit, one after the other.

Pat arrives early in the afternoon in a flurry of impatience. 'This had better be important, you know. I've got Humphrey's cousins staying with us at the weekend. And my Ocado delivery is booked for six, so I mustn't be late getting back and you know what the traffic can be like around Guildford in the rush hour…'

'Yes, dear, I quite understand. I can see you're in a frightful hurry. There's always such a lot for you to do before Christmas. Everyone's at it here as well, you know.'

Pat scoffs. 'It's hardly panic stations here, is it? Not exactly what I'd call mad preparations.' She looks around the drawing room at the few who are sitting in their armchairs. Some are dozing after their good lunch. There was a choice of roast pork or chicken curry, followed by rice pudding or apple tart. Evelyn complained because fish wasn't on the menu, even though she has already had fish this week, so she had a cheese omelette.

'So what exactly did you want to see me about that couldn't be said on the phone?' Pat is sitting down, but perched on the edge of her seat as if she is ready to fly away the minute Evelyn has spoken.

'It's lovely to see you, dear,' Evelyn says. 'I always prefer to talk about serious matters face to face.'

'Yes, it's lovely to see you too. But there had better be more to it than just wanting to see me this afternoon. I'm far too busy just for a social visit, you know, however quick.' She checks her watch. 'I might just have time to nip into Boots before I head back so come on, out with it.'

'Well, dear, I've been doing a lot of thinking recently.'

'About what exactly?'

'Oh, about the past.' Evelyn reaches for her niece's hand. It feels calloused and there is a vestige of purple varnish on the nails. They'd be in much better shape if she pushed back her cuticles after a bath, just like Mama had shown Evelyn when she was young. Evelyn's nails are still perfect pink and white ovals.

'What about the past, Aunt? I'm much more involved with the present occupying all my time right now.' Pat pulls her hand away and rummages for a remnant of tissue tucked up her sleeve.

'Yes, dear, I know. Such a busy life you have. But I've been thinking a lot lately, about all sorts of things that happened in the past, and I think I may have remembered something that would interest your nice young man. You know, the one you brought to visit me the other week.'

'Young man? Oh, you mean Inspector Williams?'

'Is that his name, dear? He was asking me such a lot of questions. I think I may have been a bit muddled at the time when he was here, but now I think I might have some answers for him so I think you should ask him back for another visit.'

Pat is staring at Evelyn and rolls the damp tissue into a ball in her hand. 'What kind of answers? I'm not dragging him all the way over here if you're just going to get silly and cause a fuss all over again.'

'Oh, I wouldn't do that, dear. I think he'll be very pleased to see me. In fact, I've written it down here, in my diary.' Evelyn pats her handbag and when Pat reaches out for it, she says, 'No, it wouldn't make any sense to you. I have to tell him myself, face to face.'

'Can't I tell him what it's all about so he knows it will be worth his while?'

'Why? Do you think he's too busy Christmas shopping to come and see me?'

'No, I just want to be sure he won't be wasting his time again.'

'Then tell him I've remembered what happened to that man he was asking about, Stephen Robinson. Tell him I've remembered and it's very important.' And Evelyn holds her handbag tight with both hands, while Pat's mouth falls open.

Part Six

And on the Sixth Day… (3,4,4,3)

Chapter 45

12 November 1945

Darling Hugh,

I think you would have found it hard to contain your laughter, my darling. You always were one for a huge practical joke! I can't quite believe how I kept up the act and managed to escape that horrible place. I just hope no one ever gets to hear about it and wonders how I've ended up without a baby after my phantom pregnancy!

So here I am, fully recovered from my supposed morning sickness, on my way to Wildflecken, the refugee camp where Brian Joliffe thinks I can help. It might be challenging there, but it surely can't be as bad as the Forbidden Village, can it? I have already met my travelling companions and one of them is a nurse who says she is expected to be occupied day and night, delivering umpteen babies. I didn't dare tell her that I had pretended to need similar services recently!

All my love, my dearest,
    Your Evie
    Ps I love you
    Xxxxx

Chapter 46

Eva, 13 November 1945

In the Night

As the wintry sun began to dip, their truck rattled through miles of dark fir trees until they finally came to the camp and Eva was reminded of T.S. Eliot's poem about the Three Kings, 'Journey of the Magi': But they were not the Magi, it was not yet Christmas and they had not arrived bearing gifts; they could only bring hope to Wildflecken, known to all the aid workers as the 'Wild Place'.

The snow had come early that year and lay thick on the ground, ice forming in the ruts made by the constant movements of supply trucks. As they drew to a halt, the lorry's exhaust billowing clouds of fumes around them, Eva could make out dark figures pulling makeshift sledges towards them along the frozen track, spilling like black ants out of the austere blockhouses in the middle of the camp.

'Stay right here. I'll tell them we don't have anything,' Ken said. He'd driven all the way from Frankfurt, telling them on the journey how the camp operated. It was familiar territory for him, this hearty Australian, but to Eva and the others it was an alien landscape, not just because of the snow and because they were far from home, but because this had been right at the heart of Hitler's heartless empire. Wildflecken, once a secret SS training base, so secret even its name didn't appear on any maps after 1938, was now a resettlement centre for thousands of displaced persons, all desperately hoping to find their lost relatives and return to lost homes.

Ken returned to the cab, clapping his hands together in their sheepskin mittens, his breath clouding the windscreen. 'I've sent one of the men to fetch the Chief, then he'll show us where to go.' He looked over his shoulder at the expectant crowd, all bundled into assorted scarves, shawls, hats and army greatcoats. 'Just look at those Poles. Bloody resourceful fellas, they've sawn the frames off their iron beds to make runners for their sledges.'

They watched the figures retreating, but a few lingered, stamping their feet, wrapping their arms around their bodies. 'What are they waiting for?' asked Brigitte, the Swedish Red Cross nurse assigned to the maternity unit in the camp. On the journey she had told Eva around forty-five births were expected shortly. 'And more to come,' she'd added. 'Every time another train arrives, there will be more babies, some in arms, some yet to be born. All frail, all malnourished. It will be hard work.'

'They're waiting for anything,' said Ken. 'Anything they can lay their hands on. There's plenty of food here. Down in the kitchens,' he waved into the distance, 'they're baking nine tons of bread a day and we're getting weekly deliveries of provisions and coal. But so much is lacking. The welfare section found a dozen sewing machines the other week, but they're no good for anything without needles. And there's a desperate need for welding rods but none to be had. We've got people out scouring for supplies all the time.'

'So how many people are there here?' Eva asked. 'I thought this camp had two or three thousand refugees.'

Ken's laughter was explosive. 'You can add a few noughts! Didn't they tell you we're housing more than twenty thousand? And the faster we ship them out, the quicker they send us some more poor bastards.'

'I had no idea there were so many.' Eva and the other two girls peered out of the truck. 'No wonder you're baking so much bread.'

'We've got twelve kitchens and each one's got to feed fifteen hundred mouths. It's a food factory down there.' Ken blew into his gloves to warm his hands, then said, 'Friggin' place! It may not have been a death camp, but it still spooks me. The sheer colossal damn industry of those fellas! We found one warehouse down there full of skis. Friggin' skis, I ask you! They were going to get an elite ski troop together for their attack on Russia, but right now we need needles, not skis! Might as well throw them out for firewood.'

Eva looked at the pale, dark-eyed faces still watching them from their ragbag of clothing. These were the ones who'd survived, who'd lived despite the horrors of slave labour and concentration camps. And Eva and the other aid workers recruited by the United Nations Relief and Rehabilitation Administration had the task of helping these survivors rebuild their lives. *Here*, thought Eva, *despite the grim stories I hear, I will be healing, not hurting, like in Bad Nenndorf.* She tried to shake the image of the shivering prisoners from her mind.

Eva was billeted in a small room with three narrow beds, along with Brigitte, the nurse, and Sally, a cheerful, red-headed Scottish girl who, like Eva, had been recruited for her language skills. 'I'm sure my parents never thought I'd end up in a dreary place like this,' Sally said. 'In their eyes, Italian, French and German were all part of a young lady's cultural education, with governesses to boot!' At this, she threw herself lengthways onto the single bed with its thin mattress, springs creaking and groaning, then sat bolt upright and said, 'Right then, what have we got to drink?'

All three girls laughed as they each rummaged in their cases, bringing out a hip flask, a Thermos and a half-bottle of gin. In the absence of glasses, they stood the flask cups side by side, then poured a measure of gin into each from the bottle top.

'Between us we've got schnapps, whisky and gin here,' said Brigitte. 'Some fine cocktail that would make.'

'We could call it a Wild Place Gimlet,' Eva said, as the three of them briefly touched the receptacles together in a toast before downing their shots in one.

'I'm all for a party, girls,' said Sally, 'but I vote we limit ourselves. We may not easily get any more hooch while we're here and who knows, there may be days to come when we're going to badly need a drink. Let's have one more sip, then call it a day.'

Eva poured three more capfuls of gin, as they agreed they shouldn't mix their drinks on the first night, then they sipped slowly, Sally dipping her index finger in the Thermos beaker before sucking it with her eyes closed as if it tasted all the better for the salt of her skin. Then she said, 'If we run out, we'll just have to make our own.'

'I heard one of the men say that before it snowed, on a dark night when the moon was full, you could see a white trail of flour through the woods,' said Eva.

'Flour trail?' Sally's eyes snapped open and she sat up, careful not to spill the tiniest drop of her drink.

'Yes, from the bakery. It's the Poles, apparently – they steal flour to make Polish vodka.'

Sally laughed, 'They sure know how to have a party! We'll have to get to know them and do a deal when we're desperate.'

'Better not,' said Brigitte. 'It might be the death of you. I've heard the last illegal still they found blinded five men and they're still in the hospital.'

'Gosh, sounds desperate,' said Sally. 'Mind you, the things some of these poor beggars have seen, who wouldn't feel like drinking themselves to death?'

'But we are here to help them live again,' Brigitte said. 'We must try to bring hope, not despair. They've had enough of that.'

Then the three girls fell silent and into that silence, the silence that comes when a community, a township, a village, is switching off the lights, blowing out the candles and settling down to sleep, there came the sounds of distant cracks. The girls all looked at each other and gasped, and Eva said, 'That sounded just like gunfire to me.'

Chapter 47

Eva, 14 November 1945

When Spring Comes

Eva tidied the pile of forms on her desk and filled her pen with ink in preparation for her first morning of work. She had been assigned to issuing temporary passes for inmates leaving the camp to seek lost family members and much-needed supplies.

Hearing a tap on the door, she turned to see Ken, filling the doorframe with his bulk in his warm charcoal greatcoat.

'Did you hear anything last night? We all thought we heard gunshots.'

'No, I didn't hear a thing. I was sleeping like a baby after that long drive, but it wouldn't surprise me. It's probably the Poles handing out justice again,' he said.

Eva looked surprised. 'What do you mean, justice?'

Ken laughed. 'Look, kid, you're going to see a few rules being bent while you're here. Things are just about starting to calm down now, but they haven't yet returned to what you might describe as civilised society.'

Eva paused in the middle of sharpening a batch of pencils. 'But we're here to run things properly. There's paperwork to be done. People can't just pass judgement themselves, can they?'

'If they feel they've reason enough, they will. Some of these people went to hell and back, and want to make sure the perpetrators get what's coming to them.' Ken rolled a cigarette between his fingers and put the skinny roll-up between his lips, while he fumbled in his pockets for a light.

'You really mean they're taking revenge? They're killing people who should be held for questioning and put on trial?'

'Maybe, we can't be sure. This is a big place and there's a lot of forest out there.'

'But the Allies have agreed. There are processes. There will be more trials like Lünenburg and sentences will be passed if people are found guilty.' *At least I hope there will be after the horrors I witnessed in my previous posting*, Eva thought.

'Sure, kid, we all hope so' – he shrugged – 'but in the meantime, there's still a lot of people running around without the right papers, a lot of people with hazy, incomplete stories of where they've been and what they did, and some of them are the good guys and some of them are the baddies. It's just like the Wild West out there, kid.'

'You mean they're taking the law into their own hands, don't you? Handing out rough justice.'

'Sort of. Official justice takes time, the machinery has to be set in motion. And some of these fellas are going to make damn sure they disappear while that's happening, so maybe some of the Poles want to get on with the job and make sure the buggers get what's coming to them. The way it works is like this, someone gets wind of a kapo who beat the shit out of the poor bastards in the camps, someone else finds an eyewitness and next thing you know' – he shaped his fingers into a pistol gesture – 'pow, pow! Kapo kaput, job done.'

Eva was aghast, picturing an execution in the snowdrifts the previous night, then said, 'And we can't do anything to stop it?'

'Easier not to, I'd say. It's going to keep happening, no matter what we try and do. And it could be far worse. I met some Americans not long ago and they said in the early days they handed some of the low-ranking SS over to their former prisoners for them to execute. And of course, it could get very nasty now and again. Sometimes they did the business quick and easy, sometimes they took their time about it. The Americans once saw some revenge-crazed Poles out of the camps beat an SS man senseless, then feed him into the crematorium. They strapped him down, slid him in the oven, turned on the heat and pushed him in and out until he'd been burned alive.' He finished his thin cigarette and pulled at the wisp of paper stuck to his lip.

'That's absolutely horrific.' Eva shuddered. 'But they can't do anything like that here, can they?'

'No, thank goodness. The bread ovens are too busy feeding everyone.' He laughed at his joke. 'So, let's be grateful we only hear the occasional shot, clean and simple.'

Eva glanced again at her neat piles of paper, her ranks of pens and pencils, and said, 'I must be stupid. I hadn't really thought it through.' *Is that what I should have done? Rough justice?*

He shook his head. 'You're not the only one, kid. We're only picking up the pieces. We can't really know what it was like for them in those hellholes.'

'I've been trying to tell myself that. I want to know and yet I don't – I just want to help people get back to some kind of normal life.'

'Sure. And you'll do a great job, that's for certain.'

He turned towards the door, then added, 'And you're going to have help here, Polish aristocracy.'

'What's that?'

'The Countess, we call her. She's quite something. Many women perished in Ravensbrück, but if it hadn't been for her persistence and courage, a whole barrack of them would have. She's a tough wise old bird and she's coming to interpret for you.'

'Oh, great. Thanks, Ken. And I'll try not to worry if I hear any more shots tonight.'

He laughed and pulled his collar up around his ears. 'We'll know how busy the vigilantes have been when spring comes, when the snow's finally melted.'

It took Eva a moment to realise what he meant, then as he left, she looked out of the window at the thick forest stretching for miles around the camp and the distant slopes iced with snow. Traces of footprints would soon disappear under fresh snowfalls and what was hidden under the dark branches in the drifts would stay well-hidden until spring.

Chapter 48

Eva, 14 November 1945

Countess Komorowski

A sudden tap at the door interrupted Eva's vision of frozen corpses awaiting the thaw of spring and she turned to see an elderly woman wearing a patchy fur coat with a sheepskin thrown over her shoulders, elegant in her bearing despite the ragbag of her clothes. Her thin grey hair was tight across her temples, tied into a meagre French pleat, and she shuffled towards the desk with the help of an ebony stick, extending a veined hand in greeting. 'My dear, I am Irene Komorowski. I think you will be needing my help as you do not have Polish.'

'Ken told me I'd get some help. Are you the Countess?' Eva pulled another chair round to the side of the desk for her guest.

Irene waved her hand, 'Titles, pah! What do they matter now? You must call me Irene.'

'And I am Eva.'

An arched eyebrow queried this. 'You have family here?'

'My grandmother was Polish, but I don't speak the language. I'm really Evelyn, but when I joined up, we agreed I'd use the name Eva. It makes more sense when I'm dealing in German and Russian.'

The eyebrow expressed surprise again. 'I suppose you thought your languages would be useful here?'

'I'd hoped so. I hadn't realised that nearly everyone here would be Polish.'

'Hmm, they were Polish and they are mostly from Poland, but many are finding that their hometowns are now claimed by Russia. And that presents us with a great problem.'

'I know. As if trying to get back home, after all they've suffered, wasn't difficult enough in itself. They've lost everything, their homes, their families and now their homeland.'

'Well, we shall get on to that in good time. But for now, we have to decide whether the people we are seeing today are permitted to leave the camp and return. Shall we see who we have?'

And so it was for several days. One after another searching for this uncle, for that brother, or a cousin. A young boy convinced his parents must be in one of the nearby towns or villages, a man certain his mother had survived the labour camp, all wanted to be allowed to leave and go in search of their loved ones. Eva grew used to the stories and steeled herself to question them and ascertain their reasons for leaving because the authorities were trying to discourage trading on the black market.

One day, after hearing a particularly harrowing story from a father trying to find his children, Eva said, 'Honestly, I do wonder why we have to ask so many questions. After all their suffering, why shouldn't they get out there and find whatever comfort they can? And if they are doing a bit of trading and dealing on the side as well, where's the harm in that?'

'I know, darling,' Irene said, 'the survival instinct is hard to suppress after so much hardship. Some of them are alive now only because they seized opportunities whenever they could that got them an extra crust. Each time they found or earnt another mouthful of food could mean another day of life.' She took the sheepskin from her shoulders and laid it over Eva's knees. 'A present from a grateful friend. He found a stash of skins recently and is now making warm waistcoats and hats to sell to help his family. The Germans out there can call us "schlechte Ausländern" as much as they like, but when they want goods they can't find, they're willing to pay hard money, so who can blame my friend?'

'Wicked foreigners,' Eva murmured, translating Irene's words. 'That's so unkind. The Poles didn't ask to come here and lose everything.'

'But not all the Germans are to blame. Many have lost their families too and many are finding life hard now.'

'It's certainly very thick and warm,' said Eva, running her hand over the skin's soft cream pile.

'You want a hat, for the winter?' Irene picked up the fleece and wound it round her own head, much like a Cossack hat. 'I can talk to my friend for you.'

'No, really, you shouldn't. I think I'd better stick to the rules for now.'

'Very well, but you must tell me if you start feeling the cold.'

Chapter 49

Eva, 30 November 1945

From the East

And through the smoke and steam yet more came, clambering down from the boxcars. A ragged tide of tired, hungry refugees. Clutching sour blankets, muddied greatcoats, precious bundles and children, they trudged wearily along the railtrack.

'Brigitte, over here,' Eva yelled. 'I've got another one.'

Brigitte ran across to where Eva was helping an exhausted mother down from the train, her fractious baby clutched to her empty breasts. A new consignment of several thousand inmates had just arrived at the nearby station, originally constructed for the mighty war machine. All ages, all states of health stumbled towards Eva and the aid workers, past heaps of freshly shovelled snow.

'If only they'd give the mothers clean nappies for the journey,' Brigitte said, shaking her head. She took the baby and unwrapped the soiled rags. Eva caught the whiff of ammonia as Brigitte turned her head for air. 'No wonder he's screaming, just look at the poor thing.' His skinny buttocks and thighs were livid scarlet, the skin shiny.

'Ow, it looks so sore,' Eva said, as Brigitte gently bathed the baby's burning flesh and applied a thick protective coating of zinc oxide cream.

'He'll soon feel more comfortable. It's not the worst case I've seen,' Brigitte said. 'But some will always bear scars from this. And most of the babies are also dehydrated. Many of the mothers are malnourished and aren't producing enough of their own milk. They probably haven't been able to feed their babies for the entire journey.' She wrapped a clean nappy round the child and handed him back to his grateful mother, then turned her attention to the next screaming infant. All along the track, Brigitte's nurses were spotting those most in need, soothing babies, comforting the sick and welcoming heavily pregnant women.

Eva then ran to help a frail white-haired woman who was trying to clamber down from one of the boxcars, several feet above the track. She was probably no more than forty-five years old, but she looked like a wizened grandmother with her sunken cheeks, shrunken breasts and white head. Yet she had done her best to make herself presentable for this journey, with a knotted grey kerchief over her combed hair and a clean black apron round her waist. She extended her scrawny arm, reaching for Eva's outstretched hand, and as she did so, the loose sleeve of her blouse slipped back to her elbow. And there on her skin was the telltale mark: the eight purple numbers on the inside of her forearm.

Eva could not help a slight intake of breath at the sight of the tattoo and the woman caught her eye and nodded. 'Dachau,' she whispered.

No further explanation was needed. Eva tried to smile as she helped the woman from the train, but inside she told herself, *You mustn't look shocked, you've seen those marks before, even though you've only been here ten days. They're all around you, the ones who've survived, all with those indelible numbers.*

Another four thousand displaced people were arriving at the camp that day and all the aid workers were on hand to help the travellers disembark from trains that had transported them into hope, rather than the hell of their previous journeys. 'Go to the nurse,' Eva told a man with open, weeping sores. 'There's soup and bread over there,' she said to a family with hungry, fretful children, directing them to the steaming vat of broth.

Paperwork had to be completed and names noted, but they needed food and comfort too.

'Careful, look where you're going,' Eva cried as a man jostled her in the crowd. Anxious residents from the camp ran up and down the track, shouting names, peering into the boxcars. Each time another train arrived, they searched for the missing. Was that a long-lost cousin or brother they'd glimpsed? Was a former neighbour on this convoy, with news of their relatives? And had anyone seen their lost child?

All the men were lean and hungry, but even when they had been eating well in the camp for a while, the women still didn't lose the bulging bellies that were the result of their years of surviving on dry black bread and thin potato soup. How many repatriation forms she had already completed in her short time at the camp, Eva could not say. Every day there were questions to ask and disappointment to contend with. People went and yet more came, so still the camp was full.

When all the newcomers had been allocated their quarters, all the babies had been fed and cleaned, and all the paperwork completed, the team allowed themselves a break. 'It's never-ending,' said Eva. 'No sooner do we ship people out than another load arrives. This place never seems to get any emptier.'

'We've got twenty thousand here pretty much all the time,' said Ken. 'But if you'd seen what this country was like immediately after the war ended, you'd think this was a breeze, kid. All the roads were heaving with foreign slave workers trying to find their way back home. Everywhere we went there were distraught parents trying to find their children and lost kids trying to find their mums and dads. And on top of it all, there were goddamn scared-shitless Nazis sneaking back and trying to find a place to hide away and pretend it was nothing to do with them.'

'So, are you saying it's all calm and under control here now?'

'Not exactly, but it's a damn sight better than it was. We're bringing some kind of order for these poor bastards with only their OST cards for ID.'

'I've seen those cards, dozens of them. They've got those three stark letters on them. It just means East, doesn't it? It's like they don't belong to any known country.'

'You got it in one,' Ken said. 'They brought seven million slave workers into Germany from eastern Europe. They wanted cheap labour for their plane and ball-bearing factories, their textile mills and mines, and workers for their sugar beet and cabbage fields. And they were all given the same basic card, lumping them wholesale into one indistinguishable group.'

'Seven million... It's hard to imagine.'

'Those damn Germans didn't care where they came from originally. They didn't think of them as individuals with a past, a culture and a heritage, they were just OST – a person from the east. Their original province, their town, their village, none of that mattered to the master race. They just printed OST in thick black letters beneath their photograph. The only ones who didn't get given OST cards are those from the concentration camps and their ID is tattooed or branded on the inside of their right arm.'

Ken looked angry and flung his cigarette end angrily onto the railtrack. 'Those poor bastards were denied their identity for nearly six years, ever since the first Nazi blitz into Poland and elsewhere. And they stayed that way until the Allies renamed them. It might not seem much, calling them displaced persons, but it's a damn sight better than just OST.'

'It gives them a shred of dignity, I suppose.' Eva sighed. 'Names and identities matter. And calling them displaced persons does at least recognise them as human beings. It's a small but significant act of humanity.'

'They bloody well deserve it,' Ken said. 'There's been no sign of humanity for them for the last few years. Treated like cattle, they all were. Branded, numbered, beaten and starved.'

'I've seen it, Ken. It's unbearable. So many dreadful scars, broken noses and teeth. And the tattoos are awful, but some of them were branded with red-hot irons. They're left with the most hideous, livid red scar tissue that's disfigured the whole arm, from the wrist to the elbow. How could they have done that to their fellow human beings? They're just ordinary people like them.'

'Don't let it get to you, kid,' he said. 'We're doing good work here. We'll do our best to help them find their relatives and maybe they'll be able to go home or start a new life elsewhere.'

'I certainly hope all that tedious form-filling is going to achieve something. These people really deserve a chance to rebuild their lives and find happiness.'

Her eyes followed the lines of new arrivals, collecting their bundles of meagre possessions and trudging towards the main camp, where fresh bread was baking and warm beds were waiting. 'The wretched aftermath of war,' she murmured. 'But seeing all this, I know it's all been worthwhile. Even for those of us who've lost loved ones. It balances the books, somehow.'

'Keep your chin up, kid. And get a stiff drink when we've finished.' Ken winked at her and carried on directing the arrivals to their new accommodation.

Chapter 50

Eva, 4 December 1945

In Their Footsteps

'I've got an important new job for you,' Sally said, bursting into Eva's office. 'Put that pen down and come with me right now.'

It was the end of the morning and everyone who needed to leave the camp that day had already collected their passes. Eva put on her coat to follow Sally outside into the icy tracks that criss-crossed the camp. 'What's going on?'

'We're opening a shoe shop.' Sally laughed. 'We're going to sort out shoes, I mean boots. Come on, it'll be fun.'

'Real boots?'

'The real thing. A large consignment's just arrived and you know how much we need them. Have you seen what some of our inmates are wearing when they arrive here?'

'Haven't I just! They're making do with whatever they can find. Pieces of rubber tyres are very much in vogue this season. So are clogs.'

The girls laughed as they ran through the snow to the warehouse, where boxes of ex-army boots were being unloaded from a lorry and tipped onto the concrete floor. Camp residents were already gathering outside, hoping they would be the lucky ones to receive sturdy footwear to help them survive the long cold winter.

'We've got to sort them into pairs, if we can,' Sally said. 'It would help if we could group them by size too, but I doubt we'll be able to do that.'

'We can probably make a guess,' Eva said. 'What size are you?'

'I'm a dainty five and a half.' Sally tugged at her own boots, straightened her thick ribbed socks, then slipped her feet into a pair of large army boots from the pile. She could only take a few steps before she almost fell over, laughing. 'Shall we just say very large and medium large?'

Eva picked up two boots from the muddy pile and banged them together. The dried mud encrusted in the tread fell to the floor. 'I think we should get rid of some of this dirt as we go along – they're all thick with it.'

'Pity there's nothing smaller for our ladies. They're good boots, though. The men will be glad of them, however dirty they are.'

'Some of them are missing their laces, but I expect our resourceful Poles will soon be able to resolve that little problem with a bit of string.'

'You bet they will. They won't let a wee thing like that stop them having warm, dry feet.'

The girls started work, tying pairs of boots that still had their laces together. Those without were roughly sorted by size. After they had been working for a while, clapping the boots to shake off the mud and making groups of them, Eva said, 'It's funny, but I keep thinking of the shoots we had on the estate at home. It's the mud, I suppose. That earthy, damp smell. Reminds me of when we'd come home after a day out bagging a few pheasants.'

'You're right, it does smell a bit like that. I used to go out on the moors with my father and uncles. I thought there was something familiar about this. Pity we haven't got the hip flasks and the hot pies to go with it.' Sally sniffed the air. 'Mmm… damp, muddy leather, but there's something else as well.' And then she put her nose close to the boot she was holding. 'No, I can't quite put my finger on it.'

Eva picked up another pair of boots and banged the soles together a couple of times, but whereas most of the mud on previous pairs had dropped off at the first sharp tap, these did not release the thickly embedded dirt. She tried again without success, then turned the soles towards her and peered at the encrusted ridges.

'That's odd,' she said and she leant a little closer. She sniffed, then pulled back. 'Oh, I think I know what that smell is,' she said. 'Look!' She held the boots out for Sally to see how the tread was thick with dark, slightly sticky mud.

'I've got the same thing,' Sally said, holding out a stained pair of boots. 'Do you know what I think? It's not just mud, is it? It's blood we can smell. There's blood mixed in with the earth on lots of them.'

The girls stared at each other and then at the pile of boots. 'So that's why it reminded me of the shoots,' Eva said. 'That iron-y smell: the smell of blood.'

The girls looked from the boots in their hands down at the enormous heap yet to be sorted. 'Where have they come from?' Eva asked.

Sally frowned. 'I think I heard the driver say Normandy.'

'So they could be our boys' boots?'

'Or German. It's hard to tell.'

Eva was quiet for a moment. 'But whichever side they belonged to, they were all just young men following orders.'

'Come on,' Sally said, 'get cracking! Whether they're the boots of heroes or not, we need them for the men here. They'll be proud to wear them.'

'I'd like to think they'll walk in the footsteps of the brave,' Eva said, pulling a penknife from her pocket to fillet the blood-soaked mud from a thick sole.

Chapter 51

Eva, 24 December 1945

Silent Night

'Have you noticed how a lot of the men are cutting down trees out there today? Look, there's another couple of them. I thought they'd got more than enough firewood, haven't they?'

Sally was peering out of the window as two men struggled to carry a large fir tree between them. Further down the track, the iron bedstead sledges were being used to haul trees back to the barracks, while elsewhere, men carried smaller trees on their shoulders.

Eva joined her at the window, their breath misting the glass. She cleared the fog with her hand, watching the procession of men and trees, then said, 'Oh, of course, we're being stupid. It's nearly Christmas, isn't it?'

'You're right' – Sally shrieked – 'they're getting their Christmas trees.' She skipped around the room with joy, clapping her hands. 'We've all been so busy here, I hadn't realised how soon it was. We've got to get organised.'

That year, that first Christmas of liberation, the aid workers at the Wildflecken camp decided that every one of the residents there should receive a present. 'We're using some of the goods from the Red Cross food parcels,' Ken said. 'I know we usually split up the parcels and store them as general supplies for the whole camp, but this Christmas is special. Some of the box-tickers might not approve of this, but hell, it's their first Christmas of freedom! Let's give the poor bastards a treat.'

So the workers selected some of the more luxurious items from the Red Cross consignment, like raisins, coffee and biscuits, plus chocolates for the women and cigarettes for the men. And all around the camp the residents were also making their own preparations: sewing, cooking and singing, as if distilling all the lost Christmases denied them during the last six years of starvation and slavery into one gigantic celebration that captured the essence of every splendid Christmas they had ever known.

On Christmas Eve, Eva and Sally soon forgot their promise to Brigitte not to sample the home-made liqueurs brewed in the camp. Ducking under washing lines of damp nappies, peeling back thick blankets that draughtproofed doors, they were invited into each family's room, glowing with the firelight from a stove. In these crowded quarters, foetid with the close smell of rarely washed bodies and infrequently changed babies, people smiled and laughed and clinked little glasses of ruby-red plum brandy.

'It's delicious,' Eva said, 'but I'm not sure how many more I can manage. It's so strong!'

'I'll help you out,' Sally said, laughing. 'It's too good to waste.'

Children of all ages had their noses pressed to the windows and when she saw the girls looking curious, a proud mother explained, 'They are looking out for the first star. We cannot begin to eat our Christmas feast until the first star of the night has been seen in the sky. We call it the Little Star. It is how we all remember the story of the star of Bethlehem.'

Suddenly there was a cry from one of the children: 'It's here, it's here! The star has come!' Everyone immediately began to offer food as well as drinks. One elderly grandmother insisted they sample her beetroot soup with mushroom dumplings and another family offered pancakes filled with mushrooms and cabbage.

'However have you all managed to put on such a magnificent feast?' asked Eva, when they found Irene Komorowski graciously offering refreshments to all the visitors crowding her quarters.

'We have been making preparations for quite some time, of course. Everyone who could spare the time went out into the forests in the autumn, picking mushrooms, which we dried for just this occasion. There is food to be had, my dear, if you look hard enough, and for those who have survived these years through eating scraps from the floor, there are great riches to be found all around us.'

'But just look at this beastie!' Sally pointed to the large whole fish, laid out in resplendent glory on the table, its glistening surface decorated with thin slices of carrot and hard-boiled egg. 'Wherever did you get this?'

Irene smiled at her and said, 'Ah, the carp is always the centrepiece of our Christmas Eve meal. Until very recently it was living in the bath, so it is the freshest of carps. You must both try it.'

She cut a small portion for the girls to taste, then said, 'And you must take this too, my dears, for good luck.' She held out two paper-thin silver discs on her forefinger. 'Here, take one each and slip it inside your undergarments, against your heart, and it will bring you good luck. You must keep it there all tonight and then if you give it to someone else tomorrow, they too will have good fortune in the coming year.'

Sally and Eva stared at the little pieces of transparent silver, mystified. Then Eva said, 'What is it?'

'The scales of the carp. Do you not do this in your country?'

Eva pulled a face and shook her head. 'No, we just kiss under the mistletoe.'

The girls held out their hands and let Irene slip the scales onto their fingers, then they looked at each other, burst into giggles and simultaneously slid their hands inside their sweaters. Sally said, 'And to think I was really hoping for scent for Christmas this year.'

'Not too much aquavit this early in the evening, I hope, girls?' Brigitte popped her head round the door. 'I could hear you two laughing down the corridor.'

'Come and join us,' Irene beckoned to her. 'You must have a good-luck token too, my dear.' She offered another carp scale on an outstretched finger.

Brigitte took it, then looked at the other two girls. 'Pop it down your titties,' said Sally. 'That's what we've just done.'

They burst into giggles and Brigitte obediently reached into the sweater she wore under her nurse's uniform. 'I'll be needing some luck before the end of the night,' she murmured. 'We've got two mothers vying to have the Christmas baby, so I'd best get back and see who wins.' She turned on her heel and left, leaving a faint whiff of carbolic soap.

'And I have another gift for you both as well,' Irene said, reaching behind her chair to bring out two sheepskin hats. 'With the warmest thanks from all of us.' Sally and Eva took the thick fleeces and pulled them over their hair and ears.

'It really is Christmas at last,' said Eva and then she began, in a timid, wavering voice, to sing a carol she knew from childhood and all around her other voices picked up the same tune, some singing in their own tongue, others in German, so 'Stille Nacht' harmonised with 'Silent Night' until they all ended on the one quiet note. And in that single moment of peace Eva glanced outside, hoping that tonight would indeed be peaceful, with no revenge-hungry Poles taking shots to pierce the celebrations.

'Happy Christmas,' Sally said. 'Now let's show them that the British know how to have a good time and sing them all some of our best carols.' They broke into 'Ding Dong Merrily on High', followed by 'God Rest Ye Merry Gentlemen', and toured the barracks arm in arm, singing at the tops of their voices.

Chapter 52

25 December 1945

My darling Hugh,

How I wish you could be here to share this special Christmas with me. It has given me such hope and joy to see the happy faces all around me. They have suffered so much, but they are so brave and so optimistic. And the children, the dear children, are delighted by the smallest treat.

If we had been able to have children, my dearest, I would have wanted to spoil them with wonderful toys, but now I can see that we don't need much at all to be blissfully happy. There are sad stories all around me, but people are determined to make the most of life again. They are alive and they are celebrating with all their hearts.

God bless my darling. I hope you are celebrating Christmas in Heaven with the Angels in your realm of glory. We had so little time together and only one Christmas in our marriage, but I treasure the memory.

All my love for ever,
    Your Evie
    Ps I love you
    xxxxx

Chapter 53

Eva, 23 April 1946

Trains for Home

Eva and Sally pushed their way through the crowds of people boarding the train, carrying battered cases and bundles tied in shawls. Girls with ribboned braids twisted around their heads twirled as they danced along the station platform, their embroidered skirts billowing above starched white petticoats.

'They all look so happy to be leaving the camp,' Sally shouted above the clamour of the brass band trumpeting a triumphant farewell.

'You'd think they were all going off on holiday,' Eva yelled back, her voice competing with wheezing concertinas and the deep, stirring voices of the men singing their country's traditional songs.

Hundreds of the camp's Polish residents were finally going home. They were travelling to their homeland by train, but a train that was more comfortable by far than the ones that had forcibly brought them into Germany several years earlier, to work in punishing, life-shortening conditions. Polish flags fluttered from all the boxcars under garlands of fresh spring greenery cut from fruit trees, the bright new leaves and emerging pink and white flower buds an optimistic sign of faith in the future.

'I'm praying they'll find happiness,' said Eva. 'Who knows what awaits them in their old villages at the end of their journey. Will their homes still be standing? They may have been looted, their animals slaughtered. Their fields will be empty.'

'And what kind of welcome will they receive on their return?' Sally added. 'Those who were left behind may have suffered terribly too.'

The girls could barely hear themselves talk over the carnival of clashing music and the jostling of whirling polka dancers on the platform, all celebrating this momentous day. Everyone was dressed in his or her best clothes for this long-awaited journey. The men were smart in white shirts and black suits and many of the women wore white aprons round their waists and had covered their heads with kerchiefs of red, blue and yellow, echoing the colours of the bright flowers embroidered on their skirts.

The train was filling with people and their bundles of possessions. Eva and Sally peered inside the carriages. Each one was lit with flickering candles, mounted on every available ledge with molten wax.

And there was warmth too, with small iron stoves alight, their chimneys like bent arms punching out through a hole in the wall. Every time a stove door was opened, the light of the glowing red-hot embers glinted on glasses of plum liqueur, shining like rubies, set out all around on makeshift tables made from boxes and rough pieces of wood. 'Come,' the occupants called, 'you must have a drink with us. Na zdrowie,' they cried to the girls, inviting them to share their drinks and their happiness.

These laughing, home-going Poles were the ones who hadn't wanted US visas, or had not been eligible for them. The precious visas were so slow in coming and only those who could prove they had suffered persecution were automatically considered.

'I can't help remembering the words of those American Baptist pastors who visited,' Eva said. 'They were trying to get a bill through Congress to admit displaced persons. I heard them speaking to camp residents and they said, "You are not strangers to us. America was founded by the voluntarily displaced. We are a nation of the displaced from all the lands." It's such an enormous huge country. Surely they could relax the rules and take many more people.'

'You'd think so,' Sally said, 'but America only wants the fittest to come. They want workers who are completely healthy. They need farmers and strong labourers. Why on earth would they want many of the people here? We may have done our best to feed them up and get them fit, but after their years of deprivation so many are not good enough for the United States. Or they've got relatives who are in a poor state of health, or children with handicaps. America doesn't want to be burdened with people like that.'

'At least everyone leaving today is stronger and healthier than when they first arrived here. We're sending them back in better condition.'

'Yes, but they're not the same people who left their villages all those years ago,' Sally said. 'Look around you. In every car there are tired mothers with demanding babies and grandmothers weakened by years of starvation and gruelling labour. They may all be happy to be going home, but not everyone of them is able to dance with the energy of those girls.'

They watched as children chased each other up and down the platform, laughing. 'It's hard to believe that not so long ago, even the youngest were working in German factories,' Eva said.

'Children are so resilient. But many of them have seen terrible things during their time as slave workers. Things they may never be able to forget. Brutal punishment, even executions.'

'One boy told me the bright and clever ones were picked out and started work from the age of ten,' Eva said.

'How typically efficient of the Germans, spotting their nimble fast fingers could assemble small machinery parts with precision and speed,' Sally said, frowning with disgust.

'When we unpacked those Red Cross parcels at Christmas,' Eva said, 'they sorted and stacked the contents so quickly and neatly.'

For the camp's first Christmas the staff had decided all the residents should have a gift. Some of the older orphaned children, who had formed a group under a team leader, were entrusted with the task of splitting the consignment. The children had filed across the snowy paths from their quarters to the warehouse, singing as they marched and swinging their arms in time, just as if they were going off to a carefree summer camp of games and campfires with the Scouts and Guides. Once the task was explained to them, they had divided their group into sections, each assigned to a different item from the packages, stacking cigarettes, dried fruit, then chocolates, passing the boxes along to each other.

'They were amazing. They formed a production line,' Sally said. 'When I praised one of the older boys, because he organised his area so quickly and neatly, he cheerfully said it was, Wie in der Fabrik, fünf Jahre.'

'Like working in the factory for five years,' murmured Eva. 'But they were only children when they were sent to work there. They had no schooling, no playtime and very little food. The conditions were appalling. How could the Germans have subjected them to that?'

'Maybe there'll still be some time for another childhood when they get back home.'

'I hope the Russians don't take away what's left,' said Eva. 'They say the big bad bear is coming to get them.'

Sally put her arm round Eva. 'We've done what we can, you know. We can't stop them leaving and anyway, look at them: they're all so happy to be going back to their home country.' And they watched the joyous procession of families board the train and stayed watching as it curved around the track, the men hanging onto the sides of the cars, waving their flags and kerchiefs, until it was finally out of sight.

'Come on,' Sally said, tugging at Eva's arm, 'we've only another ten thousand or so Poles to send home and then the job will be done.' The girls laughed as they ran to the lorries, heading back to the camp and the many refugees still waiting to learn whether they would be the lucky ones heading for a new life in America or the unlucky, returning to their old homes with uncertainty and fear.

In the weeks and months to come there was joy for some when they heard their visa applications had been granted. But even for these there was sometimes bitter disappointment, when a family member failed a last-minute health check. 'I can't bear it,' Eva told Sally, after a family had failed their check. 'They almost managed to leave, they had a new life within their grasp. And now the youngest child has developed TB. They'll never have a chance now. So near and yet so far.'

'I know. It's Sod's law.' Sally sighed. 'They're paying a terrible price for their years of suffering, but at least they're alive. And if they can't emigrate or go home, they can end up staying here. Well, not in the camp perhaps, but they can still make a decent life for themselves in Germany. Look at the ones who've already decided to stay, rebuilding the old houses and cultivating land. We saw them in the village the other week, growing beetroots, onions and potatoes. They're eating well and they're safe. It's a life of sorts, not the inevitable death they'd feared. And the locals are gradually getting used to them.'

And Eva thought of the emaciated prisoners she had seen being interrogated in Bad Nenndorf, not for war crimes, but for their political leanings. 'There may well be persecution for many of them if they return to their homeland. But at least they're free here.'

Chapter 54

Eva, 7 January 1947

Off-Piste

She remembered Ken's words afterwards, about when the snow thaws in spring and how many bodies would be found once winter was over. In her first year at Wildflecken Ken had joked about the score-settling vigilantes, laughing about their unregulated form of justice, but now she too had added to the body count.

It was so stupid of me, she cursed herself. So stupid. I should never have gone out with him. Trying to help people integrate, trying to pretend we could all be civilised again. What on earth was I thinking?

It was her second winter in Wildflecken and crisp snow had covered the hills all around the camp and the surrounding forests for weeks. The air was dry and cold and when the sun shone from an icy-blue sky, Eva longed to be outside, away from her desk, away from the form-filling and the hopeful faces. Staff were only given leave for two half-days and one whole day a month and during the summer, she had walked the green meadows and cycled the local roads to discover Gemünden and the surrounding villages. At first the local people had been distant and suspicious, but when they heard Eva speaking in their own language, they became more forthcoming. They showed her their productive crops of cabbages, carrots and potatoes. But these are not for the *Ausländer*, they said, the foreigners from the camp, who they were convinced would come raiding their fields.

Among the families trying to return to normality after the years of war and shortages, Eva met Peter Dägen, who, like many German soldiers, had finally been able to come home after a term in an American camp. She first noticed him making hay in the fields in the summer on one of her regular walks, because he reminded her of Kurt Becker, the prisoner who'd died from his mistreatment at Bad Nenndorf. If Kurt had lived, he would have been like Peter: strong and healthy, with muscular arms turning the hay his livestock would need to see them through the winter.

'Guten Morgen,' she called and to her surprise he answered in excellent English.

'You work at the Wild Place,' he said.

'Oh, you know what we call it?'

He was keen to practise his English and she enjoyed making a friend away from the constant demands of the camp inmates. Getting close to the local population was discouraged and food supplies could not be shared with the Germans, but what harm can it do, Eva asked herself. They've suffered too because of that interminable war. Ordinary civilians didn't ask to be dragged into that dreadful conflict. They're not the enemy now, they're trying to rebuild their lives too. Surely we can at least all try to be friends and talk to each other.

After she'd met him a couple of times on her walks, Peter invited her to visit the farm and meet his ageing widowed mother, who had been struggling to keep the family farm going while he was serving in the army.

'We never wanted the war,' Frau Dägen said, inviting Eva to sit at the table and join them in their simple meal of black bread and potatoes. Eva made a mental note to bring a gift of food with her if she was invited back again. 'All we ever wanted was to feed ourselves and our families. And all the terrible things people are saying have happened, they were not our fault. It was nothing to do with people like us. We knew nothing about the *Lager* and nothing about what happened there. And my sister and her husband in the city were forced to join the Party. Everyone lived in fear of being singled out. They could trust no one, not even their oldest neighbours. We were more fortunate out here in the country, but in the cities, no one could escape.'

'It's all over now, Mutti,' said Peter. 'We just have to work hard and try to forget the hardships of these last few years.'

'That's easier said than done when we've lost so many of our strong, young men. How will our country ever prosper again? So many gone, never to come back. And now we are worse off than we were before. Such hardship we have now. At least we have eggs from our hens, but our cow is dry and we cannot buy butter. Did you know that people in the village have to fry their pancakes in castor oil and our coffee is made from acorns?'

Peter's mother continued to complain to her patient blond son as they ate, but Peter kept reassuring her that all would be well in good time. Eva felt at ease in their simple but welcoming home and her sympathy for the ordinary German people, who had been forced into a system and a war they had not wanted, began to grow. The Allied forces had all agreed not to give German civilians any kind of aid, but what harm could there be in talking and listening and maybe attempting to understand why it had all happened?

Peter showed Eva around the small farm, pointing out the dilapidated barn he planned to mend, the rotten fences in need of replacement and the fields yet to be tilled. 'We will all have to work harder now we are at peace,' he said, rolling his shirtsleeves back over his strong bronzed arms, 'but it cannot be worse than the war. I hope I will not have to stay a farmer, but for now I must help my mother. If we can grow our own food, we will survive.'

So it did not seem strange that in this second winter, after visiting the farm several times and hearing Peter talk of how he hoped to leave one day, Eva should accept his offer to be shown the best ski trail in the nearby mountains. She was not a very experienced skier and had been reluctant to go any great distance alone. So far she had only explored what would be classified as nursery slopes near Wildflecken, using a pair of skis from the large horde of Nazi supplies at the camp and wearing an odd assortment of sweaters, a dark brown tweed jacket and a large but practical pair of men's cord trousers, held up with a leather belt in which she'd had to make several extra notches.

She hitched a lift on one of the regular supply trucks going past the village and met Peter at the once-popular resort, now deserted. 'These aren't the best ski slopes Germany has to offer, but they're the nearest,' he explained, leading the way to the swaying chairlift. 'If you want really good skiing, you'll have to go further to the Alps.'

Eva sat down beside him. 'I realise that, but I can't get away from the camp for long. I'm not due extended leave till the spring so I'm very happy to make the most of what we've got here.'

The chair rose higher through the sparkling air and she was looking forward to having a good run on the fresh snow. All around was new, clean and white, as if the snow had wiped away all the horror of the last five years. At the top, Peter pointed towards Aschaffenburg to the west. 'There are even better slopes over there, but this is the most convenient one for us. Are you ready?' Eva hitched up her loose trousers again, hoping they wouldn't fall as she skied, then nodded.

They began snaking their way down, Peter at speed, Eva more slowly and cautiously, but gradually growing more confident, invigorated by the sting of cold air on her cheeks. As soon as they reached the bottom they both wanted to go back again and they made two more descents before Peter said, 'One more and then we call it a day, yes?'

The sky was just beginning to assume the pinker tones of sunset and the light would be going soon, so Eva hesitated, but then said, 'There's just about time, so let's do it.'

They began the descent side by side, then Peter swerved into a thicket of fir trees, yelling, 'Over here, this is more fun,' so Eva followed. It was much more challenging, weaving in between the conifers, and her progress grew slower and slower. The light was not so good here either; the snow was still brilliant white among the dark trunks, but very little of the last of the daylight penetrated so she didn't see him hiding behind a tree, waiting to trip her up. He must have caught the front of her ski; she tumbled head first into the soft snow.

She lifted her head. 'Damn,' she said. 'I thought I was doing so well.' She unfastened her skis, but before she could get to her feet, he was suddenly upon her. She felt his weight on her shoulders and her ill-fitting, oversized trousers were pulled down behind her. 'What are you doing?' She struggled and screamed, 'Stop it.'

He punched the side of her head so hard she gasped and inhaled a mouthful of snow. Then a harsh gruff voice, quite unlike the polite and gentle tones she had heard from him so far, spat words back at her: 'You *Englisch*. So righteous, so proud! You think we can forget, huh? I will show you what I think of you people, telling us all the time how we are in the wrong and must be punished. It will end here.' She heard spitting, then the warm wetness of his hand groped between her buttocks, his fingers probing her anus, before he forced himself into her, ripping the soft tissue to the tune of her agonised screams.

'You don't like it? Maybe this you like better.' Then he plunged again, not quite so painfully but still cruelly, into the place where she had only ever known pleasure and tenderness with her husband.

After a few quick thrusts he grunted and withdrew. It was brutal and humiliating, but it was quick. When it was over, he stood up, adjusting his clothing, and she turned her head to see him leaning against a tree, lighting a cigarette. He was nonchalant, relaxed. He might have been pausing for a rest by a lamp post on a city street, catching his breath after a tiring afternoon walk.

Eva managed to turn and support herself on one elbow. Other than the pain she felt in her most tender parts, she was not injured. She did not speak, there were no tears, but she was furious and very afraid. And despite her shock and fear, the commanding voice of her combat training sergeant came back to her: '*Grab them by the balls first if you can. Don't wait for their move, you only get one chance.*' Peter only knew her as the friendly carefree girl from the camp, who filed visa applications and hiked on her days off; he didn't know that her survival instincts had been honed by rigorous training in silent killing.

She brushed the snow from her jacket, her face and her hair. She stood up so she could fasten her baggy trousers. He stood there, carelessly smoking and laughing, telling her, 'You think we can forget how your planes bombed us, how you destroyed our beautiful cities? Dresden, Köln, all the thousands of innocent civilians you killed. Never! We hate you and I will enjoy taking my time to finish you off, you little English bitch!' She was alert to the menace in his voice, the menacing hatred that convinced her she had only minutes to save herself. Again, her sergeant's instructions reverberated like a mantra: '*Swift upward thrust, don't hesitate.*' Could she do it? Could she be sure it would save her?

Eva felt inside her jacket; she let him think she was in shock. She wanted him off guard, relaxed, assured she would not fight back. She found what she wanted and then lunged for his eyes, just as she had been trained to do. Eva plunged her sharp pencil, one of the very pencils she sharpened every day at her desk to fill in the prescribed paperwork and select those who might leave the camp, into his eye socket and up into his brain. And as he screamed and put his hands to his face, falling to his knees in agony, she aimed for his head with the end of her ski pole.

He writhed and gurgled and was finally silent. Eva listened for several minutes, but once his cries quietened, there were no other sounds. 'You foolish boy,' she whispered. 'I'm sorry, I had no choice.'

She looked down at his body, now so still and unthreatening, felt for a pulse, just to be certain, then refastened his ski bindings and threw his poles nearby. She scooped snow to cover him completely, so it would look as if he had crashed into a trunk when he went off-piste.

Her cream Aran sweater and cord trousers were splattered with droplets of blood, but if anyone noticed, she could say she had suffered a nosebleed. Eva rubbed away the worst of the stains with fistfuls of snow, then left the cover of the dark trees and glided back onto the slope, down towards the cluster of lights beginning to glimmer at the bottom of the hill as the sun finally set.

Chapter 55

Eva, 7 January 1947

What the Woods Hide

'How was the skiing?' Sally asked when she came back to their quarters from her shift that evening.

Eva was already curled up in bed, a hot-water bottle wrapped in a towel between her legs to soothe her bruised flesh. She'd run herself a scalding bath as soon as she'd returned. In the bathroom she'd scrubbed her skin, slipped soapy fingers into her sore vagina and torn rectum, and hoped she had escaped the danger of being impregnated or infected as the result of her foolishness. Wiping the steam from the bathroom mirror, she had seen bruises beginning to emerge on her neck and shoulders, but her face, though flushed with the hot water and her own tears, did not betray her. Her cream sweater, and the loose trousers that had been so easily ripped from her body, were spattered with his blood and lay rolled in a bundle at the bottom of her suitcase. The dark tweed jacket, speckled in country hues of rust and green, showed no obvious evidence of her crime and she'd hung it to dry near the stove.

'Did you enjoy yourself?' Sally asked, her words somewhat muffled as she pulled her thick jumper over her head.

'It was all right, but I won't bother again.' Eva yawned. 'The snow was a bit soft, then Peter abandoned me on the slopes and went off on his own. He wasn't impressed with my abilities, he thought I was far too cautious and slow.'

'Not much of a gent then,' Sally said. 'But you got back all right?'

'I hitched a lift before it got dark. We're lucky there's always so much transport going backwards and forwards here. It's better than a bus service.'

Sally laughed. 'As long as they don't all come along at once, like the London buses.' She bent down to rummage in her bedside locker. 'I've got some plum liqueur here. Fancy a nip?'

She poured shots into the beaker cups the girls were still using in place of glasses. 'Down the hatch,' she said, tipping it down in one gulp.

Eva sipped her drink, feeling it warm her throat, burning away her grief and filling her with a determination not to let this unfortunate occurrence, as she told herself to think of it, prevent her from continuing to fulfil her duties. She knew she could insist she had acted in self-defence, she knew there would be sympathy for her injured dignity and honour, but she also knew it would be complicated. There would be awkward questions about fraternisation and her lack of judgement, then an inquiry, possibly even a court martial. No, better never to say anything.

Instead, she just said, 'So how did you come by this delicious beverage this time, you resourceful little Scottish minx?'

Sally smiled and said, 'This bottle was a present from a very grateful father. I managed to lay my hands on some callipers for his little boy. And now he'll be able to start walking again.'

'What's wrong with him? Not polio, I hope?'

'No, thank God. But it's a pretty shocking tale all the same. The boy and his sister were hidden by a friend of the family in the tiniest little cupboard in a farmhouse. For three whole years they barely left their hiding place. And by the time the children were reunited with their parents, the poor wee laddie couldn't walk. Imagine that. They saved his life, but nearly crippled him in the process. Hopefully in time his legs will straighten out as they grow stronger, but there was no way the little mite could walk unaided.'

'So many terrible stories,' Eva murmured, closing her eyes. 'And we can only help a fraction of them.'

'I wish we could do more,' said Sally. 'It sickened me to hear about the lenient sentences that were handed out to some of those murderers in Nuremberg last year. Just a few years for murdering thousands of innocent people. If I had my way they'd all hang for what they did; every single one of those murdering bastards. Prison's too good for them.'

'Why is it,' Eva said in a quiet voice, 'that all humanity and kindness virtually disappeared? Or perhaps the capacity for cruelty is always present in mankind, just hidden beneath a facade of civilisation.'

'I know. It's bad enough to hear them claiming they were just following orders, but to hear about the sheer mindless brutality as well – oh, it makes my blood boil, it really does.'

'So many dead, so many ruined lives.'

Sally stood up and began waving her arms in the air and pacing the tiny room they shared. 'And so many getting away with it! There were thousands of these monsters and only a tiny proportion is ever going to pay for their hideous crimes. The rest will try to sneak back to their old lives, trying to pretend they had nothing whatsoever to do with the camps and the slave labour.' She screamed in frustration, then said, 'We need another drink.'

Eva gave a small laugh as she held her beaker in her cupped hands, smelling the sweet scent of plums. 'You remind me of the girls in Aldershot, where I was stationed when I was training.' She took a deep breath and then said, 'One night, news went round that a German prisoner had absconded from Puckridge Camp – that was a POW camp not far from us. All the girls in my dorm started talking about what we'd do if we came across him. We didn't have access to guns, of course, so we started laughing about how we could use the broomstick that we'd adapted as a rounders bat and whether that could do any serious damage. And then one of the girls – Betty, I think her name was – she was from an army family, said, "Girls, if we find him, we'll kill him with our bare hands." And, do you know, every single one of us there absolutely agreed with her. We were all suddenly filled with the most intense furious energy, convinced we were actually capable of committing murder if we found that escaped prisoner.' Eva laughed and shook her head. 'Poor man, he was lucky we didn't get him. I'm sure he was recaptured.'

'But I can understand that feeling,' Sally said. 'I heard similar sentiments many times during the war. We absolutely hated the Germans. But if it had really come to it, could we have actually done it, with our bare hands, I mean?'

Eva was quiet, then she said, 'It was the heat of the moment. We were all excited. But do you know, I think we could have done it if he'd turned up then and there.'

Sally sipped her drink, savouring the sweetness. 'I suppose we all could if we had to. And there are rumours of gangs of survivors out there still, plotting revenge. And who could blame them?'

Eva stayed quiet, watching the small window, through which she could see the snow falling thick and fast with fat snowflakes that would drift that night, blanketing the mountain slopes, the trees and what lay safely hidden beneath their branches. Perhaps tonight there would be the sound of gunshot again. And she knew that all that was buried in the forests around the camp and elsewhere would not be revealed until the spring.

Part Seven

Any small river found in garden (4,6,6)

Chapter 56

Evelyn, 14 March 1986

When Will There Be Bad News?

She listened to the news as often as possible, tuning in to the lunchtime bulletin on Radio 4, then again at six o'clock and finally the ten o'clock news on television. Every morning she drove to the village shop for the *Daily Telegraph*, a pint of milk, some bread and maybe a Danish pastry if she was feeling in need of a treat. It wasn't a new habit; she'd done this for years and always told the girls in the shop she couldn't do without the mental exercise of her daily crossword. But now this routine had added significance as she resolved to maintain an unchanged regular programme. And when he was finally missed, what would come first? A bulletin on the airwaves, a report in the press or perhaps, more ominously, an urgent knocking at her door?

Days passed, then weeks, then finally one Monday she caught a brief snatch on the one o'clock news: 'Concern is growing for the whereabouts of Colonel Stephen Robinson, who has not been seen at his London flat since the middle of February. Police are asking for anyone with information to contact their local station immediately.'

This is it, she thought. *Now it begins.* The next day, there was a small article on the third page of the newspaper. Amusing that, his picture on page three. It was an old photograph of him, taken, she guessed, in about 1950. It was a likeness, but not very much like him in later years, although she had recognised him instantly. The report mentioned his involvement in post-war interrogation, the court martial at which he had been cleared of any wrongdoing, a brief, vague mention of his subsequent activities, which she took to mean he was still with MI6, and then finally one sentence that she hoped would put off any investigators: 'His bank card was last used in Lymington, Hampshire, on the evening of Sunday, 10 February. Police are investigating the possibility that Colonel Robinson was intending to visit the Isle of Wight or sail over to France. His passport is also missing. Foul play is not suspected at this stage.'

Evelyn folded the paper and turned to the back page, where the crossword always enticed her with its blank white squares, waiting for her quick mind and fast pen. She smoothed the page and sat back, stirring her coffee and mentally checking all the steps she had taken. *She had been careful, hadn't she?*

On her return from Lymington that night, she had emptied his wallet and separated the contents. She had cut the plastic cards into small pieces, then scattered them in various holes she had dug around the grounds. She had removed the keys from his key ring and buried each item deep in a separate spot. If anyone had seen her digging on the edges of the lawns, they wouldn't have thought it strange. She was always planting new specimens of snowdrop and narcissus or lifting rare bulbs in the garden and surrounding grounds.

The train tickets, wallet, driving licence, passport and handkerchief were burned in a spectacular bonfire to rid the garden of the last of the winter debris, along with a man's padded coat, a tweed jacket with patched elbows, some motheaten clothes and shoes with very worn soles. A sprinkle of lawnmower oil on the pyre always ensured a rapidly consuming blaze and she had raked the ashes, just to be sure. And the small amount of cash from the wallet and his pockets she added to the church collection the following Sunday, thinking that was probably something the miserly bastard would never have done in his entire life. *Can You forgive me?* she asked in silence, as she added the money to the plate, her inner plea echoing those she had made many times in this hallowed place.

Yes, she was sure she had tidied up all the loose ends. Yet one could never be sure, could one? She could not afford to be complacent. She had no alibi for that particular Sunday, but then none of her neighbours were close by and she often saw nobody, apart from the staff in the village shop, from one week to the next. It would seem more out of character if she had suddenly begun to fill her days with activities she didn't normally undertake. No, continuing with her ordinary, solitary routine was less likely to arouse suspicion.

Evelyn sat at her scrubbed kitchen table, stirring a cup of Earl Grey tea and gazing out at the trees with their slight haze of fresh green buds above the clusters of primroses. From this time on, she knew she would rarely have visitors. She could manage to run Kingsley with an occasional visit from Sharon to help in the house and maybe she should ask Jim to come back a couple of times a year, just to prune the high beech hedges and clip the pollarded hornbeam. It wouldn't do to let the gardens become completely neglected when they'd always been such a source of pride for her and her parents before her, but she could manage to mow the lawns herself, with the help of her sturdy Westwood tractor.

She cut herself a slice of the ginger cake she'd bought at the WI market a few days earlier. They always had such good produce, quiches, bakes and preserves, and it was important to continue maintaining her normal routine. She could still carry on going to the monthly meetings of the Garden Club, show her face at the twice-yearly village jumble sales, help with the church flowers, make a spiced parsnip soup to serve at the annual Lent lunches in the village hall and help with the teas at the summer garden party at the rectory. With all these mundane, normal activities, if anyone ever came asking awkward questions, her acquaintances would all say what nonsense, she was a perfectly nice, ordinary woman of pensionable age, who kept herself to herself and was a good neighbour. No one would ever point a finger at her and say she was a cold-blooded murderer.

But, she decided, popping the last of the ginger cake crumbs into her mouth, what she must also do, as long as she was physically capable and as long as she continued living at Kingsley Manor, was survey the grounds and especially the woods every single day. It wouldn't appear irregular. In spring it would seem as if she was searching the grass for the flowers of her much-prized, newly emerging snake's head fritillary, wondering whether they had spread their elusive seedlings a little further that year. At other times it would appear that she was concerned with the state of the fences around the estate, noting where the wire had come loose or the posts had rotted. Any onlookers who knew she kept hens would think she was just checking for signs of foxes when she wandered through the woods with her sturdy walking stick. And in autumn, as she delved deep into the thorny bushes, hooking them back with her cane, they'd think she was taking advantage of the crop of juicy blackberries for pies and bramble jelly.

In the months that followed there were a few reminders of the necessity for this vigilance. A couple of times, a gnawed bone appeared on the lawn, kept closely cut so she could easily spot anything out of place. The bones could well have come from a long-dead sheep or a deer carcass, but she took no chances and buried them deep beneath the beech hedge and continued watching the woods.

Sometimes she thought about the dark forests of pine and the drifts of winter around Wildflecken and wondered if they had ever revealed their secrets when the snows thawed in the spring. But at Kingsley Manor, as time passed, in the woods where the saplings grew denser year by year and the briars and brambles sent out long thorny arms that snared intruders, the woodland floor was thick with leaves, fallen twigs and branches and nothing untoward could be seen. And Evelyn kept watch, secure in the knowledge that more than one forest had helped her hide the evidence of her deeds.

Chapter 57

Evelyn, 10 November 2012

One Small Slip

I always knew that one day it would become too much for me. How many other oldies in their nineties could make regular inspections of acres of land, the way I've done for years? Most of them are satisfied with pottering around a small suburban garden, watering a few pots of flowers, or can only manage to walk a short distance to a corner shop for a loaf of bread and a newspaper. Many old ladies – because I still can't think of myself as old – give up walking anywhere at all and replace outdoor activities with day-long television programmes, gardening with knitting and games of tennis with magazines and a well-cushioned sofa. And very few can whizz through the daily crossword, which I do religiously, along with bridge and editing the parish magazine. My mind must stay agile as well as my body.

As Evelyn grew older, her rounds of the estate became a little less frequent but they were still regular and thorough. Once a week she toured the entire formal garden, which still boasted roses and flowering shrubs in their respective seasons. The herbaceous borders were not so spectacular now that the arthritis in her knees and elbows restricted kneeling and weeding, but the garden hadn't become totally overgrown, as she had feared as she scraped at the soil with a long-handled hoe.

Once a week she toured a quarter of her acreage in rotation, walking the boundaries and the copses, including Marley's End, that particularly special wood that had provided such a useful, safe hiding place. Since the sheep had gone, the fields had become dotted with birch and alder saplings and nettles, but there were still paths well trodden by deer, badgers and foxes that Evelyn followed as she toured her estate.

The wood where he lay had grown thick with briars and fallen branches over the years and although Evelyn was sure no sign of him could ever be seen, she still felt obliged to check that he remained well hidden. She reminded herself that it was what, twenty – no, nearly thirty years – since he'd fallen, so there would be little if anything to see; a fragment of fabric perhaps, or a scattering of disjointed bones. The hungry foxes had soon found him and others helped too, birds, beetles and their larvae. All of them came to her assistance in hiding her crime.

For it was a crime, she knew full well. A justified crime in her mind, but a crime nevertheless, and one for which she would pay, causing the family, the estate, the village, great distress, if it were ever discovered. *But I cannot bear the thought,* she told herself, *that the crimes he committed would not be recognised as such if he was ever found.* Yet again, his actions would be considered in the light of the duty he had performed for his country; he would be exonerated and probably honoured. *So I must continue to be vigilant, despite my advancing years, for as long as I am able.*

But finally, one day on her regular round, although she was sprightlier than most her age and even though she was familiar with every inch of her territory, a stray bramble ensnared her ankle and she fell into the undergrowth, injuring her wrist as she tried to save herself. It wasn't a life-threatening accident, it wasn't going to keep her out of action for very long, but she recognised that it was a warning of what was to come and realised she must be even more careful.

It's lucky I've fallen here, on a thick floor of dry leaves. If I slipped in the courtyard on the granite flagstones, I'd break a leg or hip for sure. Or if I fell on the wet, mossy sleepers across the ditch, down into the channel swollen with rainwater, I could go under the muddy waters. I might even drown. She picked herself up, using her stick to push herself to her knees and then into a standing position. *I can walk, and it's only my left wrist, fortunately, but it's a sign I must plan ahead.*

After calling an ambulance to take her to the nearest A&E, where a great fuss was made because of her advanced age and X-rays were taken of arms, legs and hips to check there was no damage other than the wrist, Evelyn called Pat, her brother Charles's only child. Pat rarely visited, citing work (part-time physiotherapist), family commitments (her adult sons worked in London) and domestic arrangements (she had a cleaner and a gardener once a week). Woking wasn't even that far away, but she preferred to spend her spare time playing tennis or embroidering complicated needlework cushion covers. She didn't like visiting Kingsley Manor, because she knew that she and her family would one day become the trustees of what in her eyes was a monstrous and uneconomical time warp and every visit she made confirmed in her mind that she was going to face an unwelcome task when her aunt finally died.

'Pat, dear,' Evelyn said. 'So sorry to trouble you, but I'm afraid I've had a little fall and I had to get it seen to in the hospital. I've been X-rayed and they've put me in plaster, so I was wondering if you might be able to collect me from the hospital and give me a lift home now?'

'Oh dear, no! How on earth did that happen?'

'I just tripped in the garden earlier today.' *Just in the garden, so you think I've been pruning and weeding, not during one of my regular inspections of my victim's grave.*

'What did the hospital say? Shouldn't you stay there overnight, just to be sure?'

'Oh no, dear. They're saying it's only my wrist, nothing very serious. But I won't be able to drive myself for a bit, that's all.'

'Well, I'm afraid I can't come over right this minute. I've got to collect Humphrey from the station at seven. He's on his way back from an important conference and has a lot of very heavy luggage with him.'

'Then not to worry, dear. They can take me home in an ambulance, I'm sure.' Yes, they could, but not right away, not until an ambulance was available, so in the end, after waiting for more than an hour, Evelyn called for a cab and paid £30 for the driver, a very kind man whose English was remarkably good, to take her right to the door of her home. She invited him in to carry her shopping bag as well, even though she knew Pat would think it most unwise, as they had called into the petrol station on the way home in the dark for supplies and one of those convenience meals so Evelyn could just press a button and ping, the microwave would prepare her supper. Tomorrow she would ring the village shop and arrange regular deliveries of her newspaper and groceries. Oh, how lovely to be waited on and just call for help.

And as she ate her burning-hot chicken tikka masala and pilau rice with a fork straight out of its black plastic container, as washing up was to be avoided when one was one-handed, Evelyn thought that she wouldn't call for more help from Pat for a while. Instead, she would use the time to prepare. There were letters to be burned, jewels to sell and gifts of money and silver to distribute to needy friends and worthy causes. Pat and her family would eventually inherit, but if she could not be bothered to take a close interest and if she thought the house was full of rubbish anyway, there might not be as much as she imagined. *I'll make it easy for her*, thought Evelyn, *but not too easy.*

Chapter 58

Kingsley Manor
15 March 2013

My dearest darling,

This will be the last letter I shall write to you with pen and paper. From now on, you will still receive my letters, the letters I have written to you ever since you first left these shores to serve your country, but they will exist only in my head. I shall still compose them, sharing my thoughts, my anxieties and my misdeeds with you. I shall still sign them with love and many kisses, but they will be letters from my soul and my dreams.

Please do not be disappointed that there will be no more actual letters, scribbled in ink. I will still love you for ever and ever, but I feel the time has come for me to be more careful. This winter I had a fall, after making my regular tour of the grounds and the woods. I tripped in the undergrowth near the stile. I only fractured my wrist, but it could have been much worse so I have decided that I must prepare for a time when I can no longer be active and vigilant.

Tomorrow I shall take all the letters I have written to you over the years, all the letters in which I have confessed all my foolishness and all my actions, and I will burn them. What a pity I didn't write them in 'secret inks' as we were taught when we trained. Then they could have remained a mystery for ever! What do you think I should have used, the lemon or onion juice, egg white or (your favourite, I think) good old wee!

I shall, of course, keep every one of your loving letters, the ones you wrote to me so many years ago, but my letters of pen and ink will no longer exist. It is better that way and from now on my missives to you will come directly from my heart.

Your loving Evie, xxx
    Ps I love you

Chapter 59

Evelyn, 16 March 2013

No More

Evelyn remembered how thrilled she had been to find the shoes: black velvet, with a sturdy heel, a bow over the toes and a strap round the ankle. She had thought herself so lucky to have such fashionable shoes when leather was so scarce in 1943. And she remembered exactly when she bought them: April of that year, in anticipation of Hugh's safe return from France.

They had planned a romantic reunion at their London flat – an Italian supper in Soho, a show and dancing. Clothes were hard to find too, but she had adapted her black cocktail dress and created a sweetheart neckline to flatter her creamy skin, with two diamanté buckles from an old belt of Mama's. She had planned to curl her hair and create a victory roll to frame her face, with a teasing wisp of net attached to a darling little hat that she knew Hugh would love. But in the end, that was not to be. Hugh did not return, at least to her arms. He managed to escape, but in doing so he was shot, her darling Hugh; an incidental casualty for those who were careless with lives, a shocking tragedy for those who loved him and others like him. She never did wear the shoes in the end; she couldn't bear to put her feet into shoes that should have danced with delight while she was held in her husband's arms, but which hobbled her feet when she was barely able to walk even a step without sobbing uncontrollably.

Where did they go, those beautiful shoes? Given to a girlfriend or a charity, presumably. But the dress she kept, ripping off those ridiculous clips, restoring its sober modest neckline. All that remained of her once-glamorous ensemble was the shoebox, crammed with handwritten letters from end to end. Some were those Hugh had sent from France on tissue-thin government-issue letterhead, bearing an etching of the Arc de Triomphe and the legend, 'Somewhere in France', written sometimes in pencil, other times in pen. But there were also those she had written herself in later years, after he had gone, telling him everything, opening her heart to him and him alone, when she couldn't ever reveal her secrets to anyone else. The shoebox carried a picture of the velvet shoes, the shoes that never ran to meet him, never stood on tiptoe to reach his lips and never danced in his arms.

But now even those letters had to go. Evelyn had been attempting to tidy the house ever since she had recovered from her fall. It was a warning sign to be taken seriously; she could not know how much more time she had to prepare or to continue keeping watch.

So, on a cold but bright spring day, she built a bonfire on the old tennis court, just beyond the apple orchard, with its neglected, unpruned trees. It was sad to see them so abandoned, but they hadn't fruited well for the last few years and she really couldn't cope with applying grease bands and lopping branches any more.

And the tennis court had not seen a game for many a year. This was where she had learnt to play, with Charles yelling at her to keep an eye on the net, and later she had played with Hugh, pausing to hug and kiss him when she retrieved the ball. She could still hear the shouts and laughter if she paused and, over there, the bench where a hamper sat, with strawberries and lemonade for the players. Now, the tarmac surface, once clearly delineated with white lines renewed every season, was thickly matted with cushions of dark green moss and creeping yellow buttercups.

Evelyn gathered dry material from the borders, cutting away dead stems of delphiniums, lupins and phlox to encourage healthy new flower shoots come summer. She never cut down her perennials in autumn as so many gardeners did, reasoning that dead wood protected the plants through the winter in the frost pocket that is Kingsley, where tender plants could burn as late as mid-May during the days she had come to know in Germany as the *Eisheiligen* days, the days of the ice saints. Such a picturesque way of describing the dreaded late frosts of springtime.

She trundled another barrow-load of cuttings across to the growing heap. The pile was all tinder-dry and it was a sunny day for early March. No sign of winds and showers, perfect for spring cleaning, as Mama would say.

The previous night she'd read all the letters again, one by one, sitting at the kitchen table, a bottle of amontillado sherry helping her find tears to remember. She'd put Hugh's letters to one side and bound them with a red ribbon. *Those I'll never burn. They will stay with me for ever*, she said to herself. Then she read her own letters again, her lips mouthing some of the words and whispering others, particularly every time she read, *Ps I love you*. Those letters she returned to the shoebox, still crammed full despite the removal of the ones she'd received all those years ago from Hugh, and then she taped it shut.

And at last the moment arrived. The pyre was ready to burn as soon as she put a match to the Zip firelighter tucked into its heart. But first, she poked around the base with a broom handle, just as the old gardeners had taught her, in case a creature had crept in there for shelter while she had been collecting kindling. Nothing darted out, so she pushed the shoebox right into the centre, on top of old newspapers, stained seed catalogues and diaries from years past, then struck a match. It caught instantly and soon all was blazing with flames three feet high.

'Goodbye, darling,' Evelyn murmured. 'Ps I love you.'

Chapter 60

Evelyn, 29 October 2015

The Final Fall

Evelyn strained to reach the handle of the second suitcase on top of the high wardrobe. The first case had crash-landed on the floor, but luckily the lock didn't burst open and spill the long-forgotten contents. She stretched again, as far as she could. All she had to do was pull the leather strap towards her; then she eased it across to the side and whoosh, it slid down and onto the floor, landing with a thump. But the second case was much heavier than the first and caught on the carved pediment that adorned the front and sides of the mahogany wardrobe.

Evelyn tugged at it again. Damn it, she had to get it down today. Now she'd remembered them after all this time, she couldn't leave the cases where they were any longer. She'd almost forgotten all about them, but then the other night, when she was kissing the photographs of her two dearest loved ones goodnight before going to sleep, it all came back to her. When she had finally come back from Wildflecken, after being away for so many years, Mama was unwell, Papa was in hospital and there was so much to do, so much demanding her attention, that her cases were never fully unpacked. They were stowed away and then forgotten. A bonfire had consumed all her letters to Hugh, as well as a large number of photographs, but she had not thought about the suitcases and their incriminating contents for many years. She couldn't even be sure exactly what they contained, it was all so long ago, but she could picture a passport, documents placing her at Bad Nenndorf and Wildflecken and photographs, some innocent, some not so. Oh, and yes, a sweater and trousers with tell-tale stains that could reveal everything.

One more tug and down it must come, then. Evelyn gripped the side of the wardrobe with her left hand. That wrist had never been the same since her unfortunate fall – two years ago, was it? She pulled at the case again with her right hand and then it happened. High on the tips of her toes, she tottered on the ladder-back chair she had pulled across the room to stand on to help her reach up; she lost her balance and fell. She bumped her head on the mahogany frame at the end of the bed and hit her hip on the hard floor, only a threadbare Turkish rug cushioning her fall.

When she eventually opened her eyes, the room was dark and very cold. The blackbird who always sang just before dusk was long silent and through the window she could see the moon had risen. It had been early afternoon when she'd come into the bedroom, when she'd dragged the chair across the floor and stepped up in front of the mirrored door.

Perhaps I will die here, she thought. *I might not be found for weeks if Pat doesn't remember to phone or call round. She's never been that attentive, with her busy life and demanding husband. And it won't occur to my neighbours to check, unless the village shop begins to wonder why I'm not calling in for my paper and milk.*

What a sad end! I'll pass away unloved, unnoticed, unforgiven, in this room. It belonged to Charles once. When he was sent away to school I missed him so much at first, I crept in to feel the weight of his cricket bat, swing his tennis racket and bury my nose in unwashed whites smelling of his sweat and hair oil. But when he returned, he no longer wanted to play with me and barred the door to his little sister.

She tried to move, but her head felt heavy and her hip was hurting. *This time I've really done it. This is more than just a fractured wrist, you foolish woman! All for the sake of your incompetence. You should have cleared out those cases years and years ago. Now what are you going to do?*

She lay there on the hard floor, growing cold and thirsty, waves of pain throbbing around her hip, then suddenly she grew determined. She imagined she could hear Hugh, her darling husband Hugh, calling to her and a second voice echoed the first. Wasn't that Charles as well? Both were shouting at her, telling her not to give up, that she must somehow get help. We may have died, they were saying, but we died fighting to the end. We didn't just fall off a chair and lie there doing nothing till we had gasped our last breath.

So, with a tremendous effort, Evelyn rolled over onto her front and began to drag herself in the dark across the floorboards towards the door. There were no lights on in any rooms of the house, but she knew every tiny bit of the place and could picture each piece of furniture in all of the rooms. She pulled herself forward, one painful inch at a time, pausing to gasp for breath every minute or so as the agony engulfed her. She needed light, she needed to phone for help, but she couldn't get either unless she could manage to get as far as her bedroom, down the corridor. Then she remembered Charles's shooting stick, in an umbrella stand, along with his old golf clubs and hockey stick, in a corner by the door. Using her arms to support her body, she pulled her good leg up beneath her and managed to half kneel, her injured hip dragging her other leg behind her. Half crouching, half kneeling, she made better progress and found the stick, then jabbed upwards again and again at the light switch until finally light flooded the room and filtered out into the passageway and landing.

'Ambulance,' Evelyn gasped, after her long painful journey to the phone, dragging herself across the wrinkled rugs and dusty floorboards. 'Tell them the back door isn't locked.' Country ways are so trusting that doors stay open long after dark, thank goodness.

And while she lay waiting for help to arrive, Evelyn prepared. She knew there would be much to occupy her mind in the weeks and months to come, or however long it took to recover. There would be much to do and much to think about, but she would be ready. She logged the contents of the cases at the back of her memory and prepared her story, while outside, in the dark, a barn owl called to its mate in the first hunt of the night across the Kingsley estate.

Chapter 61

Evelyn, 15 January 2016

Where is Home?

'Honestly, Aunt, the staff in this nursing home didn't seem to know who on earth you were. I began to think I'd come to the wrong place.' Pat's face looks red and shiny, either from the sleety rain outside or the heat of the ward, Evelyn can't quite tell.

'Really, dear? What was the problem?'

'Oh, there's a stupid woman on reception who seems to think your name is Hilda. I said I'd come to visit Mrs Evelyn Taylor-Clarke and she looked down her list, then went blank and said they only had someone here by the name of Hilda with that surname. It wasn't until I told her I knew you were here, and that you are my Aunt Evelyn and I've always known you by that name, that she finally let me through. Honestly, where do they get these people from?' Pat looked around the small ward at the staff and patients, then shook her head. 'Half of them are foreign, I'm sure.'

Evelyn laughed. 'Possibly, dear. But they're all very nice and kind. I'm feeling much stronger now. I managed to walk to the bathroom on my own after lunch today.'

'But your name's not Hilda, is it?'

'No, dear, it isn't. It's Hildegarde. I expect some of them find that a bit of a mouthful.'

'Hildegarde? I never knew that. How in heaven's name did that happen?' Pat pulled off her heavy raincoat and fanned herself with a copy of *The Lady* from Evelyn's bedside cabinet.

'Hildegarde was Grandmama's first name. She was half Polish, remember? It was a family name. I was very fond of my grand-mother, but I never really liked the name, nor did Mama, so I was always called Evelyn.' *Or Evie or Eva, but you don't need to know that.*

'Oh, whatever.' Pat waved her hand in exasperation. 'I hope they're not making any other stupid mistakes. How are you feeling anyway? I've brought you some shortbread. It's not home-made, I'm afraid. I was in a bit of a rush, after the morning I've had, so I dashed into Waitrose on my way over. But I hope you like it.'

'Thank you, dear. That's really very kind of you,' Evelyn said, thinking how she would much rather have had fresh flowers, maybe freesias for their sharp lemony scent or some spring bulbs about to burst into flower, something growing and alive to remind her that there was life outside this stifling ward with its smells of disinfectant and talcum powder, and accompanying sounds of low murmuring, the occasional buzzer to summon attention and the scrape of visitors' chairs.

Pat placed the tin of biscuits on the bedside cabinet and shifted on her chair. 'But the main reason I've come to see you today is to have a chat with you about what should happen next, when the doctor says you are well enough to leave here. They think it won't be long now.'

'I'll go home, of course. It will be so nice to go home, dear. Some of the other people here really aren't at all well. And I don't like being with such a lot of old people all the time. I think I'll be much better off at home in familiar surroundings. I could take little walks in the garden for exercise. I'd soon be back to normal, you'll see.'

'Well, Humphrey and I aren't so sure, Aunt. This wasn't the first time you'd had a fall and we think Kingsley just isn't a suitable place for someone your age, living on their own.' Pat paused and then gave her aunt the most cheerful smile she could muster. 'We both think you would be much more comfortable in a residential home with staff to look after you. Some of them are really very nice and it would be so good for you to have company all the time.'

'I'm sure they are very nice, dear, but I don't know if I'd like living with other people. I'm not used to it, you know.' Evelyn continued to stare at her niece. *I knew it would come to this and I know she is right, but I don't feel I have to agree immediately. Let's see how well she makes her case.*

'But we'll be worrying all the time about you being on your own, all alone in that big old house. There are no neighbours nearby to hear you if you have another fall. And even if I could drop everything at a moment's notice and rush over from Woking, it could take me ages to get to you.'

'I could have one of those alarm things round my neck. One of the nurses was telling me that her grandmother has one. I could tell you right away if I fell.'

'Yes, you could. But that doesn't mean to say I can get to you instantly, does it? I might be up in London for the day or miles away in Cornwall. Humphrey and I often pop down there for a few days with the boat. I don't just sit at home waiting for you to call, you know. And this last time – well, the doctors say that if you hadn't managed to raise the alarm when you did, you could have died of thirst and hypothermia if you'd been lying on the floor there for a long time. It does happen, you know. Two or three nights and that would have been your lot. And then where would we be?'

'At least I'd have died at Kingsley, dear. I wouldn't have minded ending my days in my own home.'

Pat frowned, then pulled her sweater over her head, revealing a very creased blouse. *Tut, tut, it takes no time to iron a shirt*, Evelyn thought, *no time at all.*

'And if I didn't remember to call you once a week, what state would things be in by the time we found you? It doesn't bear thinking about.' She frowned some more, then said, 'Quite frankly, it simply isn't fair to me and Humphrey. I don't want to walk into the house one week and find you've been lying there dead for days. I'd feel absolutely awful and it would look as if I didn't care, when I do care about you, I care very much.'

'Well, dear, when you put it like that…'

'I knew you'd see sense.' Pat pulled a couple of brochures from her hessian shopping bag. 'There are some lovely care homes round here.' She laughed and said, 'I said to Humphrey I'm almost tempted to book a place for us both right now.'

'Surely not, dear. You've got the boys to look after you.'

Pat dismissed this with a wave of her hand. 'Oh, I wouldn't dream of it. They've got their own lives to live. Besides, when you get older, really old, you need specialised help, and adapted beds, baths, treatments, and all sorts of things. You can't easily organise all of that at home.'

'I suppose you're right, dear. I was beginning to find I needed to visit the chiropodist much more than I used to. Last time, I got rather lost driving round Petersfield.'

'There you are then. When you're in a residential home, all these people come to you there. Chiropodists, hairdressers, even doctors. You're not expected to have to go anywhere. It's much more convenient.'

'It would be nice to get my hair done. Michelle was always so understanding.'

'You'll have everything on your doorstep if you're sensible about this.' Pat held out the brochures. 'I've been to see three homes so far. They've all got rooms available. But this one on top smelt very strongly of curry when I visited. I think it was the staff they have there. Now this one,' she thrust the literature onto Evelyn's lap, 'Forest Lawns, is really lovely. I think you'd like it.'

Evelyn looked at the pictures of laughing residents, the spacious lounge, the bright dining room and the extensive gardens. 'It looks very nice. I'd like to be somewhere with a garden.'

'I've already arranged for the manager to visit you here tomorrow afternoon. She'll have to talk to your doctor as well, but once they've agreed you are fit to leave, it could all happen very quickly.'

'Do they have snowdrops there? They must be in flower at Kingsley by now, Pat. Remember how the snowdrops spread across the lawns? I do miss my garden.'

'I expect they have snowdrops. Or maybe you could advise them. You know so much about gardening, I'm sure they'd be glad of your advice.'

Evelyn was quiet for a moment, thinking what would be the best response, then she said, 'Maybe I could go there for a week or two. Just to see if I like it first.'

Pat reached across and clasped Evelyn's hand. 'You do that. I'm sure you will love it there.'

And Evelyn was silent, but she smiled at Pat as she thought, *I may not have much choice in the matter, but that doesn't mean to say I will relinquish all control over my life and my secrets from now on.*

Chapter 62

Evelyn, 2 March 2016

Who Has the Power?

It is better that I suggest it, thought Evelyn. Pat will flap and skate around the issue, even though she is an executor and a trustee. If I come up with the idea, there will be less discussion and a quicker decision.

So, when Pat arrived at the nursing home, Evelyn said, 'I've been thinking, dear, it would be a good idea, given everything that's happened, if we draw up a power of attorney. It doesn't do to wait for things to get worse and if my health deteriorates enormously' – she laughed – 'if I get a bit gaga, you wouldn't be able to do it at all.'

'Oh, I'm so relieved you've brought it up. I've been wanting to suggest the same thing, but I wasn't sure what you'd think.' Pat threw herself into a chair, dropping her bulging handbag down on the floor.

'I feel fine about it. It's a sensible step to take. You know it can't be done when someone can no longer give their consent so if I suddenly had a funny turn and lost my marbles overnight, you'd be in a terrible pickle if we hadn't done it.'

Pat laughed. 'Oh, you're not going to suddenly go downhill. You're tough as old boots, you are. But you're absolutely right, we must do it while we can. And now that you're nearly ready to leave the nursing home and move to Forest Lawns, it's perfect timing.'

Evelyn wagged her finger at Pat. 'But that doesn't mean you can go selling all the family silver, now. Not without my say-so.'

'I won't, Aunt, I promise. Though talking of family silver, I was thinking that maybe now the house is unoccupied, I ought to think about putting the valuables somewhere safe for the time being.'

'You could take them home with you, couldn't you?'

'Possibly. I'll have to have a good look and decide how much needs to be taken away for safe keeping.'

'There's a whole canteen of Georgian silver cutlery in the dresser. I should think that's worth quite a lot.'

'Gosh, I was only thinking about that silver and crystal claret jug and some photo frames. I didn't know there was more.'

'Oh no, there's lots. I'm sure there are quite a lot of pieces in the Georgian oak sideboard in the dining room.' Evelyn frowned as if she was trying to remember. 'Come to think of it, if you are going to start worrying about all the valuables, you ought to have a look at the Chinese vases and Papa's netsuke collection. They're worth quite a pretty penny too.'

'Really? It sounds like there's much more than I'd imagined.'

'And I think there are some insurance valuations somewhere in the house. Try looking in the drawing-room bureau. They might give you a clearer idea of the pieces you need to keep safe. They're not very recent, but it would give you something to go on.'

Pat looked shocked at the thought of the responsibility that had been handed to her, then said, 'Perhaps I'd better arrange to stay over there now and then. It would be a good idea to keep a close eye on the place, until we decide what to do next.'

'What do you mean, next?'

'Oh, nothing to worry about, Auntie. I just meant how we're going to manage the place long-term, that's all.' Pat smiled and said, 'You'll be going to Forest Lawns at the end of next week, won't you? So, I was thinking, you could tell me what you'd like me to bring over from Kingsley. You're allowed to take a few personal pieces, even furniture if you want.'

I know what you're up to. I know you won't love Kingsley as I did, as Hugh would have done by my side if he'd lived. You'll never live there, never bring it back to life. You'll probably sell it all. First the land and then the house. It will be like Stephen said, all sold for development, no fields, no woods. Where will the foxes go to earth then, where will the kingfishers fly?

But she said, 'Yes, it would be nice to have some of my own things with me. The manageress seemed very pleasant, when she came to see me. She said I will have to sleep in one of their special beds, but otherwise I can take anything I like. I thought I might have Mama's dressing table. It would feel more like home then.'

'And what about clothes? Shall I sort them out for you?'

'I think I need to do that myself, dear. I wonder, could we possibly go back to Kingsley, just for a morning, so I can pick out what I need? Then I could show you which pictures and ornaments I'd like to take with me too.'

Pat sighed. 'Do we really have to? You're not very steady on your feet yet. Kingsley isn't the easiest place to get around. It's full of traps and hazards with all those uneven brick floors and funny steps. I don't want you falling over again. I'm sure I could bring everything you need.'

'I'd like to try and go, dear. Otherwise you'll be going backwards and forwards with clothes and other things. I'm sure it will be much easier for you if I could pop home and choose for myself.'

'Oh, very well, but I haven't got many free days. I can only do Thursday morning this week. We'll have to do it then.' As Pat took her diary out of her handbag to check, crumpled balls of tissue fell to the floor. 'Yes, that's right. That's the only day I can do. I'll check with the staff that you'll be ready to go out by then.'

'I'm sure I will be, dear. I'm feeling much better and the physiotherapist here says I'm walking very well with the frame thing they've given me.'

Pat snorted. 'Well, they would say that, wouldn't they? The sooner they free up a bed, the better. I make my patients take it slowly – when I can get to see my patients, that is. What with you and Kingsley taking up all my time, I haven't been able to see any of my clients for weeks.'

'Maybe we could have a little walk around the garden when we go, as well.' *I'd like to say goodbye to the plants I nurtured over the years. My deep purple flag iris, my speckled hellebores and the snake's head fritillary. I may never see the like again if the home's gardens are not well stocked.*

'Maybe,' Pat said, standing up, ready to take her leave. 'But only if I'm sure you can manage it. We don't want you having another fall now, do we?'

Evelyn smiled at her niece, her wayward hair, her smudged lipstick. How did Charles manage to have such an untidy daughter? 'It's such a pity we'll be too late for the snowdrops,' she said. 'They're known as Schneeglöckchen in Germany. Snowbells. Isn't that a pretty name for them?'

'Well, I never knew that. You are full of surprises, Aunt.' Pat leant down to kiss her cheek and Evelyn caught a faint scent of sweat and fried breakfast in her hair as she did so. 'I'll give you a call later, about the power of attorney.' And she left, bumping into the swing door to the lobby as she went.

Chapter 63

Evelyn, 22 March 2016

Final Farewell

And when they returned it looked the same, leaded windows peering out from beneath the first signs of laden wisteria. Pat came round to the passenger door and opened it wide, then hauled Evelyn's walking frame from the boot and stood it in front of her. Then she looked down at the metal contraption with its little rubber wheels. 'Oh dear, I don't think you're going to be able to use this on the gravel, are you? I'd better nip inside and fetch a couple of walking sticks.' She dashed away, leaving Evelyn smelling the scent of primroses and freshly cut grass through the open door, feeling the spring sunshine on her face and hands. Then Pat came rushing back, two sticks in her hand. 'These will have to do.' She bent down and helped Evelyn swing her legs out of the car and into a standing position. 'Now, do you think you can manage?'

'Thank you, dear. I'll be fine if we take it slowly.' *Fine if you don't fuss over me and hurry me.* Evelyn took small but steady steps, looking around her every now and then, noting the tight green buds on the trees, the emerging bluebells and the dying daffodils. 'I always dead-headed the daffs,' she said, pointing with the walking stick in her right hand at the dead flowers that had been golden only weeks before. 'It helps the bulbs build up their strength so they flower again the following year.'

'Well, there's no way I'm doing that as well as everything else,' Pat grumbled. 'And I'm not getting a gardener in to do jobs like that when there's more than enough mowing and pruning to get on with, to make this place look half respectable. God knows what people will think if we don't make a bit of an effort.' She hovers in front of her aunt, watching her slow progress along the stone path to the heavy oak front door. 'Here, you can use your walking frame now. Careful on the mat, and watch yourself on the step up to the hall.'

'I know my way,' Evelyn said. 'I know every single inch of Kingsley inside out.' And as she crossed the threshold she was greeted by the instantly recognisable scent of the home she had known for over ninety years. She breathed in the timeless, ever-present smell of woodsmoke from the countless logs that had smouldered over the centuries in the inglenook fireplaces of the ancient house, seeping into every timber, every inch of plastered wall, the carpets and the curtains of every room, and she felt that she had come home at last.

'I'm sure you do know your way round, Aunt. But it's one thing being totally mobile and quite another when you're not too sure of yourself. This old place is full of hazards. You just don't notice them when you're fit and well, able to skip about.' She watched Evelyn negotiate the step and then they walked slowly but surely towards the kitchen.

'I thought we'd sit at the table in here, where it's warmer. I haven't kept the range going, but there's a small heater I found. We'll have a coffee and then sort out the bits you want to take to the care home.'

'I'd like to go upstairs first.'

'Oh no, I'm not having you do that! Those stairs are far too narrow and steep. If I get you up there, I might never get you down again. No, we'll stick to the ground floor, thank you very much. You know I didn't even want to risk you coming here. You're only just walking properly again.'

You didn't want me to see what you'd been taking away or neglect-
ing, you mean. 'Well, all right, but before we go, I'd like to take a
little walk around the gardens. Just for old times' sake.'

Pat frowned. 'I'm not sure. Maybe we could just look at the
garden from the doorway. If you fall again, I'd never forgive myself.'

No, I bet you wouldn't. That would be far too inconvenient and
take up even more of your time. Such a nuisance for you, having to
look after this beautiful house with its lovely furnishings and gardens,
all held in trust for you and your family, such a dreadful nuisance.
'Well, dear, I'll just sit here then, and tell you what I'll need.' Evelyn
manoeuvred herself around the table and onto a chair Pat pulled out
for her. 'Why don't we have a little glass of sherry as well as coffee?'

'Sherry? It's not even lunchtime yet.' Pat was clattering mugs
and boiling the kettle on the range. 'I don't think there's any in
the house and anyway, I'm driving.'

'What a pity. Are you sure there isn't any here? Papa always kept
a very good cellar. He was very fond of manzanilla. There must
still be a bottle or two down there, surely?'

Pat turned to look at her aunt and shook her head. 'You've got
to be joking. It's all gone. You never maintained the cellar. There's
nothing left down there now.'

'What, all of it, Pat? All the wine, port and sherry? Who drank
it then?'

'I'm beginning to think you probably had most of it, the way
you rabbit on sometimes. Here, have a biscuit.' Pat plonked an
opened pack of chocolate digestives on the table and two mugs
of coffee.

'Shouldn't we put them on a plate?' Evelyn peeled away the
wrapper and parted the biscuits with her fingers, looking around
the kitchen.

'No, I'm not bothering with fine china and all that palaver. We'll
eat them out the packet.' Pat broke a biscuit in two, crumbs falling
onto the sweater, thick with pills of wool, curving over her stomach.

'Well, I'd like to choose some sherry glasses to take with me,' Evelyn said. 'And maybe a decanter.'

'Oh, for goodness' sake, what on earth do you need a decanter for as well? The bottle will do, won't it? They all have airtight tops these days.'

'Yes, dear, but a decanter looks so much nicer on a tray with glasses – so do biscuits laid out on a plate.' She wondered whether to mention the sugar bowl, lumpy with coffee-soaked crystals. And it wasn't the lidded pot she and Mama had always used for brown sugar. But she noticed Pat's face and thought it better to be silent.

Pat glared. She dipped the other half of her biscuit in her coffee and nibbled. Melted chocolate coated her fingers and the corners of her mouth.

'Please don't do that, dear,' Evelyn said. 'It's not very becoming.'

Pat groaned, then sucked her fingers and scrubbed her mouth with a tissue she found tucked up her sleeve. 'I'm going to find your ruddy sherry glasses now.' Her chair scraped back on the tiled floor and she disappeared into the dining room.

'Not ruddy glasses, I want the ruby ones,' called Evelyn.

And then she had a stroke of luck. Pat's mobile phone rang. She must have put it down on the table while she was making coffee. 'Pat, it's your phone. Shall I answer it?'

Pat rushed back, flustered, holding a decanter missing its stopper. 'No, leave it alone.'

'I'll just take a little look for those glasses myself then,' Evelyn said, getting to her feet before she could protest. Pat tried to wave at her to sit down again, but was soon engrossed in her call. Evelyn shuffled out of the kitchen, through the dining room and out to the staircase. Could she really get up to the spare room and check the cases? It was a steep and narrow flight of stairs and then a long corridor to reach them. She thought she could remember what she had stowed away in them, but it was all such a long time ago, it was hard to be sure.

She stood at the bottom of the staircase, turned round and then, with a bump, sat down on the third or fourth stair. She tried heaving herself up with her arms onto the next step, but it was no good. Her arms were weak and her legs weren't strong enough to push herself up, even though she was much lighter than she used to be. And then she found she couldn't stand up again, even though her walking frame was within reach. Oh dear, Pat was going to be awfully cross with her. It wouldn't be wise to push her any further. So Evelyn stayed where she was, waiting for Pat to finish her interminable call, in which she could hear the words, 'being impossible' and 'bloody sherry' and 'when I get her back'.

From her seat on the stairs, Evelyn could see the large open hallway with its piano, polished mule chest and carved hall chairs. Beams of sunlight were filtering through the dusty windows, revealing great traceries of cobwebs adorning the lamps and cornices. Really, if Pat could fetch a feather duster she'd have those cleared away in no time. And as she gazed at the spiders' delicate decorations and the dust motes dancing in the shafts of sun, she suddenly saw Mama arranging a huge vase of white and purple lilac on the piano, where she always liked to place her flowers, their perfume filling the room. And then Papa was there too, pouring champagne as guests arrived for the many parties her parents held, which filled Kingsley with laughter, gossip and music. Evelyn sighed with the memories; Kingsley was so alive then and so happy.

'What on earth are you doing there?' Pat burst through the doorway. 'I hope you weren't thinking of going upstairs.'

'No, dear,' Evelyn said, as Pat hauled her to her feet. 'I just felt like sitting down for a moment.' She pointed to the cobwebs. 'We ought to sweep those away while we're here. It would only take a minute.'

'Oh, I haven't got time for that now. We need to find you those glasses and get going.'

'But I want to tell you what else I need,' Evelyn said as Pat guided her back towards the kitchen.

'We can do all that in the car. You can make a little list for me. I've got to get back right away. Humphrey's just phoned to say he has to bring a client back for early-evening drinks, so I need to rush home and straighten up. I didn't have time this morning, because of coming to see you.'

'Are you giving them sherry?'

'Probably not. I expect Humphrey will want a beer after a hard day – he usually does.' Pat waited till Evelyn was settled at the table once more, then disappeared into the dining room again and returned with a couple of little glasses with red stems. 'Are these the ones you wanted? There isn't a full set, but I think I can find four.'

'Yes, those will do for now. I'm hardly going to be giving parties at the care home, am I, so I'm sure I'll manage with four. And we can always come back for more.'

Pat shook her head, then found newspaper to wrap the glasses and bundled them into a carrier bag. 'Leave the coffee,' she said. 'I'll clear it up next time I'm over here.'

But you won't, will you, thought Evelyn as she stood up again and began the shuffle back towards the front door. I noticed the other dirty cups in the sink, the rings on the table, the sugar-encrusted spoon in the bowl. You don't love Kingsley the way we did. Hugh and I planned to live here. We had such grand plans.

Outside, Pat was anxious to steer Evelyn straight into the car, but while she was unlocking the doors and fetching walking sticks to replace the aluminium frame so Evelyn could cross the short stretch of gravel to reach the car, she tottered into the courtyard garden. In its sheltered embrace, the iris were emerging with strong green spears, tiny violets clustered in shaded corners and the magnolia blooms, in their full pinky-pearl glory, crowded their gnarled branches.

And as pigeons cooed and a pheasant cried across the woods, in response to these familiar sounds, Evelyn whispered, 'Goodbye, Kingsley.'

Part Eight

What a small bird needs (4,5)

Chapter 64

Eva, 15 May 1947

When It's Time

It was Brigitte who finally said something one evening as they prepared for bed. Her nursing training, her experience perhaps, intuitively told her why Eva had been so off colour in recent months. 'Sweetheart,' she said, 'please don't think I'm prying, I am just concerned for your health, but you have not seemed well for some time. You were sick for some weeks a while ago, but you've not got thinner. In fact, you look as if you have been eating a lot of potatoes.'

Eva had known for a while that she would not be able to hide it much longer. In the early stages, when she was nauseous and tired, she could easily claim it was an infection picked up from the latest trainload of arrivals in the camp or something she'd eaten, but she knew it would eventually become obvious. Her uniform was growing tighter, but she felt well and her cheeks were blooming.

'Has anyone else said anything?' Tears began to spill and Eva wiped her eyes on the cuff of her pyjamas.

'Only Sally. We've both noticed.' Brigitte came over to Eva's bed and sat beside her, putting an arm round her shoulders, her starchy carbolic scent reassuring Eva of her practicality and good sense. 'In this little room, with all of us dressing and undressing together, it's hard to hide anything from each other. How far gone are you, do you think?'

'About five months.'

'Then it's a little late to do anything about it.' Brigitte shook her head. 'You should have told me before.'

'But you deliver babies, not, well, you know…'

'That's true, but I understand how women's bodies work. And as much as birth is a miracle, it can also be a curse.' She put both hands on Eva's shoulders and looked at her calmly with ice-blue eyes. 'Have you thought what you will do?'

Eva shrugged and shook her head. 'I will have to go home, I suppose.'

'To your parents? Will they help you?'

Eva put her head in her hands. 'No, I couldn't go back to them. They'd be horrified. I'll have to find somewhere to stay in London and manage somehow.'

'And then what? When the baby comes, will you keep it?'

'I don't see how I can. I'm widowed, I have to earn a living. And anyway, I don't even want it.' She spat the last words with vehemence.

'Do you want to tell me who is the father?'

Eva wrenched herself away from Brigitte's embrace and rolled over on the bed to face the wall. 'It's no one special, no one I'll ever see again.'

In a quiet voice, Brigitte said, 'You must do whatever you want. But please don't put yourself or the child at risk. It is too late for that. And I can help you when it comes.'

Eva rolled back and stared at her. 'With the birth, you mean?'

'Yes, with that, of course, but also, if you are not going to keep the child yourself, then I can find a good family for you. There are many people who have lost children during the war or find they can no longer have their own. It is not difficult to find a healthy newborn a good home.'

'They wouldn't have to know anything about me, would they?'

Brigitte smiled. 'They don't have to, if you don't want them to. There are honest, decent couples here, who will soon be going to their new homes, who would be glad of a child to complete their family. You would be giving them hope and a reason to build a good life for the future.'

'I would, wouldn't I? Hope.' Eva fell silent, chewing her lip, then said, 'But I'd like the baby to stay here. Not in the camp, of course, I mean one of the nearby villages. I don't like the idea of it going to Poland or Canada or America, so far away from its beginning.'

'It's your decision, my sweet. I'll discreetly ask around when I'm out of the camp. I'll sign you off on sick leave when you get too big and I can find you a private corner where you can give birth. We can keep it very quiet. Would that help you?'

Eva burst into tears, but they were tears of gratitude, not sorrow. She had been so worried about her condition and knew she couldn't tell Brigitte how she had become pregnant. It was all a secret and even though the snows were long thawed, there had been no news of Peter. Eva never returned to the Dägens' farm, but she had prepared a cover story in case she was ever asked about that disastrous skiing trip. She'd simply say, 'He went off and left me' or 'I think I'd upset him', and feign ignorance of his whereabouts. The country was gradually becoming more settled, but it was still far from humdrum normal life, so the disappearance of anyone, let alone a young man who could have been involved in unregulated activities, didn't arouse suspicion.

'Thank you so much for being so understanding.' Eva grasped Brigitte's hand with its clean, scrubbed nails and held it tight. 'I couldn't think clearly and decide what to do for the best.'

'Don't worry, älskling, Sally and I will look after you. So far you seem well and healthy, so probably the baby is fine too. I'll check your blood pressure tomorrow. Let me feel your belly for now.' Brigitte leant over the bed and Eva pulled up her pyjama top and eased her trousers below the bulge. 'It all feels normal.' She stood up and gazed down at Eva, then said, 'I have to ask, have you any infection, any discharge perhaps?'

'No, nothing, thank goodness.'

'That's lucky then. But you must tell me if anything, anything at all, changes, okay?'

'I will. Thank you again.' Eva wiped her eyes with her cuff and lay back on her pillow, staring at the ceiling. There was going to be a baby, a real baby, not the phantom child of her flight from Bad Nenndorf. She and Hugh had talked about having children when they first married – he wanted three and she thought two would be plenty – but then the war started and they knew it would be better to wait until it was over. Then Hugh was killed, so she would never have his children. Tears began to form again, but she willed them away. If she couldn't have Hugh's children, she wouldn't have any. This child would stay where it was conceived, in hate, not love, but she would make sure it would find love somehow and learn to live well.

Chapter 65

15 May 1947

My dearest darling Hugh,

Until now I could not find any reason on earth for coming to terms with your death, but for once, I now find myself feeling glad you are not here at this time. If we had still been together, I know this misfortune could not have occurred, and if it had, I would have been ashamed and distressed. As it is, I am thankful you are not here to be humiliated by my fall from grace. But I think you would approve of the arrangements I have made, which will ensure neither of our families will ever be disgraced and embarrassed. When I eventually return to England after the birth, the child will be settled with a local family here in Germany, where it will learn to think, live and speak like a true German, but hopefully, a better, kinder one than many of recent times.

I think it is for the best. After all, I only ever wanted your children, my darling, no others. Our children would have brought us such joy and we would have taken such pride in their achievements, however slight. If only we hadn't waited and I had given birth to a honeymoon baby, as many of our friends did, then I would have had a part of you with me for ever.

Please forgive me for my carelessness, my dearest, and for my foolish trusting nature. I will do my best to make you proud in some way or other, I promise.

Your ever-loving Evie, xxxx
    Ps I love you

Chapter 66

Eva, 24 September 1947

The Time Has Come

For three weeks Brigitte hid Eva away. But she was sure all the other aid workers and many residents knew why she was not present at her desk. How could they not? She was ungainly, her huge bulge plain to see, impossible to disguise even with loose shirts and jackets. And all through the heat of late summer she had felt slow and cumbersome, burdened with this most unwanted child.

'Don't leave me,' she cried, after four hours of labour.

'It won't be long now,' Brigitte said, wiping her forehead. 'You're nearly there.'

'I can't do it. The pain is terrible.'

'You can do it. And it won't last much longer. Then it will all be over.'

Sally held her hand. 'You're being so brave. I'm going to make you a special cocktail when it's all over.'

Eva managed a weak laugh. 'If there's something to celebrate.' And then her words were carried away on another wave of pain.

Brigitte and Sally were her accomplices in this hidden tragedy. They brought her food when she was too tired to walk to the canteen, they found her larger clothes to disguise her bulk when her own became tight. They even managed to locate talcum powder to soothe her chafed thighs in the summer heat. And when Brigitte gave her a small bottle of castor oil, saying, 'You must rub this on your belly,' Sally laughed and said, 'Then I shall have to donate a few drops of my precious Soir de Paris to add to that foul potion, so you don't end up smelling like a fishwife.'

Would the oil do the trick? Could anything eliminate all signs of the calamity that had befallen her, she wondered as she massaged her taut, swollen stomach in the weeks before the birth. Would she be able to forget it all when this was over?

Her friends were loyal and never asked questions. Sally had only once said, 'You know, if you ever want to talk about it, I'll listen. You do know that, don't you?' And both of them had shielded her from prying eyes and awkward silences. But she guessed that her secret was more widely known and when Brigitte came back to their room one day with a package of dried leaves wrapped in a square of rag, she realised Irene Komorowski knew too. 'She told me to pour boiling water on these,' Brigitte said. 'To make you Himbeereblatte Wasser.'

'Whatever is that?'

'Raspberry leaf tea. It is for the contractions of labour. Many women say it makes them come more easily.'

'So, she knows about me?'

Brigitte shrugged. 'She must do. But she didn't hear it from me.'

'What did she say?'

'Nothing. She just gave me this and said she hopes you will be well soon. She didn't say why she was giving me the leaves, but I already knew their purpose.'

'But it's obvious, isn't it? Everyone must know.'

Brigitte put her arms round Eva. 'Maybe they know, maybe they don't. But nobody cares. People here have their own worries.'

So she had made the tea and drank the bitter liquid during her final weeks, thinking she was willing to drink anything that would help her get through this ordeal more easily. But it didn't seem to work. 'Bloody tea,' she yelled as yet another contraction seized her. 'Fat lot of good that did.'

'Shhh,' Brigitte said. 'You're nearly there.'

And then finally, with screams from her and encouragement from her friends, it was all over. She could hear the cries of the baby and the murmurs of the two girls and as she raised herself on the pillows, she found herself wanting to see. 'What is it?' she managed to gasp. 'Can I see?'

'Are you really sure?'

'Yes. I have to.'

So Brigitte leant over her with the little bundle wrapped in a towel and Eva took it from her.

'It's a girl,' Sally said. 'She's beautiful.'

'She is, isn't she?' Eva said, peeling back the wrapping. As she did so, a little fist grasped her finger. 'Oh, she's so strong.'

'She's a very healthy baby,' Brigitte said. 'She'll thrive. We'll sort out a bottle for her as soon as we can.'

Eva continued staring at the new being in her arms. She didn't look like him. She was not a figure to hate. She was newly made, innocent of all sin, deserving of love. There was a smear of blood on her head, which had a dark slick of wet hair. Eva stroked her cheek and the baby turned towards her, mouth open like an eager fledgling. And instinctively, Eva bared her breast and allowed the baby to begin suckling.

'Are you really sure you should be doing that?' said Sally. 'It will make it much harder for you to part from her.'

'Let her,' Brigitte said, putting a hand on Sally's arm. 'It's only natural.'

'She's hungry,' murmured Eva. 'She needs me. I didn't know she'd need me.'

Brigitte and Sally looked at each other, but Eva did not notice; her gaze was entirely on the baby held close to her breast. 'I know I must let her go eventually, but for now, she's mine. My baby. And I am the best person to care for her.'

Chapter 67

Wildflecken
1 October 1947

My darling,

I have not felt this much overwhelming love or this much anguish since I was informed of your demise and although this time it is not a death I am mourning, it is painful and distressing in an entirely different way. The child came into this world healthy, I held her briefly and now she has gone to live apart from me.

My head tells me that this is the only solution, that I could not keep her, that it is better she has a good life, not knowing anything of the manner of her conception. But my heart is torn in pieces again after feeling her soft skin, her downy head and hearing her cries.

Although the act of her creation was violent, her birth, albeit painful, was wonderful. She is perfectly formed and though I had expected to feel indifference or even disdain for this child of that terrible man, I could not. I was sure I would not want to look at her or hold her, but when I saw her in Brigitte's arms I held out my hands to cradle her. Then I looked into her innocent eyes and saw only trust and unquestioning love, which I felt equally in return.

But today, after feeding her from my breast for seven days, I have kissed her for the last time, smelt her milky scent for the last time and let her fingers grip mine for the very last time. She has gone to her new home and I am totally bereft. But, my darling, I will grow strong, for your sake and for the sake of all who have made sacrifices during these difficult and trying years. I have given her away to grow up with loving parents and eventually I will leave this place and never see her or know of her again.

Your loving Evie, xxxx
    Ps I love you

Chapter 68

Eva, 24 December 1950

Christmas is For Children

Eva shrank back into the furthest shadows of the candlelit church, hiding behind the many families gathered for this special service. She could see the little girl chattering to the woman who held her hand. Her blonde hair was twisted into pigtails beneath a woollen bonnet, her chubby legs wrapped in hand-knitted stockings and her body buttoned up in a warm grey coat sewn from a thick blanket. She looked strong, healthy and well cared for, and Eva longed to pick her up, breathe the scent of her skin again and kiss her cheeks.

Eva could not stop watching her, drinking in every second, knowing she should never have put the child born out of hatred to her breast. Ever since her birth, Eva's head had been filled with thoughts of her daughter, perhaps the only child she would ever bear.

The pain of her first suckling was nothing to the pain I've felt since giving her away. No mother, anywhere, under any circumstances in the world, can ever find it easy to abandon their own offspring. Parents in London evacuating their children to unknown families in the countryside, far from the threat of bombs, persecuted Jews in Europe waving goodbye to the Kindertransport, not knowing whether they would ever meet again. But none of them could have done it without stifling their cries as their hearts tore into pieces.

She continued gazing at this little blonde being of her own flesh and blood, born through sweat, agony and tears, born out of a brief but unforgettable moment of brutal hate. She was not to blame. She was innocent, oh so innocent, from her very first breath.

I thought it would be easy. I thought because she wasn't Hugh's child and, especially because she was the product of such a cruel attack, I could discard her, give her away without a second thought. But she looked at me with her puzzled eyes when she was born, when I held her for the very first time. I should never have held her, never put her to my breast, never felt the softness of her skin, the warmth of her breath and her sweet scent, but my instinct was to protect her; she was so new and so vulnerable.

It was Christmas again and snow had fallen, just as it did every year at that time. In the camp there were freshly cut fir trees, excited children and the smell of that year's batch of plum liqueur. And in the local Catholic church in Gemünden on that Christmas Eve, where Eva watched from her dark corner, there was the perfumed haze of incense mingling with musty woollens as people came to prepare for the celebratory feast that awaited them later that night.

But I should never keep coming back to see her. I knew from the very start I should have just turned my head away from that plaintive newborn cry, but it was so needy, so pitiful. But I looked and I touched and then I couldn't pretend she didn't exist. And now I long to slip her hands out of her red mittens, just for a moment, so I can look again at the perfect pearls of nails on every finger. I wonder, if I tipped her chin, are her eyes still blue? And I yearn to take off her bonnet, uncoil her plaits and feel the silk of her hair in my fingers.

If she had been stillborn or had died soon after her birth, it would have been easier. That would have saddened me, a new life so quickly gone, but then I could have forgotten about her. Then she would never have been more to me than a tiny crumpled newborn, not this laughing dimpled child, growing more full of life with every day, every month, every passing year.

And of course my biggest mistake was pressing Brigitte to tell me where she had been taken. I should never have asked, but I simply had to know. I had to be sure she would be safe and would be loved. And once I knew she was so nearby, I couldn't help walking past their cottage, strolling beside their fence to see her in the garden playing with a ball or singing to herself. And in the summer, I saw her pick raspberries with the woman she calls *Mutti*, eating the berries that stained her mouth and her white dress. It saddens me that she can never speak to me, kiss me or call me Mummy.

Eva stayed at the back of the church, hidden partly by the dim light and also by the heavy scarf pulled low over her forehead and tied tight under her chin. She didn't speak to the child, nor to her adopted parents, but she heard them speaking to the little girl, just as she had many times before. That was how she knew the name they had given her daughter. 'Lieselotte,' she mouthed. That's what they named her. Sometimes they called out 'Lottie', too, and 'liebchen'.

She watched the little family greeting neighbours with warm smiles, shaking hands with the priest and then departing. They appeared to have no other children, just Lieselotte, who grasped the hands of her adoptive parents and trotted between them, chattering about the supper of carp, fried potatoes and *Lebküchen* she had helped to make. *And I will never share her Christmas celebrations, show her how to roll pastry for mince pies, give her a stocking filled with secrets or cook her roast turkey, and she will never know the joy of finding a sixpence in her plum pudding.*

As she watched them go, committing every happy skip and every laugh made by that golden child to memory, Eva became aware of an old woman in a threadbare coat and shawl staring at her with an intense gaze, her eyes absorbing her. Eva lowered her head, as if in prayer, but was conscious that she was still being watched and after a minute or two, looked up. The woman was now standing close by. In a feeble voice, she croaked, 'Peter, wo ist Peter? Ich habe mein Kind, mein Sohn, verloren.'

She reached out with a weak scrawny hand, trying to grasp the sleeve of Eva's coat, but Eva turned away and pushed past her, pulling her scarf across her face, and left the church, disappearing into the chattering crowd on their way back to warm homes for their Christmas feast. As she hurried away in the cold air, which promised a clear night filled with stars for the children to claim as theirs, she couldn't help but feel pity for Peter's mother. 'I'm sorry,' she whispered as she walked with brisk steps along the snowy roads. 'I'm so sorry I can't comfort you and tell you that your son is dead and you now have a grandchild you will never meet. We're both mothers and we've both lost our children. I know I should tell you, but I can't. Please forgive me.'

Part Nine

At the end of the day… (3,6)

Chapter 69

My darling one,

I will soon be returning to England for good. Our work here is nearly done and Mama needs me at home. She has not been herself ever since Charles died and I feel it is my duty now to be there with her.

The child thrives, so I can leave here knowing that my work is done there too. Without revealing myself to her or to her parents, I have walked through the village often and have seen her growing strong and sturdy. She will have a happy life and be loved, I am sure. It pains me to think I may never see her again, but I know I must go. Besides, Kingsley is calling me and I long to see trees in bud in an English spring. But in due course, I hope I can make another contribution to improving the good of the world. As I thought at the time, Bad Nenndorf was an evil place and there has been an investigation, but Robinson has been acquitted of any wrongdoing, despite what I and others there witnessed. I am frustrated that he has been let off without severe admonishment or punishment, so I will think carefully about what else I can do to rid this earth of the man I blame for your unnecessary death. I despise those who hate mankind and cannot love their fellow human beings.

Your loving Evie, xxxx
    Ps I love you

Chapter 70

Eva, 30 May 1951

Leaving At Last

'Na zdrowie,' Irene Komorowski said as she and Eva clinked their glasses of plum brandy. 'To your health, my dear, and long life.'

It was time at last for all to go home. Eva and her friends had done all they could and the Wildflecken camp was destined to cease healing and feeding the deprived and displaced, stop mending broken souls and become a base for American soldiers raised on golden breakfasts of orange juice, easy-over eggs and sweet waffles awash with syrup. Hundreds of thousands of lost souls had come to Wildflecken hungry and forlorn, broken in both body and spirit, but thousands had also left full of hope for the future.

Brigitte and Sally were now long gone and with them her secrets. Both had tended to Eva when she was heavy with child and held her hand as she laboured, coaxed her through her pain and held her in their arms, her tears soaking their uniforms, when she was parted from her baby. Brigitte left to continue working with the Red Cross and wrote saying that she was helping new mothers in other war-torn areas and was responsible for drawing up policy guidelines for the organisation. Sally hugged Eva the day she left to return to Scotland, saying, 'Come and see me when you get back. There's always a spare room for you.' But that was two years ago and now Sally was married with a baby of her own and Eva did not want to visit her and be reminded of her own childlessness.

One of the few remaining Wildflecken inmates to whom she still felt close was Irene Komorowski. The Countess was not only too old to leave, she was also too ill and so too were several of the women she had protected and kept close by her side since they had first been incarcerated at Ravensbrück. Tuberculosis had finally snuffed out any hope they might have had of making a new start across the Atlantic, although early on a handful of the women had been fit enough to escape to Canada, which was recruiting seamstresses. Irene had urged them to go when they had nervously asked about this distant country. 'Take it, take it,' she had said, in front of Eva, when the offer came through. 'You have the chance of a new life now. You must go. I will be happy for you.' Some went, some stayed and now those who had declined to accept the posts would stay in Germany for ever, their chance to return to villages annexed by Russia snatched from their grasp and the opportunity to make a new life in a new country denied them by declining health.

Eva did not know for certain if her efficient form-filling, her patient questioning, her interpretation had ensured that all the people she had encountered in the last six years would go on to have a happier life; all she could know was that for the most part they had a chance of a safe life, free of persecution and abuse. They had been rescued from misery and might now be able to achieve happiness and maybe even prosperity.

'Would you really have wanted to return to Poland?' Eva asked Irene on the last evening out of many, as they sipped damson plum liqueur by the glowing light of the stove in Irene's room, the walls draped with richly embroidered shawls just like the one she wore over her shoulders.

'Poland, my homeland, yes, but not Russia. We have no love for the Russian bears. Nor they for us.'

'But you must miss your country and your family very much.'

Irene shrugged her shoulders. 'My family is here now, there is no one waiting for me back there. My aunts and uncles were left behind, but all of them and also the cousins who were taken with me are long gone.' She waved her elegant but bony hand towards the door and the room beyond, where her countrywomen were cooking cabbage dumplings and brewing tea. 'My girls are all the family I have now, these women and the others who are staying. We have a little Poland here.' She laughed and tossed back her drink, then poured more into their glasses.

'No matter how hard we tried, we could never get rid of you all,' Eva laughed. 'Even though we did our best.' Eva and the other aid workers had been given a target of producing 10,000 visas a month, but in the last few months of operation they had only processed half that number, as the remaining residents of the once-teeming camp of many thousands were either too old, too ill or too resigned to their fate to win the fabled prize tickets for America or Canada.

And now she too had to leave. She had not returned to London once during her time at Wildflecken, nor had she visited her family in the furthest green hills of Surrey. *I could not face their continual questions about how I coped after Hugh's death*, she thought. *And I could not bear their tears once Charles, my older brother, had died. But above all, I wanted to stay as long as possible to drink in every snatched moment of my one and only child's life. The only child I will ever have.* She hugged that secret tight within herself.

Whenever she could, Eva walked or cycled to the village, ostensibly to visit some of the former camp residents who had decided to settle in the locality, in reality to catch a glimpse of Lieselotte running around in the cottage garden, out walking with her parents and, now that she was nearly four years old, playing with other children nearby. Her occasional periods of leave were spent walking in the mountains, and she and the other girls went to dances at the British army bases, where they met officers in need of company and where the NAAFI ensured they were well fed.

Could I have found someone else? Eva often asked herself this question. *But the memory of Hugh and everything else is too much to inflict on a new love. Besides, I'm not sure I have any love left to give.* So she flirted, laughed and danced the lindy hop with enthusiasm, but always left the dance hall alone to return to her hard single bed.

A smiling woman entered the room from next door, bearing a large plate, which she offered to Irene and Eva. 'Kielbasa,' she said, pointing to slices of dark red sausage flecked with fat, and 'Ogórki kiszone,' indicating the pieces of green pickled gherkin.

'Eat,' said Irene. 'Then we can toast some more. It is better with vodka, but I know how much you like this,' and she poured another drop of the scarlet liqueur into Eva's glass.

'So, do you really think you'll stay here for the rest of your life?'

'Why not? I have all I need here and' – Irene waved her hand towards the window, which overlooked the forests and land around the camp – 'there is even a place out there where I will finally lay my head to rest in peace among my fellow countrymen.'

Eva knew what she meant. During the years the resettlement camp had been in operation, residents who died were buried in a Polish cemetery within the camp boundaries. Some inmates had never been able to recover from their time of terrible deprivation, some had suffered terminal illness and some had simply grown old and died waiting for their turn to leave. And maybe, Eva thought, somewhere among those burial plots, there are also bodies that didn't die a natural death, unless those still lie undiscovered among the dark trees all around the camp and across the countryside.

'But can you bear to stay here, in the country that has hurt you and your compatriots so much? I get so angry thinking of the Germans who were sentenced at the early trials, who are now being released. You can't say they've properly served their time. And there are those who were never put on trial, never accused, who've slipped back into their civilian lives unquestioned. Don't you ever feel you want to do something about it?'

'My dear, there was a time when I did. But now I have little time left, I ask for peace. I don't want to end my life disturbed by thoughts of hatred and vengeance.'

'I'm not sure I'm ready for that. I haven't made my peace yet.'

'But you will be going soon too.' Irene smiled at her and patted her hand. 'There is no more work for you here now, it is time for you to go home.'

Eva sighed and shook her head. 'I know. I'm leaving the day after tomorrow. But I don't know what I'll do next. Seeing shows in London, afternoon tea at Fortnum's, polite cocktail parties and dinners with my parents and their friends… it will all seem so utterly pointless after what I've seen and heard here.'

'You have a sweetheart waiting for you, I expect, and your family, they will be overjoyed to see you again.'

'My parents will be pleased, but there's no one else.'

'So what will you do? It will be strange, I am sure, just to go home. And you are a clever girl. You must continue working.'

'I think you're right. But I don't know what yet. Being here has shown me how little people need to make a good life. I don't need very much. And besides…' She hesitated, pictures of Hugh and the tortured prisoners in her head, alongside a laughing fair-haired child. 'I once made a promise, several years ago. I swore I would do more to make amends but I haven't been able to fulfil that promise yet.'

Irene's reddened eyes regarded Eva's frown and she said, 'You are a good person, my dear. You will do what you must do, God willing.'

'Thank you. And do you know, you are one of the people who has inspired me most. You kept up the spirits of all the women with you in Ravensbrück and showed them how to survive. You are wonderful.' Then Eva leant over and kissed the old woman on her dry, papery cheek. 'I'll miss you and this extraordinary place when I'm back in London.'

And Irene reached down beside her chair and said, 'Then you must take this to remind you of us. A single sip, or even just the smell of this, will bring you back to us here, to Wildflecken.' She laughed and handed Eva a small bottle of fiery crimson liqueur.

Eva read and translated the handwritten label, tied round the bottle's neck. 'Wild Place Slivovitz,' she said and laughed. 'Then I'll never be able to forget you or the camp. A part of me will always feel it belongs here.'

Chapter 71

Eva, 10 September 1951

Germany

This has to be the very last time, then never again, Eva promised herself. *Just once more and then I'll go back to England. I know I can't stay here in Germany for ever, I know I have to leave her. She's nearly four now, she may have started learning her numbers and letters at kindergarten and soon she will grow up. It can't hurt to see her while she is still so young, can it, while she still reminds me of the baby who nuzzled my breast before we were parted? She went without a murmur, wrapped in her soft shawl, while I wept.*

So Eva returned, not to Wildflecken, which the Americans had started adapting as one of the bases for their Cold War operations, but to Gemünden, the village near the resettlement camp. Wearing cat's-eye sunglasses, a chic silk scarf tied over her hair, Grace Kelly-style, she hoped she would not be recognised in the new cotton dress she had bought with bartered cigarettes. She drove from her guesthouse in the next village along the country roads she remembered so well from hours of carefree hiking on her days off, during that first summer.

And on the way she passed the ski resort that she had only ever visited once, that fateful day. She tried not to think about what lay hidden in the dark green forest on its slopes, but she couldn't help glancing through the window at the thicket of trees as she drove past. No one had ever come to the camp looking for Peter and she had never heard any enquiries about him. He was just one of thousands of disturbed young men, recently returned from the war, who couldn't settle back into the lives they'd led before the conflict.

When she reached Gemünden she wandered like a tourist around the picturesque beamed cottages and rested for a while at a table outside the inn, where she asked for *Himbeerwasser* and *Apfelküchen* in a distinctly American accent. She sipped the raspberry-flavoured drink through a straw, ate a couple of forkfuls of the cinnamon-spiced cake, looking across the village square. The distant tinkle of cowbells drifted from the meadows around the village and stray chickens clucked as they scratched and pecked in the dusty road.

Surely, in her new disguise, no one would realise she was the girl in a uniform who had filled in the forms and stamped the applications at the camp. And if Peter's mother was still alive and should come into the village to sell eggs or buy flour, she could never associate this fashionable figure with the girl who had hiked to the farm in sturdy leather boots and corduroy shorts.

After her refreshment Eva strolled along the little alleyways and lanes, snapping with her new camera: a quaint rustic doorway, a window box filled with red geraniums, a neat row of beanpoles. And finally, she saw her. A chubby blonde girl, plaits wound around her head in the traditional style, dressed in a dirndl skirt and a white blouse. With dimpled arms half covered by short puffed sleeves, she tossed a ball to another child in the cottage garden. She laughed, she ran, she jumped as she caught the ball bouncing on the path.

She's happy here and she's healthy, she has a good life, Eva thought. How I long to scoop her up and whisk her away with me. No one would see, only the other child would know a strange woman had taken her. I could run, run to my car. We'd be gone in minutes and then we'd be together for ever. But I can't. Her family love her and she loves them, that's clear. How could I destroy the life she knows, where she belongs? If only I could kiss her, if only

I could hold her once more, but I know I can't. All I can have are my memories of her and a picture I can keep for ever.

Snap went Eva's Box Brownie camera. Snap of the garden, snap of the ball, snaps of the golden hair, the cheeks, pink from running and jumping in play.

Now I shall have her for ever and always. And if I can't kiss the real child, feel her soft cheeks, her silky hair, smell her sweetness, I can kiss a photograph and know that I let her stay and be happy.

She took snap after snap until her film was all gone. The children were still playing and when the ball rolled into the dusty, unmade road, Liese chased it out through the open garden gate, stopping by Eva's feet. She looked up at the well-dressed woman who had been watching their game.

Eva tucked the box camera strap over her shoulder and bent down to pick up the ball. She held it out, thinking, *quickly, take her, then run.* But as the girl held out her hand, Eva caught sight of a movement out of the corner of her eye. The door to the cottage opened and a woman's voice called out, 'Lottie, hier bitte.'

Eva took one last aching look at her daughter, skipping over the grass to her adoptive mother. Then she forced herself to turn away and as her steps gathered pace, she bit her quivering lip to stem the tears coursing down her cheeks, knowing she would never see her child again.

Chapter 72

Eva, 20 February 1952

The Final Return

Eva took a taxi from the station and as she stepped out, woodsmoke and wet leaves scented the air. She was home with her cases and her memories. And after all those years away, how little had changed. Mama was older and sadder, Papa was older and frailer, but Kingsley Manor still frowned beneath its drapes of wisteria and climbing roses. And in the gardens carpets of snowdrops still scattered the lawns with their modest white heads of blossom and pheasants still cried in alarm as she walked the grounds. The woods and copses seemed strange at first, but then she realised it was because all the oaks, beech and chestnut were bare and she had become used to the ever-present dark green of the secretive forests around Wildflecken.

'You're very welcome to stay here with us, darling,' her mother said when she talked about finding work in London. 'We'd love to have you living back home. Anyway, you don't have anywhere else to live after the mansion flats were torn down.' Her mother was stabbing at her needlepoint, stretched on its stand, her little wire glasses perched on her nose, but when she spoke she peered over the lenses.

'I know you never approved of the flat, Mama, but I would have been quite happy to go back there if it hadn't been damaged in the raids. I need to do something constructive, you know. I have to have a life. I can't just stay here passing on your orders to Mrs Glazier in the kitchen and I certainly can't eat her lovely steamed puddings day in, day out. I'd end up being an enormous lump and it would drive me – and all of you, come to that – absolutely mad.'

'But why ever not, darling? There's plenty of room for all of us. You can have friends to visit, you know we wouldn't mind. We want you to be happy, darling. And you'd be such good company for Marion. It's been so hard for her being alone with dear little Patricia since Charles was killed. I know she'd appreciate having you here.'

Eva paced up and down the room, from the crackling fire to the breakfront bookcase and back again. *I can't bear to see the child. Pat, just three years younger than my little girl. And I can't explain. I can't tell Mama she really has a second granddaughter and that it breaks my heart every time I see or hear small children.*

The gilt ormolu clock tinkled. It was four o'clock and dusk was falling. Mrs Glazier would soon enter, pushing the tea trolley as if she was offering a selection of delicacies worthy of tea at The Ritz, when all post-war rationing could offer was toast with a scraping of margarine and a mean smear of bramble jam. Eva was already missing the good bread baked at Wildflecken and the hearty meals served by the NAAFI in the British army bases in Germany, where she had lingered before finally coming home.

'But, Mama, times have changed and I have changed. I know before the war it wasn't unusual for unmarried or widowed women to continue living with their parents, but it doesn't feel right now. I've been alone ever since Hugh died and I'm used to being on my own now.'

'Well, darling, all I can say is I lived with my family till I married and no one thought that was at all strange.' She tucked her needle into the canvas and removed her glasses, staring at her daughter almost as if she no longer recognised this strong independent woman who had left England a saddened widow.

'But that was then, Mama. Women are much more independent now. They don't want to go back to just being stay-at-home spinsters and housewives, you must realise that. And in this last war, women did jobs that would have been unthinkable for them in the years before.

Look at what they've been able to do. They've driven ambulances, they've worked on farms as land girls – why, they've even become bargemen, delivering coal and timber, and lumberjacks as well.'

'Yes, darling, I've heard all about that. Quite unsuitable occupations. And really, the clothes they wore. We saw some of those lumber girls in the village, a group of them giggling in their most unladylike breeches. They made quite an exhibition of themselves. Everyone noticed them and thought it was quite shocking.'

'Oh, Mama, you shouldn't be shocked. They were dressed to do an important job. Everyone has had to adapt, you know. And I can't go back to living here quietly for the rest of my life. Maybe eventually I will, but for now I need challenges and I need purpose.'

'So what does that mean, dear?'

'I'm joining the Civil Service.' Eva saw her mother's thin pencilled eyebrows suddenly arch. 'No, don't worry. It's nothing to make you ashamed of me.' *You'll never know what would make you feel ashamed. I've made sure of that.* 'I'll be working in an office in London. It will be safe, steady work, with a good salary, and I won't have a problem finding a flat somewhere.'

'But what will you be doing in the... Civil Service?' She emphasised the last two words as if they had an unpleasant taste.

'Oh, just typing and filing, I expect. That's pretty much all I've been doing for the last few years, so I'm quite used to it. But I'll come home at weekends, I promise.' She knelt down in front of her mother and held her hands. 'If I'm living in London, I'll be able to pop into Peter Jones for you, as often as you want. You'd like that, wouldn't you?'

'Darling, that would be marvellous. Then I wouldn't have to send off for my silks and wools. I can't go into town as much as I'd like now that your father isn't as well as he used to be.' She pulled a delicate handkerchief from her sleeve and dabbed her eyes.

'Mama, I'll do whatever I can for you. After all, what are daughters for?'

Chapter 73

Kingsley
14 December 1967

My dearest darling,

I should be sad, but somehow, strangely, I'm not at all. I cried a little when Mama died and I managed to look sombre enough during the funeral, but now that it is all over, I am feeling quite content. Kingsley is now mine, all mine, and I can enjoy it properly.

Mama and I tolerated each other well enough, but she never let me forget that in her eyes, I was just a sad widow, a woman who had to work for her living. And her constant references to you, my darling, such as 'if only Hugh had lived' and 'it would have been wonderful to have had more grandchildren', were all said with a dab of the eye and were so irritating.

As far as she was aware, she only had one grandchild, Charles's daughter, Pat, and she didn't make an enormous effort with her, so I don't see how she would have enjoyed having more. I know she assumed I would remarry one day, but how could I ever replace you, when you were the only man I could ever really love?

And now Kingsley is mine. Now no one can tell me how to enjoy its delights. I had always imagined that we would live here together, but in a few years I shall be able to retire with a full pension, plus whatever the state deems to give me, and I shall indulge myself. I don't want to have an extravagant retirement; I shan't make a fool of myself as an elderly woman on world cruises, dancing with the entertainment staff paid to pay compliments to the lonely. I shan't force my views on good solid volunteers in charities, the church or parish council, like many other retirees, I shall just continue to sing in the church choir, contribute preserves for the WI monthly market and join the village garden club. My indulgence will be Kingsley and its gardens. There will be more snowdrops, more hellebores, delphiniums and phlox; I shall become a horticultural addict.

But I have also not forgotten my promise. He is still alive, I know that. He received an honour at the beginning of the year, a small one, but an honour he does not deserve nevertheless. I shall watch and wait and one day I will have a chance to fulfil my promise, I'm sure.

So all my love, my darling, for now.

Your ever-loving Evie,
    Xxx
    Ps I love you.

Part Ten

Staring you in the face! (4,2,3)

Chapter 74

Mrs T-C, 30 November 2016

Bathtime

She tries not to think about being naked in front of the care home nurses. Her once-athletic body is wizened, reduced to slack skin and bone, mottled with purple blotches and the brown stamps of age. No silvery stretchmarks are visible on her abdomen though; those faded long ago.

She slips off her lambswool cardigan and white silk blouse, then tries to undo the buttons on the side of her tweed skirt. No, that is too difficult with her stiff arthritic fingers. She will need help with that too now.

'Mary,' she calls, 'I'm ready for you.' She leans on her walking frame and eases herself onto the high padded seat in the bathroom. Thank goodness she has one of the few rooms at Forest Lawns with an adapted bath. She never could bear showers, damping one's hair and spoiling it in between one's weekly shampoo and sets.

Mary kneels on the floor to remove shoes and nylon popsocks. Evelyn would prefer to wear tights or even stockings, but they simply aren't practical any more. She once tried wearing stockings with elasticated tops, 'hold-ups' the department store assistant called them, but they failed to grip her shrunken thighs and wrinkled their way down to her knees when she stood up.

'We'll have to ask the toenail lady to call in and see you again,' Mary says. 'She'll be in on Tuesday.'

Evelyn's toes are claws with thick ridged nails, but her hands, though veined and bruised, still have oval nails, buffed to a shine the way Mama taught her so many years ago, when nail varnish was considered vulgar. It's one of the few aspects of her body that still pleases her, that and her silver hair with its neat curls, and her Cupid's bow lips, always emphasised with Estée Lauder's Rebellious Rose lipstick.

'Shall we have lavender or peony bubbles today?' asks Mary, holding two bottles of foaming gel over the bath.

'Oh, I think I'd like to try that new lily-of-the-valley for a change instead. It reminds me of my youth, you know, when I wore Muguet. Such a lovely scent. Muguet des Bois… Hugh, my husband, loved it.'

'We'll use that one then. You'll be smelling like a spring garden in no time, won't you?' And Mary holds out her hand to help Evelyn stand up as she slips the remaining garments from her frail body, then guides her into a sitting position on the moulded bath seat, with a towel round her shoulders to keep her warm while the bath fills. Evelyn would prefer to have her bath straight after breakfast or just before bed, but bathtimes at the home have to be scheduled around staff availability, not residents' preferences, so her bath is run just before lunch. *But then I shall be clean, sweet-smelling and well-fed for my visitors this afternoon. I'll take a nap after lunch and wake refreshed to face my inquisitors. I'm quite looking forward to it now. They'll interrogate me, but it won't be like the awful interviews I witnessed years ago, where the prisoners were cowed and broken; I'll be in control, not them.*

As the water tumbles down, frothing into scented bubbles, Mary repeatedly checks that it is neither too hot nor too cold. 'I used to love to swim in cold water,' Evelyn says.

'You never!'

'Oh yes. They thought it was good for us. They said if the Germans caught us, they might push us into freezing cold showers, so we all got used to it, just in case. But this is just like Goldilocks,' says Evelyn.

'Goldy what?' Mary asks above the sound of the bathwater running.

'Goldilocks and the three bears. You know, dear, one bowl of porridge was too hot, then one was too cold and one was just right, like the temperature of the bathwater.'

'You always make me laugh, you do,' Mary shakes her head and hands Evelyn a clean flannel. 'There now, it's full enough. I'll do your back and you do your bits.' She puffs out her cheeks. 'Tell you what though, this room's too hot for me. It might be just right for you, but I'm sweating like a pig.'

'I'm sorry, dear. That's the trouble with having to wait for the bath to fill up. But I'm lovely and warm now, so why don't you open the bathroom door for a little bit? Let a bit of fresh air in?'

Mary opens the door and fans herself with a spare dry flannel. 'Phew, that's better! Now let's get you all cleaned up.' The two of them rub away in silence. Mary reaches down into the water to scrub Evelyn's feet and soap her legs.

'You'd never think I was quite a good cricketer in my day to look at me now, would you?'

Mary laughs. 'Go on with you, Mrs T-C. You'll be telling me you played football as well next.'

'I played cricket with my brother Charles. He was a terrifically fast bowler.'

'We did rounders at school,' Mary says.

'Gosh, I haven't played rounders since… oh, since the war. We didn't have any cricket kit with us at the time, so we made up games of rounders. We had to make do with an old tennis ball and a broom handle. Such fun it was.'

'Where was this then?'

'In Camberley, during our training. We were all young girls, some straight from school – I think I was the eldest. I was widowed by then, so I was a bit of a mother figure to the younger ones, I suppose.' Evelyn laughs as she wrings out her flannel. 'Such high spirits all the girls had.'

'I bet you were a one, eh? Probably the worst of the lot.'

'I don't know what you mean, Mary. I was perfectly well behaved. I had to set an example to the other young girls. So young, no more than teenagers.'

'Get away with you! I bet there were some lovely young men around in those days, all smart in their uniforms. We've all heard the stories.'

'Well, we did meet up with some rather nice pilots later on. Especially the Polish chaps, they were quite charming and awfully handsome. They told us such extraordinary stories about how they'd escaped from Poland to reach this country. Some of them had walked all the way to France. Imagine that. Astonishing, isn't it?'

'Blimey, Mrs T-C! Walking halfway across Europe? I get puffed just walking round Guildford on my day off.'

'They were very determined men. And many of them skied across the Alps on their journey.' Evelyn is quiet for a second. 'I did a bit of skiing in Germany after the war – Skilaufen, we called it.'

'I bet that was something. All those snowy mountains and lovely scenery, eh?'

'It was most interesting,' says Evelyn. And after a moment's pause she adds, 'It's a time I can never forget.'

Chapter 75

Mrs T-C, 30 November 2016

The Truth

'I'm having visitors this afternoon, Mary. I'd like to see them in the library on my own, so could you see that we are not disturbed?'

Evelyn shuffles along the dark patterned carpet in the corridor and stops by the gilt-framed mirror on the wall. She pats her curled hair and studies her grinning reflection so she can check no spinach from her lunch has caught in her teeth and that her lipstick hasn't smudged. It hardly matters, does it, applying cosmetics, having one's hair set? She knows she has not made a great impression on the male sex for many years, yet she still wants to look well groomed. She shuffles a little further, then sits waiting in the muffled book-lined room for her guests, waiting for the sound of voices, hearing only the steady ticking of the mantel clock echoing her heartbeat.

'Here we are, Mrs T-C,' announces Mary in a loud voice, ushering in Pat and Inspector Williams. 'Now, shall I fetch all of yous some tea and cakes?'

Her visitors both look as if they'd rather rush away unfed and unwatered, but Evelyn says, 'That would be lovely, Mary. And would you have any mince pies for us today, perhaps?'

'We won't be staying long, Aunt. This isn't a social call, you know.' Pat is shrugging off her grubby raincoat.

'No, dear. But I do like to be hospitable to my guests.' Evelyn smiles at both of them. 'Please take a seat, both of you.' Pat shakes her head in annoyance.

'I understand you wanted to see me, Mrs T-C,' says the Inspector. 'You've remembered something, I believe?'

'Yes, that's right,' Evelyn says, diving into her handbag. 'Now, where have I put it?' She glances up to see Pat rolling her eyes. Perhaps it would be fun to tease them a little. Not for long, just for a few minutes. It would be a shame not to use this opportunity, as it will probably be the last time she can play the game.

'I'm sure I had it right here a minute ago.' She removes the contents of her bag, very slowly, one by one. A pen, two newly sharpened pencils, a powder compact, a lipstick, a clean handkerchief, a small pack of tissues and a purse. Then she delves deeper and brings out a slim black diary and a pencil sharpener. She looks over at Pat and dangles the handkerchief in front of her: 'You'd better have it, dear. I know you never bring a clean hankie with you.'

Pat snorts, but takes the piece of lacy white fabric and sits wringing it tightly in her fingers. 'I hope you remember where you said you'd written this vital bit of information. You'd better not be messing around with us today and wasting our time. We're all far too busy for that.'

Inspector Williams leans forward, his arms on his knees. In a soft voice, he says, 'Do you want to tell me what you think you've remembered?'

Evelyn flicks through the pages of her diary, turning them one at a time. 'Oh yes, here we are,' she says. 'Stephen Robinson.'

'That's right. I was asking you before about Colonel Robinson. Have you remembered meeting him again?'

'I think so.'

'And can you tell me when you think that was?'

'I'm not sure exactly when. Is that important, Inspector?'

'It might be. But why don't you just tell me what you've remembered anyway?' He smiles. He is such a nice-looking young man. Evelyn finds him very pleasant and understanding, quite different to Pat. She wouldn't mind spending more time with him, but the game must come to an end at some point.

Evelyn looks down at the page in her diary. It's almost completely blank; there are no words written there, just the letters SR. But then she really didn't need to write anything down, she remembers it all too well. Then she looks up and smiles. 'Yes, I will tell you what I've remembered. I think you said that he had disappeared a long time ago and nobody knows what has happened to him.'

'That's right, I did say that, when we last met. He never turned up again. We believe he left his flat one day in early 1986 and disappeared. No one's heard anything and nothing has been seen of him, ever since.'

'Well, I know what happened to him.' Evelyn drops her diary back into her handbag and then adds the other items, one at a time, deliberately placing everything in the right compartment and fumbling to fit her pencils into a narrow pocket. She hears Pat heaving theatrical sighs as she does this, but doesn't react to her.

'Really? And are you going to tell me what you know?'

Evelyn completes her repacking, clicks the handbag clasp shut, then smiles, as if she is going to deliver a wonderful surprise. 'Because you've been so kind and patient, I am going to tell you. You see, I remember what happened quite clearly. I couldn't possibly forget.' She pauses for a moment, then says, 'I killed him.'

Both the detective and Pat are wide-eyed, then Pat speaks: 'Really, Aunt! Now you're being ridiculous.' She turns to her companion. 'She's playing games again. I knew this would be a total waste of our time.'

But Inspector Williams holds up a hand warning her to be quiet, then says, 'Now why do you say that? Why do you think that you killed him, Mrs T-C?'

'Because I remember doing it. I remember it very well.'

'Are you sure? Now think very carefully before you answer.'

'Oh, I'm quite sure, Inspector. I remember it as if it was yesterday.'

'Do you mean there was an accident, with one of the guns?'

'Oh no, not at all! It was quite deliberate. I'm a very good shot.'

'So tell me how it happened, then.' He has lost his smile and assumed a serious face. Pat is frowning and tutting under her breath.

'He deserved it. He wasn't an honourable man, whatever anyone else might think. He was responsible for the deaths of many innocent men, including my darling husband, so I shot him.'

Pat gasps and holds her hand to her mouth, then exclaims, 'This is getting out of hand! She's an old lady, in her nineties. She doesn't know what she's talking about.'

But Inspector Williams cautions her again with a slight wave of his hand and says, 'And can you remember when you did this?'

'Oh, I'm not sure exactly when. It was years and years ago.'

'And where did this murder take place?'

'At Kingsley.' She hears Pat gasp again. 'I left his body in the woods at Kingsley, but I doubt you'll find anything there now. It was all a terribly long time ago.'

Then the Inspector sits back. He pulls out a file from his briefcase and presents Evelyn with the pictures of the sweater and trousers he had shown her before. 'Does the murder of Colonel Robinson have anything to do with the bloodstains we found on these items of clothing, madam? They were found in the suitcase stored at your home.' He points to the ringed stains in the pictures: 'Could this be Stephen Robinson's blood?'

Evelyn laughs. 'Oh goodness me no! That's not his blood. That's someone else's entirely, from many, many years ago. Oh no, I was much more careful this time round.'

'This time?'

'The second time. The time I had to deal with the nasty Colonel.' Pat is muttering behind her. She can hear her quite clearly.

'And the time before?'

'Oh, that wasn't planned. It just happened.'

Inspector Williams looks stern. 'I see. So, you appear to be telling me that you have killed more than once? Am I to understand that you are saying that you have committed two murders?'

'Oh yes, just the two. I was trained to kill, you see. We all were.'

Pat stands up. 'That does it, I'm not having any more of this. She's finally lost her mind. Can't you see it's all nonsense?'

'It's the truth, dear. The truth, the whole truth and nothing but the truth.' Evelyn laughs after this statement, recalling all the many courtroom dramas she has seen in films and on television during her long lifetime.

And then Mary pushes open the door to the morning room, backing in with a loaded tray that rattles as she waddles across the carpet, saying, 'The mince pies had all gone, but I've found yous some nice shortbread.'

'How lovely, Mary,' Evelyn says. 'I'm quite peckish after all this talking.'

Pat and the Inspector stand up and move to a corner of the room, speaking in hushed voices. Evelyn can't catch every word above the clatter of the cups being set down, but she hears Pat say, 'But the property is going on the market early next year. I can't have this going on.' And he replies, 'Don't worry just yet. Searching those woods needs a lot of manpower. I'll have to have a good reason to do that.'

And Evelyn takes a piece of shortbread and thinks that just this once she will try dunking it in her cup. Just this once. To celebrate.

Part Eleven

Keep your mouth shut or they'll give you away (4,4,4)

Chapter 76

5 December 2016
Am I mad?

My dearest darling,

I think you too would find this all quite amusing. I've so enjoyed playing my little games with Pat and that nice policeman and now I have the chance to have one more turn. My time in this wonderfully kind care home would have been quite dull if I hadn't had this interesting diversion. Do you remember how when you came home on leave we loved to play charades? This has been like one long game of charades, one long Christmas party.

And now I feel fairly sure that they are all beginning to suspect that I really am demented, so if I throw the dice just once more, I think I will be able to convince them that my mind is in pieces and then they will never believe anything else I say.

But I will never tell them everything. I will never tell them I still write my letters to you in my head and I will never tell them about Liese, my darling little Liese. She is our little secret.

Goodnight, my darling, I will see you very soon.

With all my love,
    Your Evie, xxx
    Ps I love you

Chapter 77

Mrs T-C, 10 December 2016

Fire, Fire

Evelyn gazes at the tiny black and white photograph of the little girl. The surface is cracked and creased from handling, from the thousands of times she has held it and kissed it. The gloss of the print has worn away with a thousand or more kisses, but still she looks upon that smiling face, caught in a moment of happiness many years ago.

'Goodbye, my darling,' she whispers. 'It is time. I have to let you go now. I'm sorry, but I'll never forget you. I will always be able to see your face when I close my eyes.' She traces the child's features with the tip of her finger: the plaited blonde hair, the dimpled cheeks, the sweet mouth. 'You are part of me, but I must let you go. I can't bear the thought of Pat finding you once I've gone. She'd recognise you, match you to the photo in the biscuit tin, then she'd ask questions, think disturbing thoughts, reach worrying conclusions. No, it is better this way.'

And then she holds the picture over her metal waste bin and lights a match. She lets the flame lick the corner of the little snapshot and watches it catch and burn. Then, as it curls, she lets it fall to join crumpled envelopes, used tissues and cotton wool, which all burst into flames. And in among the debris lie the torn pieces of the insurance valuations Pat had found at Kingsley, with their incriminating notes in his handwriting. As the fire flickers and smoke rises, Evelyn stands back a bit, then lowers herself into her armchair. They'll be here soon: the smoke alarm will rouse them. She laughs to herself. It reminds her of the madness of Mrs Rochester in the attic in *Jane Eyre*.

Bleeping escalates to ringing and in seconds all the home's alarms are shrieking in terror. Within minutes she hears steps thundering along the corridor, confused shouts, frantic knocking on doors nearby, then finally Mary bursts into her room, turning on the light: 'For the love of God, Mrs T-C, the fire alarm is going off! We must get you out of here right away.' She takes Evelyn's elbow and eases her out of the armchair, guiding her towards the walking frame.

'It's all right, dear. It's not much of a fire, there's no real danger.'

'Of course there's a fire. The alarm is screaming blue murder. And there's smoke in here. Come on, I must get you out to safety.'

'No, dear, it's not a real fire. I was just burning a bit of rubbish.'

Mary looks in the metal waste bin. The flames have died down, but the ashes are still smouldering. 'Oh, my goodness, you can't go doing that in there! You'll have us all burned to death in our beds.' She grabs the bin and dashes into the bathroom, where Evelyn hears her running the tap, water gushing and splashing.

'There's no need to do that, dear. It's out now.'

Mary pops her head round the door. 'I'm making doubly sure. You could have burned the place down. Whatever next, Mrs T-C?' She opens the bedroom window and fans the curtains till she is satisfied that the smoke has gone, then leaves the room. Evelyn can hear her calling down the passageway: 'It's all right, everybody. Mrs T-C has been having a little bonfire up here, but there's no damage. Everyone back to bed now.'

She returns and helps Evelyn into bed, then shuts the window. 'That wasn't very clever now, was it? We'll have to have a little talk about this in the morning.' She looks around the room and sees the box of matches left in clear view on the dressing table, next to Mama's silver-capped cut-glass cologne bottle. Putting the box in the pocket of her tunic, she says, 'I'll take these for now, if you don't mind. We don't want you playing with matches any more tonight now, do we?'

Evelyn closes her eyes as Mary turns out the light and shuts the door. She can hear rapid steps outside, more doors banging, staff uttering soothing assurances and the general sounds of everyone settling down again for the night. She knows what will happen in the morning. There will be a management meeting. The doctor will be called, the memory assessment team will gather, they will question Evelyn and they will give their verdict.

If her prediction is correct, they will decide that both her behaviour and her memory are unreliable and that this means she is showing distinct signs of dementia. Then they will consult Pat, who will confirm their diagnosis with her account of recent meetings and a report on Evelyn's 'ridiculous behaviour'. Then Pat will contact Inspector Williams, who will… what? Ask her more questions? Her, an unreliable witness? Arrest her? That would be amusing. She could tease him some more; pretend she'd forgotten she had already confessed to her crimes. She could tell him she is waiting for a reply to her letter from her husband and isn't the post shocking these days, or she could say she is leaving this hotel and refuses to pay the bill because the service is not what it used to be. Oh, please fetch the handcuffs, Constable! I've been such a naughty girl today. And she chuckles to herself as she begins to fall asleep.

Chapter 78

14 December 2016

My dearest darling,

I've definitely done it now. The fire was a masterstroke, as well as solving a little worry of mine. They haven't told me officially of course, I've just overheard them talking, but I know that a memory assessment is going to take place very shortly. Pat has only been in once since the fire and she spent less than five minutes with me. She practically threw down the pencils and talcum I'd asked for, then spent the rest of her time in the manager's office. I feel a little guilty as I know she must be very busy with her own preparations for Christmas, but really, I can't help the timing of this. If that nice detective hadn't been so persistent, I could have waited until after Christmas. It would have been much more convenient for everyone, I'm sure. But there we are. Needs must.

We'll be together again soon, my darling.

All my love for ever,
    Your Evie xxx
    Ps I love you

Chapter 79

Mrs T-C, 19 December 2016

Ask Me Another

There are two of them and Pat. They all stare at her, daring her to remember. It's rather amusing, thinks Evelyn. So easy to fool them.

They sit in a barren meeting room at the care home under stark white lights, reminiscent of the interrogation centre, Evelyn remembers. She and Pat are on one side of the table, the two professionals on the other, files and notepads spread before them. It's like an important career-changing job interview or an audition for the lead role in a major film and it's one she must pass. She needs to convince them beyond all possible doubt that her mind is impaired, that her memory is unreliable.

The first few questions are far too easy. They don't ask about the fire, they say, what is the date today? How old are you? What did you have for breakfast? Who is the prime minister? But after that it becomes a lot more entertaining.

'I'm going to show you a series of cards now,' says the memory assessor, an overweight woman with stringy grey hair, who looks as if she might be losing her own memory soon. She sets out a row on the table in front of Evelyn, as if she is dealing a round of poker. 'I'd like you to look at each one. Take your time, then I'm going to ask you to read them aloud.'

Evelyn looks at the four cards. Each one bears a word in large print – saucer, dominoes, postcard and school. She reads them out and decides to adopt a suitably frail, stumbling voice, aiming to convey anxiety and uncertainty, the qualities she feels are most appropriate for the role she is hoping they will award her.

This is going to be far too easy. Evelyn has always had a good memory and when she trained years ago, they all undertook memory-boosting exercises to help them retain vital information. Even until recently, she has ensured that her memory has been stretched with frequent exercises. When she shuffles around the Forest Lawns public spaces, she notes how many leaflets are on the hall table, whether there are any new posters pinned on the noticeboard, which china shepherds and shepherdesses are slightly out of place on the mantelpiece and how many framed pictures are left askew on the walls after the cleaners have finished dusting. She creeps along the corridors to the residents' quarters, memorising names and room numbers. She is alert, her mind is retentive and she almost wishes she was being given a harder test of her skills, to demonstrate her ability, but nevertheless, she acts her part and stares at the words.

The assessor smiles at Evelyn. She taps the first card and says, 'Can you tell me what category you would put this word in?'

Evelyn smiles back and thinks, what a stupid question. The woman has pointed at the word saucer. If Evelyn weren't wishing to fool her, she would say it was a common noun, of course. That would stump her. She probably doesn't know the difference between common and proper nouns. She probably wants her to say crockery or china, but instead, Evelyn says, 'Are we going to have tea soon?'

The woman doesn't smile. She points again: 'And this one?' The word dominoes is indicated. Evelyn shakes her head. Then the woman moves on to the other words and with each one, Evelyn gives a confusing answer. Then the assessor says, 'I'll give you a clue. Which one of these is a game?'

Evelyn wants to laugh, but takes a breath to help her keep a straight face. *But this is the game. This is a wonderful game. I've been playing it for weeks and it seems that I might be winning.* 'Oh, I don't know,' she says. And so it continues with all four words. Evelyn guesses that the word postcard is a fence and the word school is where to see the doctor, and pretends she has no idea what to do with the saucer.

Then the woman says she is going to ask Evelyn to remember these words in a few minutes and turns the cards face down on the table. Evelyn strains to prevent her laughter. She often plays patience and pairs in her room with an entire pack of playing cards, so four is hardly challenging.

She is then asked to spell world backwards. Evelyn's spelling has always been excellent and is sharpened with her daily crosswords, but she manages to stumble and mutter, 'D-O-L?'

'And could you count backwards from twenty for me, please?'

Again, Evelyn bites her lip and maintains her composure, then jumps from twenty to twelve to ten and five. This is going rather well. They must be convinced by now that her mental powers are diminished.

So when the woman asks her to recall the words that were printed on the cards, she enjoys staring blankly and saying, 'What cards?' She can hear Pat sighing in the background, which is rather irritating. *I'd like to see what her memory is like at ninety-five. Pathetic, I bet, with the amount of alcohol she drinks all the time at home. I know she does, I can see it in her mottled complexion; nothing like as good as mine at her age.*

And she takes note of the look that is shared between all three members of her audience and knows that she has given an award-winning performance. She must have got the part by now: the Demented Duchess, the Mad Marchioness. The assessor is scribbling on her forms and the doctor is nodding at Pat, who is shaking her head with a weary expression. Evelyn studies their faces. *They should be applauding and asking me to take a bow. It isn't easy pretending to be something you aren't.*

And then she decides to give them all something to liven up their morning. She stands up, levering herself into a standing position by pushing her hands down on the table, then sweeps away the cards, scattering them all over the dark patterned carpet. 'I can't stay here all day, I'm going home now,' she says. 'I've got a bus to catch.'

She turns, supporting herself with the back of the chair, and is about to sweep the water jug off the table as well when Pat catches her arm, rather too firmly, Evelyn thinks. 'We're not finished here yet,' she says in a grim voice. 'Sit down again.'

'But you're making me late for the coffee morning. I promised I'd be there to organise the beetle drive, I have to go now.'

'No, Aunt, we're staying here.' Pat manoeuvres her back into her seat. 'The doctor hasn't finished talking to you.'

Evelyn decides her newly acquired role merits one last flourish. 'You're all dismissed,' she says with an imperious wave of her hand, a gesture she had seen from Mama on many occasions when she was dissatisfied with the work of a cleaner or gardener. 'I'm dismissing the lot of you. You're wasting my time. I'm a very busy woman, you know.'

Pat glances apologetically at the two professionals, who are trying to complete their notes. 'Maybe I'll just pop outside and see if someone can bring in a tray of coffee and biscuits. That usually keeps her quiet for a bit.'

'I want fig rolls!' shouts Evelyn. 'You know how I like fig rolls. Don't let them fob you off with Garibaldi.'

Chapter 80

23 December 2016

My darling one,

You won't have to wait very much longer, my darling. They are watching me closely now, but I will get away soon, don't you worry. Everyone here talks of nothing but Christmas, so they have almost forgotten me for the moment, but I know it won't last. I have planned how I will be able to come to you and it won't be long now, but I may not have many opportunities, so I must come while I still can.

They asked me lots of questions the other day and it was such fun, I tell you. I had no idea it would be quite so easy, not at all challenging. They asked me to look at words on cards, 'flashcards' we used to call them, for a few minutes, then see if I could remember any of them about five minutes later. It was just like the parlour games we used to play at Kingsley all those years ago. You do remember how good you were at charades and Gin Rummy, don't you, darling? And of course I remembered every single one of the words, but I had to pretend I couldn't and then I told them I wanted to go home. How I stopped myself from laughing, I honestly don't know.

I also said Harold Wilson was the Prime Minister, that I hadn't had any breakfast (it was mid-morning by then and I'd actually had a very nice poached egg on toast in my room) and then I pretended not to recognise Pat, and asked if she could go and fetch Mrs Glazier, so I could plan the menus for the week with her. I suppose that could have been a little upsetting for her, but do you know, I didn't mind doing it one little bit as she was so unhelpful during my last visit to dear Kingsley. I could see her looking cross and confused, but that didn't stop me.

There were lots more questions too, all of which I could have answered, but it was getting a bit tedious by then, so I decided I wouldn't answer another thing, made a bit of a fuss and insisted I had to leave. Pat went off to fetch coffee and I told her to get fig rolls, then I made another scene when she came back with Garibaldi. I've been getting a bit tired of the Christmas shortbread and mince pies they keep giving us here, so I don't think it's unreasonable to ask for something different for a change.

Oh dear, darling, look at me rabbiting on about biscuits! We won't do that when we meet up, I promise. But you will be amused to know that I finished the meeting with a little song. That funny George Formby one you always liked about bumping off your wife! 'She's Never Been Seen Since Then', I think it's called. I couldn't remember all the words, but I thought it was an appropriate tune in the circumstances. Such fun!

So goodbye for now, darling, we'll be together again very soon.

All my love,
    your Evie xxx
    Ps I love you

Chapter 81

Mrs T-C, 24 December 2016

Give Me Moonlight

Evelyn wakes at midnight, her alarm clock chirping in her ear. She has allowed herself to sleep for three hours, to be fresh and alert for what must happen next.

All is quiet after the rush of the day. Concerned relatives have visited before departing for their own Christmas festivities and ever-patient carers have soothed those left behind. The minds of the care home staff are full of thoughts of carols and crackers for now, but after New Year, they will remind each other that she is unreliable. When the holiday season is over, they will review security, move her to the dementia wing, where doors are always locked and inmates closely supervised, and she may never be free again.

Before she woke, she had been dreaming and in her sleep a voice had been calling to her: 'Evie, Evie, come to me. I need you.'

She is sure it was Hugh she heard calling; his voice was clear and urgent. It was not the way she remembered him speaking to her all those years ago, but it was most definitely his voice. He had sounded distressed, as if he really needed her help.

She presses the button to elevate her bed so she can sit up, then switches on the bedside light. The care home is silent. No other residents are calling or bleeping for assistance, no soft footsteps are padding the corridors tonight and no alarms are going to start ringing till first light.

Outside, in the extensive gardens, she hears the screech of a vixen. Could that have been the sound she'd heard as she was dreaming and translated into Hugh's voice in her sleep? How can she even be sure she would still recognise his voice, echoing over the years, more than sixty years since he had been killed?

She swings her stiff legs out of bed and hauls herself to standing with her walking frame. Step by slow step, she inches towards the window. 'It's time, Hugh, darling. I'm coming to you now,' she whispers.

The curtains are slightly open and a bright sliver of light gleams through the gap. She pulls them further apart and sees that the full moon is shining in all its silver brightness over the gardens, so although it is the middle of the night, there is very little black in the picture before her, but various tones of charcoal grey and dark green, with every shrub, border, path and curve of lawn clearly defined, as if it was a dimly lit overcast day and not the witching hours of night. And there must have been a frost too, as every leaf is shimmering with silvery ice under the gaze of this bright light.

It is Christmas Eve. Evelyn remembers that first Christmas at the end of 1945 in Wildflecken; the excitement of not just the children but also the adults, tasting foods long forgotten as well as the sweetness of liberation. And tonight, children who have not experienced privation will still be waiting with excited impatience; they await gifts of toys and sweets, smuggled to their beds while they sleep. And perhaps, although it is not an Anglo-Saxon custom, they have been watching at their windows for the first star of Christmas, the way they did at Wildflecken all those years ago. Evelyn searches the sky. There must be stars up there, but she can't see them from her window. 'Hugh, let's go out and look at the stars together,' she murmurs.

Evelyn finds her thick dressing gown and slippers and leaves her room. No one challenges her as she creeps along the dimly lit passageway. No one sees her pass through the dining room, festooned with paper chains and Chinese lanterns, nor through the hall with its tall Christmas tree decked with the glass ornaments of childhood and sparkling with coloured lights. She can hear the murmur of the night staff drinking tea and chatting in the kitchen at the far end of the corridor, but none of them sees her punching the numbers into the keypad at the entrance to Forest Lawns. One, two, three, four… How lazy of the management to never change the code. She had double-checked again earlier that day and yes, it was still the same as when she had first arrived.

Her fingers are rewarded with a small buzz; the door swings open and then she is outside, feeling the fresh chill of the night air sting her cheeks and freeze her lungs. The garden is clearly lit by the moon shining on the path like a beacon, calling her to walk along its length. She shuffles along the paving stones to an open area of lawn, where she finds a bench and sits down.

There are no overhanging branches, no intrusive lights, so now she can see the full expanse of the night sky, the moon surrounded by a dusting of diamond stars, all twinkling, all claimed by children all over the world, as their very own Christmas star this holy night.

'Good night, Lieselotte,' she whispers. 'Happy Christmas, liebchen. I hope you have been happy in your life so far. Perhaps you have had children of your own and now are blessed with grandchildren. I'd like to think you have known the joy of young lives and I wish you a happy life when I've gone.' She smiles and hugs herself. 'Hugh, I'm coming now. Hold out your hands for me, darling.'

She fumbles in the pocket of her dressing gown for the button, the very special button that was issued to all of the young men and women during their days of training. It has been waiting in her dressing table drawer for just the right moment ever since. If the poison has lost its potency after so many years, then she is sure this wintry night will claim her. She begins humming under her breath and gradually adds words to the tune, 'Stille Nacht', her frail voice drifting away on a wisp of frosted breath in the chilly air.

And then, smiling, she takes the tablet, closes her eyes and welcomes the chill of the night to hold her still at last in a final embrace, beneath the icy moon and stars.

Solutions to crossword clues

1 Quiet! Tall gin mixer required for full menu (3,6)
  All things

2 Clever and good-looking (6,3,9) Bright and beautiful

3 Animals have strange cuter ears (9) Creatures

4 Grand tea cooked in mall. Different size portions
  (5,3,5) Great and small

5 Eric's partner in Louis's world is both clever and
  brilliant (4,3,9) Wise and wonderful

6 And on the Sixth Day… (3,4,4,3) God made them all

7 Any small river found in garden (4,6,6) Each little
  flower

8 What a small bird needs (4,5) Tiny wings

9 At the end of the day… (3,6) The sunset

10 Staring you in the face! (4,2,3) Eyes to see

11 Keep your mouth shut or they'll give you away
   (4,4,4) Lips that tell

A Letter from Suzanne

I want to say a huge thank you for choosing to read *My Name is Eva*. If you did enjoy it, and want to keep up to date with all my latest releases, just sign up at the following link. Your email address will never be shared and you can unsubscribe at any time.

www.bookouture.com/suzanne-goldring

My journey into writing this novel began when two elderly ladies giggled like schoolgirls and gave me tantalising glimpses of their wartime lives. I knew then that there was an important story waiting to be told. However, discovering exactly what they had done for MI5 and MI6 proved more difficult than I could have imagined, as they and the other women I interviewed clammed up when pressed for information. They had all been trained to keep their secrets well hidden and so the idea began to grow.

Evie's letters to her husband Hugh developed from a cache of flimsy wartime correspondence I transcribed after it was discovered hidden in a shoebox at the back of a wardrobe. Written by my great-aunt Nora to her young husband Fred, known as 'Tiny', they captured the determination and optimism of the British at war and gave me Evie's voice. Then, when I discovered that my aunt had worked for the United Nations Relief and Rehabilitation Administration (UNRRA) in post-war Germany after Tiny was killed retraining with the RAF, I knew I finally had my story.

Volunteering for a local residential home where the elderly are cared for with the greatest patience and respect helped me to understand how Evelyn would adapt to her new environment. And talking to the residents, writing their life stories and running their book club showed me that an agile mind can often still inhabit a frail body and how important it is for the elderly to retain freedom of choice and maintain their dignity.

To learn more about the training of SOE agents, I visited the Secret Army Exhibition at Beaulieu in the New Forest in Hampshire, which revealed the mysteries of coding, silent killing and secret inks, which were further explained by the very modest Shelagh.

In writing *My Name is Eva*, I have been supported and encouraged by members of the Elstead Writers Group, Melanie Whipman, the Ark Writers and my Vesta friends – Carol, Denise and Gail. I am also indebted to Sandie Baker and Rose Carter, who introduced me to a local care home, where I've met many wonderful residents and members of staff and where I have enjoyed many cups of tea and home-made cake. For police procedure, I am grateful to Mr Jolly, who, despite being told I only needed him to check the police interviews, read the entire novel and announced he couldn't fault it.

My thanks go to all those who read and commented on my first draft: Stella, Jacqui, Richard, John, Chris, Sally, Kathy, Len, Jenny and my supportive husband, Mike.

And finally, many thanks to my very patient editor, Lydia Vassar-Smith, who listened to me.

While writing *My Name is Eva*, the following books were helpful in my research: *The Spy Who Loved* by Clare Mulley, *The Debs of Bletchley Park* by Michael Smith, *Forgotten Voices of the Secret War* by Roderick Bailey, *Auschwitz* by Laurence Rees, *The Wild Place* by Kathryn Hulme, *Alone in Berlin* by Hans Fallada, *Cruel Britannia* by Ian Cobain and *Love and War in the WRNS* by Vicky Unwin.

I hope you loved *My Name is Eva* and if you did, I would be very grateful if you could write a review. I'd love to hear what you think, and it makes such a difference helping new readers to discover one of my books for the first time.

I love hearing from my readers – you can get in touch on my Facebook page, through Twitter, Goodreads or my website.

Thanks,
Suzanne Goldring

　　　　　　　　@suzannegoldringauthor

　　　　　　　　@suzannegoldring

　　　　　　　　www.suzannegoldring.wordpress.com

CPSIA information can be obtained
at www.ICGtesting.com
Printed in the USA
BVHW082155031219
565541BV00001BA/137/P